When Condors Call

A Novel of Peru

Inge Bolin

When Condors Call

Cover Design: Andrea Bolin

Library and Archives Canada Cataloguing in Publication

ISBN 978-0-9866298-0-8

Chaska Publications

Nanaimo, British Columbia

chaskapublications@gmail.com

To the patients who courageously fight leishmaniasis

To the people who work on finding an ethical cure

And to those who support their efforts

Table of Contents

Todos Santos

Lightning flashed through dark clouds concealing Huaman Orqo, the sacred peak where eagles soar. A clap of thunder followed. Another fiery zigzag line hissed across the sky brightening it for a few seconds. Then a deafening thunderclap wiped out the splashing sound of a tropical downpour that had transformed the muddy road into immense puddles of turbid water.

"It is close, very close," the bus driver said in a shaking voice as he parked his ancient vehicle near the plaza of Qoripampa. With fear etched on their faces the passengers looked out at the violent sky. Some made the sign of the cross. Others reached with trembling fingers into their *ch'uspas* and *unkuñas* to find coca leaves in these small woven bags. Arranging them into *k'intus*, each made of three coca leaves, they blew across the surface of the tiny bouquets, hoping to appease the mighty thunder god so he would spare their lives.

"A bad omen," Ica heard an old woman murmur in Spanish mixed with the Quechua language of the highland Indians.

Another woman turned around and stared at Ica's face, framed by blond hair. She reached back to drop a *k'intu* into her hands. "Offer this to Qhaqya," she insisted in a friendly, but determined tone of voice. "You, too, must save yourself from his deadly strikes."

The fiery spectacle continued, but gradually the thunderclaps withdrew. The danger moved away. Ica knew that at this altitude of more than three thousand meters above sea level in the high Peruvian Andes, lightning bolts kill enough people and animals each year to instill terror throughout the villages.

The passengers slowly started to recover, emitting sighs of relief.

"No se preocupe, el trueno ya se fue," an old man assured Ica with a forced smile, telling her not to worry since the thunder had moved away. She nodded with a smile. The driver announced that passengers who stay in Qoripampa must now disembark. Ica stood up to pull her two bags from the overhead rack. As she turned her head toward the back of the bus she noticed a man alone in the last row of seats. He was hunched over with a worn brown poncho pulled across his forehead. An old gray scarf covered his nose and mouth, merely allowing his eyes to be seen. Why does he sit there alone, while other passengers crowd together in the front rows, she wondered. With trembling fingers this man tried to stuff coca leaves back into his *ch'uspa*. He, too, must have appeased Qhaqya, Ica thought to herself.

The two passengers who had been sitting beside her also turned to the back, wondering why she stood there motionless, gazing at the veiled man with a puzzled expression on her face.

"He is ill," one of them whispered. "He has *espundia*."

"It's bad, it's contagious, it disfigures the face," the other one affirmed in a barely audible voice.

"Can it be cured, is there a hospital?" Ica asked in a whisper.

"No hospital, we have no hospital," the passengers beside her responded.

"Is there no help? He should be ...," Ica wanted to persist but was interrupted by the bus driver who urged her in a friendly but firm tone of voice to disembark quickly, so he could make up for the time lost while waiting for the thunderstorm to move on.

As she reached for her bags, the veiled man was about to scoot to a seat by the window. His abrupt movement caused his scarf to slip down to his neck, exposing profound lesions around his nose and mouth. Frozen in place, Ica stared at him, pain written on her face. With a rude gesture of his hand, the passenger beside her made the sick man sit down. Nervously he adjusted his scarf, looking at Ica with an expression of shame and despair in his dark brown eyes. She thanked the passenger who helped her pull her bags down and hurried to the front of the bus.

"*Adiós y buena suerte,*" the driver called out with a friendly but concerned expression on his face, wishing her good luck as she jumped from the bus onto the muddy ground.

"Thanks," Ica responded, waving at him and the continuing passengers. Except for the man hunched over in the last row, they waved at her curiously as she walked along the dirt road fronted by simple one-storey adobe houses. She was glad to be back on her feet. It had taken that rusty, mustard colored, old bus almost seven hours to make it from the city of Qosqo to Qoripampa.

The downpour had stopped as quickly as it began. The sun's rays had emerged from behind dark clouds, dancing on the surface of the mud puddles. Lush vegetation and the humid earth released an intense aroma announcing the height of the Andean spring.

Looking across stone fences built around small adobe homes, Ica got a glimpse of side yards full of flowers, herbs, vegetables and fruit trees, with chickens and piglets now frolicking in the mud. Some escaped to the road. Certainly people cannot be far, she thought, but why is this place deserted?

After passing a few houses she came to a corner and entered what looked like the main plaza. Even this central meeting place was empty except for a lonely dog sniffing the corner stone of the statue of a peasant woman. The animal took a brief look at Ica, then continued on its round, little impressed by the new arrival.

She placed her two duffel bags on the bench beside the statue. The fact that no one was there to meet her came as no surprise since she had not been able to announce her early arrival to the Rodrigues family. But why was nobody stirring in this village? Not a soul who could show her the way. The few streets had neither names nor numbers. Still, she found the village charming with its earthen houses nestled against green hills and surrounded by precipitous mountain slopes and snowcapped peaks in the distance. She liked the red roof tiles of some houses and the simple grass roofs of others. Even the weather-beaten wooden doors she found attractive and the tiny windows, most of which lacked panes. In some ways these houses reminded her of the simple huts in the remote Swedish countryside where she had spent her holidays as a child.

She turned around to contemplate the plaza. It seemed quite large for such a small and simple village. Had this perhaps been an important center in ancient times, a place where meetings and ceremonies were held? After all, Qoripampa means 'place of gold' in the Quechua language, spoken in highland Peru at least since Inca times.

She took a seat on the bench between her bags, reflecting on the significance this village may have had at the beginning of the sixteenth century when it was still part of the ancient empire of Tawantinsuyu, known for its many achievements, including its superb organization. She knew that in 1534 the Spanish conquerors had reached these remote highlands and wondered about all that had happened here in the last 454 years. She was confident she would find out. After all she was to stay here for at least a year, until the end of 1989 or perhaps longer. This should be enough time to discover some of the secrets of this place. She smiled, thinking of the excitement this new territory had in store for her and what she would learn. Altogether this should more than make up for the lack of modern conveniences, she tried to convince herself.

Simple living was of little concern to her, but what if the villagers would not accept her? This dark thought had often crossed her mind. What if they refused to share their knowledge with her? Would she end up like some fellow students who never completed their fieldwork because the villagers would not trust them? Nervously she played with the handles of her bags and looked toward the snow-covered mountains, forcing her thoughts into a more positive direction. She imagined that eventually she would be one with the villagers, working toward a better understanding of the healing powers of medicinal plants and of good health for all.

Then her thoughts turned back to the veiled man in the bus. It struck her that he had not been accepted by those passengers who crowded into the front rows keeping their distance from him, or by the man who so rudely told him to sit down. She wondered whether he was shunned even by his own family for fear of becoming infected. How sad, she thought, the man looked young. What would his life be like if he couldn't be cured, if he were alone without hope until his end? She sighed, thinking about the sadness in his eyes. Then, with a more determined look on her face she whispered, "I must learn more about this disease."

Suddenly she noticed an old woman in her traditional outfit, consisting of several woven skirts and a colorful blouse, appear at the far end of the plaza. The woman took a quick look at Ica, then hurried down a side road. Shortly thereafter an elderly couple emerged from a tiny corner store. They also glanced at her briefly before heading in the same direction. Happy to see some life in this otherwise dead village, Ica still wondered why nobody acknowledged her presence. Would her worst fears come true? Would she be rejected by the villagers, would she be asked to leave? She looked at her blue jeans, her white runners and her blue, hooded rain jacket with lots of pockets. Would even her clothing be unacceptable in a traditional village? But then again, she had been assured that the Rodrigues family was well known in Qoripampa and happy to have her stay in their home. With this in mind she smiled, envisioning what she could learn about herbal medicine from Don Rodrigues.

She now noticed more and more people appear on the far side of the plaza, then walk away along the same road as did the others. She began to feel uncomfortable sitting alone in the middle of the plaza. Reaching for her bags she was ready to follow the locals wherever they went, when she felt a light pull at her hair and heard a giggle. She turned and gazed into the faces of three grinning boys, who she guessed to be about ten years old.

"Gringa, de dónde vienes?" one of the youngsters asked without inhibition.

Relieved that her presence was at last acknowledged, Ica still wondered what to think of the curious, somewhat impertinent expressions on the faces of these boys. Why would they dare to refer to her as *gringa*, not the most flattering term for a foreigner, and bluntly ask where she came from.

One of the boys took a seat beside her on the bench, while the others hovered over her shoulders asking endless questions in Spanish. "Why did you come to our village? Will you stay long? What did you bring in those big bags?"

One boy touched her shoulder-length hair, asking with a grin, "How come your hair looks like the yellow *ichu* grass that covers our high meadows in the dry season?"

The other two boys stared at her closely, wondering, "Why are your eyes the color of green mountain lakes?"

The three boys giggled, shaking their heads.

"*Qué no molesten la visita,*" the serious voice of a slightly older boy echoed across the plaza telling the three youngsters not to annoy the visitor. The boy came closer greeting Ica with a big smile and a handshake.

"My name is Victor. Don Rodrigues told me a Señorita Ica would arrive tomorrow. I'm glad you came early," the boy said in passable English. With a movement of his hand, he motioned the younger boys to leave.

"*Gracias,* Victor. Thanks for coming," Ica said, smiling with relief.

Insisting on carrying both her bags, Victor led the way toward the river. They arrived at a simple, but comfortable looking two-storied house, made of adobe blocks of mixed earth and straw dried in the sun. The walls, painted in light brown color, contrasted with the white window frames and the red tiles on the roof.

"This is the home of the Rodrigues family," Victor said with pride. He explained that no one was at home since today was Todos Santos, All Saints Day, when the villagers assembled by the graves to pass the day with the returning souls of their dead relatives.

"Please tell me about it," Ica said with curiosity.

"I'll take you there and you'll see," Victor answered with a flash in his eyes that did, however, not hide a tinge of sadness. He deposited Ica's bags in the living room, offered her a glass of *chicha blanca,* a delicious drink made from corn and *quinua*, and off they went.

They headed for the outskirts of the village where the cemetery lay high above the sacred river Willkamayu. On the way, some villagers overtook them. Ica noticed that they looked at her with shyness, nodding their heads and murmuring, *"buenos días."* Others kept their eyes fixed on the ground as they passed. Victor explained that the entire village had cooperated in cleaning the cemetery, burning old grasses and shrubs and getting everything ready for this important event. "People get along fine on Todos Santos, but this is not always the case," he added in a tone of voice that left no doubt that he knew his village well.

They passed fields of corn, beans and potatoes that had been planted over a month ago. Halfway up a nearby slope Ica discerned a small adobe church, carefully whitewashed. Narrow window slits without panes appeared on the four sides of its steeple. A cross atop its red tiled roof jutted into the blue sky, contrasting with the eucalyptus trees in the hills beyond the church.

"What an idyllic place!" she exclaimed, enchanted by the site.

"Yes, it is... most of the time," Victor responded. In a serious voice he whispered, "More than 600 people live in our village and problems do arise. Should you ever get in trouble, I will help you. I know what's going on here and you can trust me."

Ica squeezed his hand, smiling back at him, "Thank you so much, you're wonderful."

As they arrived at the gate of the cemetery, Victor cautioned, "Señorita Ica, please wait, I'll tell the Rodrigues family about your arrival." He walked alongside the graves where people made offerings to their deceased relatives. Shortly thereafter he returned with Don Rodrigues, a tall, wiry man with a black mustache. He looked more like his Spanish than his Quechua ancestors.

"*Bienvenida*, Señorita," Don Rodrigues exclaimed, welcoming Ica while holding her hand with a friendly smile on his brown, weather-beaten face. "Sorry I did not meet you at the bus stop. We expected you tomorrow. Todos Santos started yesterday with the 'Day of the Living' and today we celebrate the 'Day of the Dead'." Releasing her hand in a graceful manner, he added with pride, "That's how we honor our deceased relatives."

Ica nodded. "I'm so glad you invited me."

"It's our pleasure," Don Rodrigues responded as he led her into the cemetery to meet his relatives who had assembled by the family grave.

He introduced Ica to his wife, Doña Nilda, a plump, pleasant looking woman with a broad smile on her brown face, to their beautiful daughter Francisca and to grandpa Rodrigues. They welcomed their visitor with a handshake, complimented her on her good command of the Spanish language, and invited her to join them in honoring the souls of the deceased.

Ica was relieved to be accepted in such a warm and friendly manner and for being allowed to participate in this rather intimate celebration for the ancestors.

The family had spread a cloth on the grave. On it they had placed the favorite foods and drinks of their beloved grandmother, who was at the center of the celebration since she had died less than a year ago. Corn, potatoes, sugar cane, beer made of fermented corn, called *chicha*, sparkling drinks, and flowers had been arranged artistically across this makeshift table. Breads of many different shapes and sizes, resembling dolls, alpacas, llamas, sheep, cows, horses, and dogs were especially plentiful.

"These are the gifts for my wife. She died six months ago," grandpa said with sorrow, adding, "Some gifts are for our other loved ones who passed on within the last three years." Coming closer to Ica, he murmured, "We believe that the souls of our relatives who are not fondly remembered, are disappointed and must return to the realm of the dead unhappy and unable to find a place to rest." He shook his head as he added with concern, "We want to ensure this does not happen."

Formally, yet intimately, Don Rodrigues thanked the spirit of his dead mother for the help and guidance she had given the family throughout her life. Doña Nilda and her daughter whispered as though in a dialogue with grandmother's spirit. All family members joined in placing bouquets and chains of flowers on the grave. Then grandpa took over, praying with great emotion for the welfare of his dead wife's soul.

Ica sensed an atmosphere of harmony and solidarity in this cemetery where some families had hired musicians to play for the deceased on flutes, violins and harps. Grandpa explained that sometimes a family may ask a gifted villager to give a speech in honor of the dead.

Turning toward Ica, grandpa Rodrigues confided that the customs on Todos Santos retained some elements from ancient times when the Incas honored their dead and symbolically fed and entertained their mummified bodies on the main plazas of their large empire.

Ica observed families praying silently. In the far corner she spotted Victor sitting beside a grave, his elbows perched on his knees with his head resting in his hands. His pleasant features had assumed a somber look, his eyes were sad. Why is he alone, she wondered? By whose grave is he sitting and why has he nothing to offer?

As she scanned the cemetery, she noticed a young man standing with several people by a grave a short distance away. He gazed straight at her. As their eyes met, he looked away. This young man, muscular and rather tall for a Quechua native, with a strikingly handsome face, watched her again. His expression was determined, somewhat curious, but not inviting. Ica felt uncomfortable. She turned her back on him to escape his glance.

Most of the food items in the cemetery were now distributed to the musicians. Some families left their offerings on the graves. After relaying more good wishes to grandmother's spirit, the Rodrigues family was ready to leave. On their way through the cemetery they introduced Ica to friends and neighbors who welcomed her with warmth and kindness.

In the lower part of the cemetery Ica saw Victor still sitting by a grave without a headstone and lacking offerings of food and drink. Only flowers and blossoms had been carefully spread across the grave. She noticed tears flowing down Victor's cheeks. At that moment a middle-aged man approached the boy and sent him off with a rough gesture. Everyone else headed home.

As soon as they arrived at the Rodrigues' home, Doña Nilda gave Ica the tour of the house. A large entrance area, carefully whitewashed, with an array of coat hangers on the walls and enough space to deposit any kind of luggage, led to different rooms with heavy wooden doors. Everyone left their muddy shoes on the stone floor by the entrance, putting on woolen slippers.

Ica followed her hostess into a spacious living room. She approached one of the two large windows that allowed a view into a backyard of fruit trees, bushes and a vegetable garden. A third window faced the earthen road that passed through the entire village. Adobe houses, smaller than the Rodrigues home, lined the road.

She looked up to the high, whitewashed ceiling of the living room, then admired the dark brown wooden floors, polished to a luster. She imagined family and visitors, occupying the worn chairs and benches arranged along a very large rectangular table, having dinner or conversing over tea. Two couches with brown velvety covers met in a corner flanked by two side tables. This place conveyed a feeling of coziness. She walked toward a large wall closet that stood along one of the whitewashed walls and was filled with dishes, plates, glasses, and souvenirs. She smiled as she noticed that within this room every flat surface above the floor was decorated with candle holders containing partially consumed candles.

Given the size of the room with ample seating space, Ica imagined the Rodrigues family in engaging conversations by candle light with healers and herbalists from this and other villages. She was eager to participate in such sessions, learning the secrets these people used in healing their patients.

Slowly moving toward the couches Ica stopped, fascinated by the photos of her hosts' extended family that hung along the wall. Some had faded and looked very old. Her eyes came to rest on a newer photo in color, showing Francisca and a young man hugging with big smiles on their faces. Doña Nilda approached.

"Is this Francisca's brother?" Ica inquired.

"No," Doña Nilda responded with a sigh. "It's a man she used to love. Perhaps she still does." Shrugging her shoulders she revealed, "They have done good work together. He appreciates her, that's all."

Ica took a closer look. This man resembled the one who had stared at her in the cemetery.

Doña Nilda took Ica by the arm, leading her out. "I will tell you everything about our family, our ancestors and some of the famous healers you see in these photos. But it will be another day when we have more time."

"All this is more than I expected," Ica stammered. "What an interesting family, what a beautiful home."

"Wait until you see the kitchen and outhouse, they are nothing to brag about," Doña Nilda responded in a friendly, yet slightly embarrassed tone of voice. They entered the kitchen. A robust wood-burning stove in the corner, a large table and chairs arranged around it, with pots, pans and cooking utensils hanging above several cupboards and a set of baskets to keep non-perishable foods were all it contained. Beyond the kitchen on the outside Doña Nilda pointed to a cemented platform with a built-in sink and a single faucet. "Here we wash dishes and clothes and get ourselves ready in the morning." She took a couple of steps and pulled a plastic sheet from a pole, revealing a make-shift shower. "If you are brave, you can shower here, but the water is very cold." She sighed. "Will we ever get electricity in this forgotten village? And, there's the outhouse," she said apologetically, pointing to a small hut by the fence.

"That's fine," Ica responded. "When I went with my parents to the tropical forests, we led an even simpler life. But it was exciting!"

"I'm relieved," Doña Nilda said laughing. "You must tell me more about your adventures, but now we must hurry on." She showed Ica the doors to the family bedrooms and the laboratory where Don Rodrigues worked with medicinal plants, and then took her upstairs where three more rooms were located. She opened one of them and asked her guest to step in.

"This is splendid!" Ica exclaimed. She had not expected to find a bright, freshly painted room in this well kept but rather old house. She walked to the window that opened into a backyard from where the aroma of many different herbs entered the room. In the distance she saw fields, rolling hills and snow-covered peaks, partially concealed by thick clouds. The gurgling sounds of the Wilcamayo River mixed with the warm, whistling wind that tossed the rainclouds across the sky.

Several young piglets scurried from the road through the fence into the Rodrigues backyard. Too large to follow, mother pig nervously paced along the fence, grunting at her offspring. Chickens competed with an array of birds for the worms the water-logged earth had brought to the surface.

"What a wonderful place!" Ica exclaimed.

"It's fine in the late afternoon, but wait until you have passed a night here before you make up your mind about the peace you may get," Doña Nilda responded in a teasing tone of voice.

"What happens at night?" Ica asked with increased curiosity.

Doña Nilda placed herself in the middle of the room, pointing to different directions as she explained, "First several packs of dogs bark across the village. I'm sure they communicate with one another. After they have finally worn out their vocal cords, it's early morning and time for the roosters to take over. Soon thereafter, still before dawn, our peasants start to hustle along the muddy roads, eager to reach the distant fields before the sun burns too hot on the steep paths they must climb."

Ica listened with a grin on her face. "So I shouldn't expect a dull moment while I live in this cozy village?"

Doña Nilda nodded with a smile. "Make yourself at home," she suggested. "Our son Rodrigo lived here before he moved to Lima." She closed the door behind her.

Ica looked around the room. She loved the warm tone of the maize-colored walls that contrasted with the dark brown wood of the furniture and floor. The bed, night table, desk, closet, shelves and drawer chests were arranged in an orderly fashion. Slightly worn from years of use they gave a warm feel to the room and so did the thick blankets, woven from alpaca wool that covered the bed. Ica was moved. This room had the best view and had been lovingly renovated.

She started to unpack. There was plenty of space to arrange her clothes, books, and miscellaneous personal items. Carefully she took a large envelope from one of her bags. She pulled out several framed pictures, one with relatives in Sweden, others with student friends at the Alexander von Humboldt University in Germany and the University of California. Pictures of her dogs and other pets followed. Then her eyes rested on a photo of her parents in the Amazon rain forest. She kissed it and put it on one of the hooks that stuck out from the middle of the wall facing her bed. She placed the other pictures around it, then sighed deeply, recalling the good and sad times of her life, the struggles it had brought her and the triumphs. She realized she had made mistakes in the past and hoped that thirty years of experience would come to her aid now. She was ready for a new beginning and perhaps could finally pursue the work her parents had been so eager to accomplish in South America, but were denied by their fatal accident.

As she put the pictures that did not find a place on the wall back into the envelope, she noticed that in one of them her former boyfriend smiled out from among their student friends. She thought she had discarded all the photos of him, but there he was, looking like an intelligent young man and no one could have guessed what was hidden behind his smile. He had a sense of humor that made him the center of every party. She shuddered remembering how he used to put his arm around her when he told those funny stories and she recalled the day when he had asked her to marry him after they had known one another merely as friends for a few months. He wanted her to wait until he had finished his degree in a field related to medicine. He had never explained to her or any of their friends what his work involved, nor the exact location within the medical compound where he was working. "I help humankind," he often said. With pride he used to add, "I do good work and someday I will be honored for it. I'll surprise you with a breakthrough. Just wait a little longer."

Ica shook her head, emitting a deep sigh as memories poured into her mind she had been fighting to forget for so many years. She trembled as she thought back to the day when she had tried to find him in a building attached to the faculty of medicine at her university. She had wanted to deliver his birthday card signed by their common friends and arrange a time when they all could celebrate together. With a pained look on her face she remembered walking through empty hallways that led to a dark enclosure where dogs were crammed into small cages. The animals looked at her with pleading eyes, yelping and eager to get released.

An adjacent door with a sign, "No Public Access," was partially open. She remembered looking inside to see whether someone was present to tell her where to find her friend. With horror she recalled seeing dogs strapped into metallic holding devices and onto dissection tables. Men in white lab coats with scalpels and injection needles in their hands, hovered over the terrified animals. Some of them yelped in excruciating pain. She had almost fainted when she recognized her boyfriend leaning over a dog in agony. This man she had trusted had an expression on his face that she had never seen before. "My God, that's vivisection," she had stammered, "humanity's darkest sin.... and he's one of them."

She had slammed the door shut, ran along the corridors and outside.

In severe shock she took to her room for a long time, refusing to see anyone. At last, with the help of her friends, she moved to a different city, hoping never to see him again and to forget that he existed. Her friends had promised to keep her new residence a secret.

Separated by time and space from this horrifying discovery, her body still trembled at the thought that she had a boyfriend who was capable of such despicable and dehumanizing acts. She stood up, tears running down her cheeks. She took a deep breath and walked to the window, forcing her thoughts into a different direction. This nightmare will never haunt me again, she promised herself as she grabbed the picture and tore his image. Then she reconsidered and destroyed the entire picture for fear that the gap between her friends would again remind her of this cruel, cowardly and dishonest man who dissected live animals, helplessly strapped into metallic devices in the name of science.

Ica had received several grants and awards and was eager to continue her work on herbal medicine. But what she had seen in this lab behind closed doors and in labs at different universities and medical research facilities in other cities affected her former positive outlook on life. Over and over again she had asked herself, how such gruesome torture could take place even in societies where most people seemed kind and compassionate and where good scientists knew only too well that experiments involving the torture of millions of animals are not only immoral, but also without medical value. Some have even caused deaths as their results were applied to humans. Ica knew that wise people throughout the ages had condemned such crimes against life itself. Yet, the torture continued, mostly hidden from the public eye. It became increasingly harder for her to endure such hypocrisy. Trust no longer came easily. Since the shocking revelation in the vivisection lab, she had never considered marriage, or even a close relationship with a man. Nor did she forgive herself for not having rescued the dogs from their horrendous fate.

Now, separated by time and living on a different continent, Ica contemplated the last rays of the sun piercing through the cloud cover. "I'll be alright here," she said with a sigh. "I know I'll be alright."

Slowly she continued to arrange her room. She washed by the well in the small courtyard. As night began to fall, Don Rodrigues, Doña Nilda and Francisca were ready to follow the invitation of the Avaron family who lived on the other end of the village. Ica was not in a festive mood, but Francisca convinced her to come along. Together they left the house.

Feeding Forgotten Souls

The village was wrapped in darkness. The clouds in the night sky looked ominous as they were tossed about by an increasingly fierce wind. Dim candle light streamed through the windows of the adobe houses where families continued celebrating in honor of their deceased relatives.

The Rodrigues family with Ica in tow approached a rather large two-storey house with a wooden balcony, carved in the colonial style. "They live here," Francisca whispered in a disapproving tone of voice.

The extended Avaron family welcomed their visitors into the dining room of their home lit by many candles and two kerosene lamps. A large wooden table, covered by a white, embroidered tablecloth, was loaded with a variety of spicy dishes, and many shapes of bread. Silver cutlery lay beside porcelain plates and crystal beakers. Beautiful *qantu* flowers, dedicated to the dead and considered sacred since Inca times, adorned the table. The chairs were carved from the wood of the rare mahogany tree and matched the arms on two large couches and several wall units. A wide door frame separated the dining room from the living room which was furnished in a similar fashion, with couches, armchairs and side tables. Ica was surprised to see such luxury in a village that had given her the impression of relative poverty.

Mr. Avaron's mother, who had also passed away since last year's Todos Santos, smiled from a photo on the wall above the table. Her spirit was believed to return to the house for a few hours to be with her living descendents who were honoring her memory as they did in the cemetery, offering the foods she had cherished most in her life.

"Doña Doron de Avaron and my grandma were friends," Francisca whispered while the other people were engaged in conversation. "They were good people, helping the poor whenever need arose. But the old lady's descendents ....," Francisca did not finish her sentence, instead a ray of contempt crossed her face and Ica understood. "That's why grandpa did not come along," she added. Still whispering she said, "Our grandma did not want us to hold a dinner for her soul. Before she died, she asked us to give all the food to the orphans and the sick, and that's what we did. We visit here only to honor the memory of Doña Doron de Avaron."

Soon visitors and hosts were seated around the long dining room table. Don Avaron and the younger male members of the family offered drinks of wine and *chicha* to the adults. As different soups and spicy treats were brought to the dining room, the kitchen door swung open. Ica noticed a boy washing dishes in the kitchen sink. She was both surprised and relieved to see that it was Victor. Knowing that he was safe, she enjoyed the lavish dinner as did the rest of the group who complimented their hosts and the servants for their cooking.

"Please let us all move to the living room," the lady of the house, dressed in her best silken clothes, suggested to her visitors after everyone had finished eating. As soon as the last person had left the dining room, Victor entered from the kitchen and quickly stuffed an assortment of left over breads into his pockets. His hands trembled as he thought of his mother and grandmother who would not have accepted this kind of behavior. But he had to do it. At that moment Don Avaron's daughter returned to the dining room catching Victor in the act of filling his pockets.

"Thief," she whispered angrily, not to alert the visitors. "Get out!"

Victor ran out the door and into the pouring rain. Although he was used to nights without light, he could barely see his hands in front of his face. He had to pass through two gates to get to his hut at the lower end of the Avaron property.

Slowly he moved through the first gate. He let out a shriek as his hands touched a warm, wet body. Instantly he remembered the *pishtaco*, a dangerous spirit that stalks his victims at night. But quickly he realized that he had touched one of the cows that had moved from its flooded enclosure to the less waterlogged path. As he hurried through the second gate, a flash of lightning illuminated the landscape for a few seconds. Now he could see the Avaron's private bakery. The cinders in its large oven emitted a reddish hue and right across from it was his little hut. He opened the door from which hung a broken lock. Exhausted he fell on the wooden platform that served as his bed. His clothes were soaking wet and so was the bread. The neat shapes had given way to an unrecognizable mass. Rain dripped from the roof and accumulated in a mud puddle in the middle of the room, while tears ran from his eyes. He would have given anything for a hug from his mother and grandmother, whom he remembered with fondness. But they were dead and without an offering of food, their spirits were left to wander unsatisfied, finding no peace.

Back in the Avaron home, family and visitors enjoyed the delicious *sank'ayllo*, a corn beer that had been boiled with coca leaves, alcohol and sugar. They toasted to their ancestors, most of all their grandmothers, who had died within the year. Everyone was content that the souls of their beloved were honored and fed, allowing them to rest in peace.

Hosts and guests also used this get-together to exchange views about their crops and how to combat diseases that attacked their cows and sheep. Both families used to own haciendas, landed estates that had been expropriated during the agrarian reform in 1968. At that time Peru's haciendas had been distributed to landless peasants, but most hacienda owners retained more land than did the average villager. This was alright for the Rodrigues family whose life style was not lavish. But the Avarons, still upset by the expropriation, clung to their former way of life in every way they could. In contrast to the Rodrigues family, they showed little concern for the less fortunate of their village. In fact, they used young orphans like Victor to work for them in return for food and a leaky roof over their heads. These children could not afford to complain, and few villagers were aware of the treatment they received.

The clock ticked away and it was close to ten o'clock when Doña Nilda looked at Ica. "We had better head home, you must be tired," she suggested.

As the others were saying their good bye, Ica whispered, "I would like to say good night to Victor. He looked so desperate this afternoon. I really want to see him," she pleaded. Don Rodrigues who had overheard her concern consented to accompany her to find Victor after they had left their hosts. Doña Nilda and her daughter headed home.

The rain had stopped. Don Rodrigues knew that Victor lived in the lower part of the Avaron property. With the help of a flashlight, they found the bake house where the dying cinders still gave off some light. They knocked at the little hut across from it. Within seconds Victor emerged, his face lighting up as he recognized his visitors. They embraced in the local fashion and entered. Standing in the mud puddle in the middle of Victor's hut, Don Rodrigues' eyes followed the beam of his flashlight around the room. He was displeased with the sad condition under which this eleven year old lived. Although Victor had been working with him sorting and cataloguing herbs for several months, the Rodrigues family was unaware that this young boy had no decent place to stay. Victor had never complained.

"Put on dry clothes," Ica suggested. "You will catch a cold. You are dripping wet."

"I have no other clothes," Victor answered, "only this." He pointed to a pot on the ground, where a shirt was soaking, waiting to be washed.

"You must come home with us. This is no place to live," Don Rodrigues urged in a friendly but commanding tone of voice, tinged with anger. He exited with Ica and Victor.

Back at the Rodrigues house, Doña Nilda led Victor upstairs to a small simple room adjacent to the one Ica had occupied just a few hours before. A broad smile crossed his face when he saw the furniture - a comfortable looking bed, a closet, shelves, a small table and two chairs. Francisca brought clothes that used to belong to her brother who now resided in Lima. "I had no idea he lived like that, I should have been more observant," she said looking with disgust at Victor's wet and worn clothes. "But I am not surprised." Turning to Victor, she affirmed with a triumphant look in her eyes, "You will live with us from now on. I will tell the Avarons tomorrow morning."

"Living here saves you a trip across the village when you help us with the herbs," Don Rodrigues remarked with a smile, as he spread a blanket over Victor's bed. "And tomorrow we all will work together. We have piles of herbs waiting to be catalogued and processed."

"Let Señorita Ica rest for a day," Doña Nilda suggested, pulling her husband's sleeve.

He looked at his wife with a grin. "My love, it seems to me that she is more eager to start than any of us."

"I can hardly wait," Ica responded, laughing and settling the family dispute.

They hugged, wishing one another a good night and retired to their rooms.

Victor placed his head on the soft pillow, a feeling he had not known in a long time and pulled the blanket up to his chin. His happiness would have been complete, if only he could have helped the spirits of his mama and grandma on this Day of the Dead. As he was about to cry, an idea flashed through his mind.

As soon as no one stirred in the house, Victor put on his clothes and took the moist bread crumbs out of the wet pants he had worn before. He knocked on Ica's door, then carefully opened it. "I must go to the cemetery," he whispered. "I must bring something to eat for the spirits of my mama and grandma."

" Let's go tomorrow," Ica suggested yawning. "It's already so late."

"It must be today on the Day of the Dead," Victor insisted. "The spirits of the dead will depart at midnight, I must go now." He hesitated, then moved closer to her. "No one may see me make my offering."

"What do you mean," Ica wondered.

Suppressing tears, Victor whispered, "Some people believe that my mother committed suicide. They say that when this happens, there is no salvation." He sighed. "I know this is not true." In a more determined tone of voice he asserted, "But I also know that without an offering of food for her and my grandma, their souls must search for happiness until the end of time."

"I'll come with you. You cannot go alone," Ica cautioned as she pulled a sweater and pants over her sleepwear. "Do you have anything to offer?"

Victor showed her the moist bread crumbs.

"Let's take these instead," she suggested as she handed him the fresh breads she had received from the Rodrigues family in the afternoon. Victor grinned with joy. They tiptoed down the stairs.

"Wait," Ica cautioned, "We better tell Doña Nilda that we will be gone for a while, just in case ...."

"We may not tell anyone," Victor interrupted, as he opened the door for Ica, then scooted out himself, carefully closing it behind him. "People say it's very dangerous to go to the cemetery on Todos Santos when the souls are about," he explained. "They would never let us go."

They left the Rodrigues home quietly and entered into the night.

The rain had stopped and the wind had scattered the clouds revealing a full moon that spread a silvery hue across the landscape. With light steps, not wishing to awaken anyone in the small houses along the way, they hurried toward the cemetery.

Victor broke the silence and confessed in a whisper, "I'm sorry, Señorita Ica. I'm sorry I had taken bread that belonged to the Avaron family. I never steal, but I cannot leave the spirits of my mama and grandma another year without bread on the Day of the Dead. My grandma died last year and my mama died some years ago. I want them to rest in peace." He looked at Ica. "Many in this village do not know my grief. I only cry in my little hut when things get too bad. But I want to tell you. I need to tell you what happened to me, because I know you will understand."

They hurried along their way and Ica listened intently as Victor recalled the frightening day five years ago when his mother returned from her fields on the steep slopes of Mount Yaucat. She was bleeding severely from the side of her head. He could see her staggering down the path where she collapsed. Two men picked her up and carried her toward her house. Victor was horrified. He ran to meet her. He was only six years old at the time, but he remembered the terrible moment when the men laid her down on the ground. She was gasping for air as she desperately tried to tell him something. But she closed her eyes forever, unable to utter a word. He yearned to hear her beloved voice. He needed to know what she was trying to tell him. Trembling he hugged her dead body and kissed her cheeks, hoping she would regain consciousness. He held her hands as they started to become cold. He looked toward the sky praying to the Apus, the great mountain gods and also to the God he had learned about in school. But neither granted his wish. His mother's hands became colder. Sobbing he lay down on the ground, begging Pachamama, the great Earth Mother, not to take his mama back into her womb but to return life to her as she gives life to all creatures and every plant. But his prayers remained unanswered. None of the deities listened and life became almost unbearable in the longing for his mother.

For years he tried to find out what really happened to her. Did she have an accident or had someone tried to kill her? But why? She never harmed anyone. His grandma said that mama knew much about the village, the region and about healing. She was always at the Sunday market selling the medicinal herbs she had collected, and items which she brought from as far as Lake Titicaca. Victor had always gone with her on these adventurous trips, since he was a baby tucked into a shawl on her back from where he could view his universe.

After his mother's burial, his father left. Victor hardly re-membered him as he had often been gone trying to earn some money in the cities. People said he finally went to the *selva*, the jungle region, to find gold. He was never seen again.

While his grandmother was still alive, things were not so bad. She was a pleasant old lady who passed most of her time beside the earthen stove cooking potatoes, corn and other vegetables that grew in her backyard. She fed Victor when he came home from herding the neighbors' sheep to earn some money to keep their lives going. Grandma knew much about the time when the Incas still roamed the region and left ancient cities as testimony of their existence and work-manship. He loved to listen to her stories and legends from times long gone. Legends about the Apus, those honored mountain deities, about Pachamama, the Earth Mother, who gave birth to her human children, nourished them through-out life and took them back into her womb after death, while their spirits soared to the highest mountain peaks.

Most importantly, grandma helped Victor overcome the pain of losing his beloved mother by reminding him of the wisdom of their ancestors. He remembered her saying: "As soon as the most cherished memories of your mama have become deeply embedded in your mind, you will be happy again. As you think of her with love and joy, you will always be together because you will have become one with her spirit."

But one day, almost a year ago, Victor came home from herding sheep and found grandma beside the stove, slumped against the wall, motionless, with her mouth open. He was afraid, seized by a sense of hopelessness and wished that he, too, could be with her and his mama in the safe womb of the great Earth Mother. Being without close relatives, the Avaron family had allowed him to sleep in their little shack by the bake house. In return for much hard work he received food and a leaky roof over his head.

Ica suppressed her tears.

Victor confessed, "For some time I remained sad, but then I had hope again. I wanted to make my mama and grandma proud of me. I knew that they healed many people with medicinal plants. I also wanted to learn more about herbal medicine. When Don Rodrigues found out about my interest, he let me help him and taught me more about herbs." He looked up at Ica with a proud smile. "Don Rodrigues knew my mama. He said she was very knowledgeable and taught him a lot about herbs and healing. Now he teaches me what she taught him. Isn't that something?" He chuckled with joy. "I also got to borrow Don Rodrigues' English books and now I can talk with you. We have a secret language few in this village know." He held up her hand in a gesture of solidarity.

"You are a wise little guy," Ica affirmed, giving him a hug.

As they turned a sharp corner, they saw the cemetery stretching half way up the hill in the light of the full moon.

"We are almost there," Victor uttered, fear showing on his face. "I hope the souls will remain calm.... we shouldn't be here at night."

"They will rest in peace," Ica remarked in an assuring tone of voice and only slightly worried.

"On the Day of the Dead they are everywhere," Victor asserted, "right until midnight."

Ica nodded, respecting his beliefs.

They approached the cemetery in silence when they heard the sound of steps seemingly coming from a side alley. They held their breath for a moment, then they turned around. No one was in sight and the noise stopped. Again the same sounds echoed along the alley. Now at the gate, Victor pushed down its handle. The gate opened. He uttered a sigh of relief.

"No need to climb over it," he whispered.

They entered slowly and carefully closed the gate behind them, tiptoeing alongside several graves. They stopped at the grave that was barren, except for some wilted flowers Victor had strewn across it in the afternoon.

He fell to his knees, touching the ground. He prayed for the welfare of the souls of those he loved so much. He opened his bag and cautiously placed the differently shaped breads on the ground. In a dialogue with his beloved mama and grandma, he asked their souls to rest in peace. He sang a song in Quechua that he used to sing with his mama. Then he kissed the earth and got back on his feet, tears flowing from his eyes. He turned to Ica, "Thank you for helping me feed my ancestors. Thank you so very, very much."

Back at the gate, Victor turned around, looking at the moonlit graves. With his sleeve he wiped the tears from his eyes, smiling at Ica. Equally relieved she looked at him and at her watch. Midnight had just arrived and the souls were about to return to the world beyond.

Victor opened the gate and quietly closed it behind them. As they passed the same dark alley, they again heard the sound of footsteps. A young man approached. In the light of the moon Ica recognized the face of the man who watched her so intently from a gravesite in the afternoon.

"*Como está*?" she called out to break the silence, asking how he was doing.

"You don't know our local customs," the young man responded in a serious tone of voice. "It's dangerous to enter the cemetery at night, especially on Todos Santos." Turning to Victor he said, "You should know this better than anyone else."

Victor nodded, admitting that the spirits are about and that the *uraña wayra*, the dangerous wind of the night, can kill.

Looking at the young man, Ica added, "Thanks for telling us, but you could be a little friendlier. By the way, what are you doing out in the middle of the night?"

The man almost smiled, but managed to keep a serious face. "Buenas noches," he said as they reached the Rodrigues house from where he disappeared in the night.

"Don't worry, he won't tell anyone," Victor assured Ica. They tiptoed back into the house and went to sleep.

Herbs that Speak

Ica rose early the next morning ready to organize her botanical work sheets. She was happy to finally be able to work with South American plants. After failed attempts at studying modern medicine and zoology, she had finally followed in the footsteps of her parents and studied botany at the University of California, earning a bachelor's degree. Under the supervision of a noted botanist, she had done comparative field research in Indonesia which earned her a master's degree and brought her some international recognition for her discoveries. Her published articles had also caught the attention of Don Rodrigues who had taught university courses for several decades and was a well known and respected expert on the curative powers of Andean medicinal plants. He had recently retired from most of his teaching responsibilities and could now spend more time on his research on medicinal herbs and the manufacture of natural medicines which the poor so desperately needed. Given his in-depth knowledge and wide reputation, Ica was happy to be able to work with him in Qoripampa doing her Ph.D. research on those plants that are used in the Andes to treat local diseases but of which the curative powers are unknown in the outside world.

Soon Ica heard others stir in the house. The smell of baking bread and freshly brewed coffee floated into her room, indicating that breakfast was ready. Then Doña Nilda's voice, *"El desayuno está servido!"* echoed through the house. Within minutes, the various doors within the house opened and everyone appeared in the living room with a big smile, hugging and wishing each other a good morning and a successful day. They sat down at the large oval table where bread, butter, jam, eggs, herbal tea for Victor and steaming hot coffee had been placed around a large bowl filled with oranges, bananas and other fruits. Ica was astounded and Victor was overwhelmed to see such a variety of foods.

"This is the kind of breakfast we eat on special occasions," Francisca said with an air of pride. "Otherwise we eat potato soup with seasonal vegetables, just as our peasants do."

"Both sound fine to me," Ica responded with a radiant smile.

"A feast," Victor added. "What a wonderful feast."

Everyone gave thanks to Pachamama, the Earth Mother, for providing the delicious foods and then began to eat.

Don Rodrigues was in a good mood. Not only because he and his family had slept like logs during the night, hearing neither the door open nor close after midnight, but also because he was excited to have a new colleague with a keen interest in his favorite topic.

Victor looked happy after last night's excursion to the cemetery. Having satisfied the needs of those he loved most, he had gained new strength and was ready to go further in the footsteps of his mama. He wanted to learn much more about herbs and ways to cure. Ica was relieved to see Victor so content. She noticed that with such a positive air about him, he looked quite handsome despite the fact that his growth had been slightly stunted and several of his fingers had not grown straight due to years of excessive work as a young child. His eyes radiated kindness and curiosity and his enthusiasm was contagious.

With breakfast over, everyone helped Doña Nilda clear the table. Then Ica and Victor joined Don Rodrigues in his lab. It exceeded Ica's expectations. The lab was bright with many windows that opened, allowing air currents to dry the fresh medicinal plants. Long rows of shelves held all the materials and instruments which were required to identify and catalogue the plants and produce herbal medicine. Several large tables provided ample space to sort the plants. Don Rodrigues gave Ica a tour of the lab, then discussed the ways in which they could cooperate on various projects.

Twice a week in the afternoon patients came to the house to be treated for local diseases using the medicine produced in the lab. Several treatments developed by Don Rodrigues had been very successful and had found their way into top medical journals and some labs elsewhere in the world.

Don Rodrigues spent the day with his team demonstrating his lab method for sorting the plants in accordance with their curative powers. Ica noticed right away that Victor was very knowledgeable for an eleven year old. There were several plants new to her and Victor was always ready to explain where they grew and how they were used in the manufacture of medicine. Proudly he told her, "I learned about herbs when I collected them with my mama and grandma all over the mountains. They knew the medicinal plants very well and the diseases they prevented and cured. They told me that the herbs spoke to them," he added in a whisper.

Time passed quickly as they exchanged knowledge about ways of preventing and curing diseases and promoting good health.

"If only we had a small hospital here in Qoripampa," Don Rodrigues said with concern, "We could care so much better for our villagers and the families of the surrounding communities. Without such a facility we must send too many patients to the hospital in the provincial capital or to Qosqo. It's expensive and there is not always space for them."

"I know," Ica responded with equal concern. "Passengers in the bus in which I arrived yesterday complained that there is no hospital in the entire region."

"We'll get one eventually, but it will be a struggle," Don Rodrigues said. "In the meantime we must do our best with the little we have."

As dusk set in, the last plants were sorted and catalogued.

"Tomorrow we'll collect more plants!" Victor exclaimed with a triumphant smile. "I know exactly where they grow."

Don Rodrigues shook his head as he cautioned, "You must take care when exploring the high mountains. I will leave tomorrow before dawn. Wait till I return from the provincial capital in a couple of days. Then we will go together."

But the next day looked too good to stay home. As the sun rose in a cloudless sky, warming the air and the moist earth, Ica and Victor could not contain their desire to climb to higher places to collect those precious herbs that grow only during the rainy season. They ate breakfast with Francisca who agreed that during those months when the rains are heavy, a sunny day must be used to advantage. She would have joined them, but had to attend a meeting in a small town to the south, where she was one of the leaders of a movement against peasant exploitation that had spread through many villages. As they were ready to leave, Ica asked Francisca to inform Doña Nilda about their excursion when she came back from the market and off they went.

Victor beamed with joy as he introduced Ica to his favorite places and to some of his friends they met along the way. People welcomed her with affection. They looked surprised to see a foreigner, but did not ask why she had come.

Higher up the slopes became more precipitous. Victor noticed a patch of very special herbs on a nearby outcrop. Oblivious to the fact that the earth was waterlogged, he stepped on the outcrop and reached for the plants.

"Look Ica," he called out. "This is ...."

His voice died as the earth and rubble gave way under his weight and he tumbled downhill in an avalanche of mud. Ica hurried down the meadow alongside the mudflow, her heart pounding as she found him covered by mud and stones. With all her strength she pulled him out of the mud and onto the grass. Not knowing the scope of his injury, she knelt and immobilized his bleeding head between tufts of grass.

"Dr. Yupanqui," Victor uttered in a faint voice, his right hand still clinging to the precious herbs he had picked before his plunge. Ica did not understand the name.

"Dr. Yupanqui," Victor repeated, as he closed his eyes.

Ica looked nervously down the valley. In the distance she saw two young girls coming up the path loaded with woven bags of the kind the highland people used to carry produce to barter in the villages below.

"Please hurry and get Dr. Yupanqui," Ica pleaded as they came closer.

The girls took a glance at Victor, then deposited their bags beside Ica and ran down to the village.

Ica observed Victor's breathing and the color of his skin. Relieved that the girls seemed to know this Dr. Yupanqui, she wondered why she had not heard of him before. The Rodrigues family had told her that Qoripampa had no regular physician, only a few healers and one young doctor who had recently finished medical school in the capital. They said that he combined herbal medicine with certain modern practices and worked free of charge while spending most of his time doing research. But in the two days since she arrived, she had not been introduced to any of them and worried about their level of expertise.

Almost an hour had passed since the girls ran down to the valley. Victor's breathing had been normal as he rested beside Ica, but she was worried about a concussion, an infection, or internal injuries. Finally she saw three people in the distance hurrying uphill - a young man, followed by the two teenage girls. As they came closer, she recognized the man she had met twice in the cemetery – once by day and once by night.

He greeted her quickly, with his eyes on Victor while he opened his kit and proceeded to clean the boy's head wound. Before he bandaged it, he showed Ica the crushed leaves of a plant he called *muña*. "This plant works against infection and inflammation," he explained as he placed it on Victor's wound. He checked the rest of his body, then lay him down on half the blanket he had brought along and covered him with the other half.

"It doesn't look serious. There's a cut on his scalp, and he may have a concussion," the doctor reassured Ica, as they waited for two boys from Qoripampa whom he had asked to bring a stretcher from the first-aid station.

She thanked the two girls who had been watching the doctor with fascination. They smiled, took their bags and hurried uphill.

Ica and the doctor took turns placing cool compresses on Victor's forehead. For a while both sat in silence. Then the young doctor looked at Ica and introduced himself as Ayar Yupanqui. "Just call me Ayar," he said. As though to avoid questions on her part, he proceeded to ask how the accident occurred.

She explained.

"You don't know this place well enough to venture off alone with only a child as companion," he warned in a firm tone of voice.

Ica nodded, this time without contradiction.

"You need someone to introduce you to these mountains," he insisted, looking her straight in the eyes.

"I'll learn in time. There are many people who can teach me," she responded. Although she did not want to reject his offer to help her get acquainted with this new environment, she could not sense whether he was truly concerned about her or whether he believed her too ignorant to live in his village and would rather see her leave. But despite his somewhat unfriendly tone of voice, she noticed something in his dark eyes that suggested that his concern for her was not only superficial.

"Señorita, please tell me what it is that interests you in this god forsaken part of the Andes," he inquired.

"I want to learn about traditional ways of curing diseases with the medicinal plants that grow here," she answered bluntly.

"Why not modern medicine?" he insisted.

"Modern is not always best," she asserted. "And, as you know, it is much too expensive for people with small incomes."

Ayar smiled with a tinge of irony showing on his face. "That's an interesting point of view. You foreigners sometimes come up with the most controversial ideas."

"There are many ways of thinking in the world out there," Ica responded. "We are different in the same way as you are different here." In a serious tone she continued, "Look, Ayar, I want to learn as much as possible in the short time I can spend here. Perhaps I could learn from you as well."

He nodded, remaining silent.

Ica looked at him curiously. "Your first name is not Spanish like that of other villagers. Why?"

"Well," Ayar reflected. "My parents believed in our ancestors' way of life and their values. Ayar was the name of one of the mythological founders of the Inca Empire. I guess they had hoped that I, too, would become the founder of something worthwhile." He laughed with an expression that left no doubt that he did not consider himself worthy to become part of mythology.

"By the way," Ica interjected, "my name is ... "

"I know," Ayer interrupted, "it is Ica Jansen."

Victor stirred and asked for a drink of water, just as the boys arrived with the stretcher to carry him to Qoripampa.

Over the next two weeks Victor improved steadily in the Rodrigues home. Ayar visited him often and stuck around to talk with Don Rodrigues and Ica about herbs and their healing powers. But he never stayed for a whole evening and was seldom seen socializing in the village.

"Where does he spend all his time and doing what?" Ica thought to herself. "And why is he always in a hurry?"

Several weeks later Ayar told Ica that he had to return to the University in Qosqo to attend a conference and teach a course. He invited her to look at the plants he had collected and studied over a number of years. Ica grabbed her notebook and pen and together they went to his small adobe house, a five minute walk from the Rodrigues home.

She was delighted as Ayar showed her some rare medicinal plants that grew only in specific micro-environments. She had not come across those in her work with Don Rodrigues and jotted down their names and predominant characteristics. He gave her specimens of dried plants he had collected in regions ranging from the frigid heights of the Andes to the steaming jungles. "I hope...," he said with some hesitation ... "perhaps we might be able to work together when I return."

Ica looked surprised. He had never said anything that indicated much interest in working with her. Within the last few weeks, however, she had become used to the stimulating discussions with him and she liked the way he looked at her when he explained calmly and thoroughly the natural medicines of the Andes.

She thanked him for sharing so much of his work with her. "This means a lot to me," she confessed. "There is so much to learn about the medicinal plants of the Andes and the Amazon." Looking at him with an enthusiastic expression on her face she said, "Perhaps I can even continue the work my parents had pursued before they were killed."

Ayar reached for her hand, holding it between his. "I'm sorry you lost your parents so early."

Ica nodded, sadness showing on her face.

"What work did your parents do," he asked, loosening his grip.

"They were botanists. They studied the medicinal plants of the Amazon and the sub-tropical parts of the Andes. From the time I was eight years old I went along on their fieldwork. On our fourth trip, after a successful season, my parents were so happy." She smiled but became somber as she continued with some hesitation. "We took a small float plane from the Ucayali River to fly out of the jungle. All of a sudden, the plane began to shake and then crashed headlong into the jungle." Ica placed her hands across her face, sobbing.

Ayar came closer, putting his arm around her shoulders.

"My parents and the two other passengers died instantly," she stammered. "The pilot was severely injured and died a few hours later. I was alone until a helicopter came to my rescue two days later." She showed Ayar a scar on her upper left arm. "I escaped with only a cut. It should have hurt, but I do not remember any pain. I only felt the horror of seeing my parents dead. I was only twelve years old."

"I am so sorry," Ayar repeated in a soft tone of voice, holding her tighter.

Ica went on. "Our best friends from California, who were also botanists and colleagues of my parents, came to Peru and took me home with them. They didn't have children of their own and were happy to adopt me. They were good people who helped me get on with my life. They had such a great sense of humor. But they died in a car accident when I was nineteen." She closed her eyes. "Life can be quite cruel."

"It can bring much pain," Ayar said. "But we cannot give in."

"I know," Ica agreed. "That's why I'm here. When I was a child I told my parents I would become a botanist like them. They would be so happy to hear that I have continued on their path. But it took a long time until I dared to return to Peru and I still don't have the courage to go to the jungle. I still remember so vividly what happened. For now it's less painful to study the plants of the highlands."

"I am glad you came. You made a good choice," Ayar said, looking at her without hiding his admiration. Holding her hand, he confided, "When we continue the work of the ones we love, they become part of us. Their spirit is always present as we pursue our common goal. In this way, our loved ones never die."

She smiled at him. "I understand, Ayar. Thank you so much."

Looking at her watch she realized it was late. "I better leave. You must rise early tomorrow," she said as she reached for the precious plants he had given her. He accompanied her to the Rodrigues' house. This time the good bye was more difficult.

A Healer's Obsession

The next morning Ica rose early, ready to catalog the newly acquired plants. But she could not find her notebook. She remembered leaving Ayar's place with her hands full of the precious herbs. She must have left it there. She hurried to his house. Doña Cirila, who cared for his house and lived upstairs, opened the door.

"Ayar is gone. He took the first bus. Please come in," she said with a smile.

"I forgot my notebook," Ica explained apologetically.

Doña Cirila led her to Ayar's workplace, pushing several cats out of the way and a dog limping on three legs.

"This Dr. Ayar is really something," she sighed, petting the dog lovingly. "What a nuisance. He brings home all the sick animals he finds and keeps them forever. And I must take care of them when he is gone for months." She opened the door asking Ica to enter. "I hope you can find what you need in this mess," she said laughing as she left the room.

Ica scanned the place but did not see her notebook. She carefully moved a pile of papers strewn on a wooden desk top - excerpts from journals and books, and notes in Ayar's own handwriting. In many of his notes she recognized the word Leishmaniasis. She read the sheets on top of the pile:

"The Leishmaniases diseases - cutaneous and mucocutaneous – have plagued people in Peru for centuries. The cutaneous type – *Leishmania peruviana* - locally referred to as *uta*, affects the skin by creating ulcers. This disease, which is also found in other parts of the world, can often be cured, but it may take months or years. Much worse is the mucocutaneous leishmaniasis or *Leishmania braziliensis*, the dreaded *espundia.* This disease, which mainly occurs in Peru, Brazil and Bolivia, has already existed in Peru in pre-Inca times. Mochica vases and figurines with grossly distorted faces testify to the presence of this dreadful condition. The afflicted suffer from an erosion of the mucous tissues, especially the palate, pharynx and larynx, the nasal and oral mucous membranes. Eventually the face is destroyed and death usually results from infection or obstruction of airways or the food passage."

Ica turned the page to read, "The psychological impact on patients is devastating. They are shunned wherever they go. Many only leave the house at night, with a hood pulled over head and face."

Then she read, "Many people are afraid to come in contact with leishmaniasis patients, believing that the disease is contagious. This is only true when the open wounds of two individuals rub together. Otherwise the disease cannot be transmitted between people."

She took a deep breath and looked out the window onto a backyard of trees, their branches bent by the weight of the ripening fruit. She tried to recall what happened in the bus when she disembarked almost three months ago. The veiled man, hunched over in the very back of the bus must have had this disease. Now she recalled one of her fellow passengers telling her he had *espundia.* She sighed and shuddered at the thought of it. Now she also remembered that during her field work in Asia she heard about visceral leishmaniasis that affected the organs, but she hadn't been aware of the way this disease manifested itself in South America.

Her eyes wandered to the corner of the table. She opened a book. It showed horrifying pictures of mucocutaneous leishmaniasis at all stages. She leafed through it hastily and read: "Research is still in its infancy on epidemiology, the way the disease takes shape and progresses, and on affordable cures and medications that do not lead to serious side effects."

As though in a daze she scanned the pages and read:

"Protozoan parasites of the genus *Leishmania* are transmitted through the bite of sandflies of the genus *Lutzomyia*. A cure is especially difficult when dealing with parasites of the species *Leishmania braziliensis*, which lead to the mucocutaneous type, the *espundia*. Antimonial drugs such as Pentostam and Amphotericin B cause severe side effects.... Glucantime is effective when used at the early stages of mucocutaneous leishmaniasis, but may cause heart problems and other severe side effects. These drugs are also very expensive and thus out of the reach for most patients."

Ica noticed several articles in Spanish and English and many more pages with Ayar's handwriting. He wrote about possible ways of preventing the disease. He wondered whether people who are indigenous to a jungle region are immune to it, and suggested that in order to find out, one must do research among native societies deep in the rainforest.

Then she came across a letter written from the jungles of Madre de Dios and addressed to Ayar. It was signed "your sister Cora."

Ica read: "It is not easy to live here, it is hot and humid and washing gold is hard work. But I will not come home as you suggested. I must earn enough money for our family to survive should another drought hit us. I also want you to attend school in the valley and later study medicine. You will be a great physician."

In a letter sent at a later date Cora wrote, "Ayar, my brother, I have been feeling sick these last few weeks. I will come home to recover before returning to this green hell. Please give my love to our parents and friends."

This was the last letter in the pile. Ica wondered whether Cora made it home, and if so, where was she now?

She placed her hands on the stack of papers. All of them dealt with this terrible disease. Now she understood why Ayar remained in his room for days and weeks on end.

Below the pile of Ayar's notes she noticed the red cover of her notebook. He must have continued to work last night after she was gone. Suddenly she realized that what she had done, half dazed and shocked by her discovery, was less than decent. Ashamed to have gone through Ayar's work and still stunned by what she had learned, she grabbed her notebook and put Ayar's papers back into place.

"*Gracias,* Señora," she called out as she left the house.

"*De nada*, Señorita," came the response from the kitchen. "You are most welcome."

Ica walked back to her room, puzzled. Why would Ayar tackle such a difficult task? Why would he study such a little known disease? Yet, she understood why he wanted to combat it. She, too, had been seized by a sense of urgency as she wanted to help the young man in the bus. The thought of him suffering without help had never left her. In Ayar's case, the concern must be even deeper and long standing. She wondered about Ayar's sister. Why had he never mentioned her name?

The days and weeks passed quickly as Ica worked with Don Rodrigues, Victor, and sometimes Francisca, cataloguing herbs, learning about their healing powers and preparing herbal medicine for the poverty-stricken patients of Qoripampa and surrounding villages. With Don Rodrigues Ica began to discuss leishmaniasis more frequently and the need to find an herbal cure.

"I agree, we should put more effort into treating this devastating disease," he often said with concern. "Most patients with *espundia* are sent to the capital for a cure, but the hospitals are overcrowded and we should begin to cure them here. It's easier for those hospitals to get the modern medication than it is for us, but they, too, run out of it periodically." In a worried tone of voice he uttered, "The climate is changing. It's getting warmer and the sandflies start to occupy new and larger territories. They are coming closer." Walking over to Ica, he whispered, "Our Dr. Ayer has been at it for some time. He does research on the whole complex thing. With his talent and dedication he may find an herbal cure, sooner or later."

Ica began to find herself thinking more frequently about Ayar. Sometimes she felt a longing for him that she did not want to admit to herself, let alone to others. "Work comes first," she reminded herself over and over again.

Life in Qoripampa had been good so far. Ica found a deep sense of accomplishment working with Don Rodrigues, learning about herbal remedies and witnessing the successful treatment of patients. She also became acquainted with the joys and sorrows of village life. Food was never plentiful, but villagers were less affected by the harsh economic times than were the poor living in cities.

From time to time, the calm of village life was interrupted by news about the Shining Path movement that was spreading through Peru. As terrorist activities intensified in specific regions of the country, Ica received letters from family in northern Europe and from friends in California where she had moved with her parents two years before their deadly accident and where she had pursued most of her studies. Family and friends urged her to come home and so did the professors of her doctoral committee at the university. But she felt she could not possibly leave at a time when she was learning so much and feeling so comfortable among the people of Qoripampa. She assured family and friends abroad that neither her village, nor the province had yet become a target of terrorist activities.

Ica was intrigued every time visitors arrived at the Rodrigues' home from the high mountains. They told her about health and healing in their remote villages. One day Doña Nilda introduced her to Juana, José and Mateo who periodically left their high-altitude community of Ritipata to work for a while in the valley and to exchange alpaca wool, dried alpaca and llama meat, and freeze-dried potatoes for other produce. They told Ica about herbs that grew only at high altitude and ways of curing patients that were not widely known. Her wish to visit Ritipata which literally means the 'high snowy place', became stronger as she found out more about this region where people referred to themselves as the sons and daughters of the thunder god. On their next visit to the Rodrigues home, Juana and her nephews invited Ica to travel with them to their remote village.

"We will return to our *ayllu*, our village, our family, when the new week begins. Please come along," Juana suggested. "We will arrive in time for the ancient fiesta of Para Raymi." With an enthusiastic spark in her eyes she approached Ica, telling her in a barely audible voice, "It's a celebration in honor of the rain and other cosmic forces. We pray for the life force in the universe to rejuvenate itself, so it will flow with renewed energy and sustain all life. Please celebrate with us."

"You will like it," José told Ica in a whisper, then added, "People down here in the villages and towns call us *indios* because we live in earthen huts. They look down on us because our lives are simple and we own little. They say we are ignorant, but they are wrong." With his head held high, he added, "You will see, we know many things, important things which our ancestors taught us."

"I would love to visit your village," Ica said with enthusiasm, accepting the invitation.

Mateo proposed that Ayar come along. The others nodded in agreement, unaware that he was gone. They seemed to know him. Where was the connection, Ica wondered.

A week later, Ica was asked by her neighbors to join the dances in the village plaza that took place every Saturday night. Francisca agreed to accompany her to this event, although this kind of get-together had never been one of her priorities. She was much more interested in supporting peasant struggles for better living conditions in the villages within the province. But tonight would be an exception. In no time she was ready to go, with her face washed and her hair brushed. She had never gotten in the habit of wearing makeup or festive clothing.

Ica had set aside the clothes she found most attractive for the occasion and was ready to put them on when Doña Nilda entered.

"Be careful, young lady," she said, only half joking. "You are already too pretty for the boys in this village and many look at you with longing eyes. With these clothes you will attract even more of them."

"Francisca is pretty, I am not," Ica said laughing. "She looks like a princess with her pitch black hair, dark eyes and perfect complexion, while I look plainly common."

"You do not look common to the people here," Doña Nilda contradicted. "In fact you look....."

"Ravishing," Francisca added. "That's why Dr. Ayar has eyes only for you and no longer notices me or any other girl in the village."

"That's not what I've observed," Ica said with a smile. "But if you both think I should put my old clothes on to avoid any problems, I will do so." She threw a long green cotton dress over her body and combed her hair.

"Looking like this, neither of us will get a dancing partner," they joked, ready to join the neighbors for the dance.

At that moment they heard a knock on the door. Ica opened.

"Ayar," she called out with her mouth open in surprise, and her eyes sparkling as she saw him standing in the entrance.

He gave her and Francisca a polite hug. "I am back for a while. The university is on strike again, after just a few weeks in operation." He looked at Ica with a grin.

"Is this such a happy event?" she asked laughing, without showing her excitement about his arrival.

"Not really," Ayar answered. "But it was to be expected."

Francisca interrupted to say that she would go ahead to meet the neighbors who had been waiting.

"See you at the dance," Ica said, waving at her.

Ayar approached her. "I received a small grant for the research I proposed. We could do it together," he said with a flash in his eyes.

She reflected on the kind of research to which he was referring. Could it be about leishmaniasis, the dreaded *espundia*?

Ayar saw the questioning expression on her face and explained in an apologetic tone of voice, "I should have told you earlier about the work that has kept me in my room. Only visits to patients could bring me to leave it and ...." looking at her with affection, "... our short get-togethers."

He brought a chair and asked Ica to sit down, pulling up another one for himself. "Let me explain," he said in a soft tone of voice. "I've been working for years to find an affordable cure for terrible diseases called ...."

"I know," Ica interrupted. "The leishmaniases diseases, *uta* and the terrible *espundia*."

Ayar looked surprised.

"I'm sorry, I read your notes," Ica stammered. "The day you left I had to retrieve my notebook which I had forgotten in your room. I am sorry; I was overwhelmed and could not stop reading."

"Are you interested," Ayar said with his eyes sparkling. "We could make a great team."

"Let me think about it," Ica responded. "It would not be easy. Let's go to the dance, I promised I'd be there. Tell me more about your work later tonight."

They joined in the dance on the plaza. It lasted half through the night. *Huaynos*, love songs from Inca times, played by a band of six young villagers, accompanied their steps. Ica was surprised to see Ayar dance with enthusiasm and a kind of charm she had not noticed about him before. As they danced around the square, they were greeted by their fellow villagers, whose gestures revealed that they considered them valued members of the community.

Ica suggested they join Francisca and their neighbors for a chat and to exchange dancing partners from time to time for politeness sake, and to prevent gossip that they might be more than just friends and colleagues.

In the early morning hours the musicians packed away their instruments. Tired, yet energized, the dancers left the plaza.

"Let's talk about our work tomorrow," Ayar suggested.

"Oh, I must tell you something exciting," Ica remembered. "We are invited to join Juana and her nephews on their trip to Ritipata. We will leave early on Monday."

Ayar did not respond.

"Their village sounds intriguing," Ica resumed. "Their medicinal plants are unique, and these people know about ways of healing that don't seem to be known elsewhere. And there will be a great fiesta." She beamed with a contagious enthusiasm.

But Ayar was not thrilled. Instead his face became somber. "It's dangerous to go to the high mountains during the rainy season, very dangerous," he uttered in a tone of voice that clearly showed his disapproval.

"I promised Juana and her nephews that I would come with them," Ica asserted. "The fiesta must be very special. It's ancient and it sounds mysterious."

She stopped walking and looked into Ayar's eyes. "I must go with them, I promised."

"Don't go," he warned again. "The mountain sides are steep, landslides are frequent and these people's culture is very different. You may not like it and the altitude can make you sick in that village that reaches up to almost five thousand meters above sea level.

"If the doctor comes along, I'll be o.k.," Ica teased with a mischievous look on her face. But Ayar remained sour.

She was perplexed. Why would he act so contrary to his normal self? What was he afraid of? She knew that something was wrong, but Ayar gave no indication that he was willing to talk about it. They said good night in front of the Rodrigues home.

Early the next morning Ica made preparations for the trip. She bought enough provisions for herself and her companions and added some of Ayar's favorite foods in the hope that he would change his mind and come along. But he did not appear all day. In the late afternoon Victor discovered that he had been called to a neighboring village to attend to an ill child. He returned home after midnight.

At 3 a.m. he was still unable to sleep. Ica's excursion to Ritipata lay heavily on his mind. He knew that the inhabitants of the high villages are not very talkative in the presence of outsiders. But he was well aware that during the upcoming fiesta people would open up as they sang, danced and laughed for days on end, and they would be talking. If he came along, Ica would surely discover that this was the village where he was born. She would find out everything about him, about his ancestral roots, so deeply embedded in Ritipata. She would find out that he grew up in a tiny hut, where a family cooks, eats, and sleeps on an earthen floor, devoid of anything "civilized." He was not ashamed of it. He admired his parents and others for what they were and what they had done in their lives. But he shuddered thinking of Ica's reaction as she would witness a population arrested on the first step on the ladder to success as seen by an "advanced" society. In his country, a person's pedigree had to be devoid of the "primitive" in order to be accepted outside the village. He never used to worry what other people thought. He knew he could accomplish what he set out to do. But would Ica be able to accept his roots?

He thought back on his relationship with a fellow medical student from the city of Arequipa who ditched him the moment she found out that he came from a society of herders who lived in abject poverty. This episode meant nothing to him now. He was glad to be rid of this empty affair. But what if women thought alike when it came to this? He knew he would have to tell Ica the truth, once and for all. But the fear of losing her was terrifying. During the weeks he was gone, he had yearned for her every day. He needed her. He decided to meet her at dawn and perhaps, if he was lucky, she would remain in the valley. With this in mind he fell into a deep sleep.

Ritipata

Qoripampa awoke to another misty morning. Heavy clouds concealed the mountain peaks. It had rained all night and a light drizzle continued to fall on the water-logged soil. The wet and slippery path would make the ascent to Ritipata more difficult. But this did not disturb Juana and her nephews José and Mateo who arrived punctually at 4:30 a.m. at Don Rodrigues' house to load their two horses with the bags Ica had filled with provisions and gifts. They were happy to return to their mountain home after three weeks in the valley where Juana had been weaving for various families. José and Mateo had worked in the fields earning small wages.

Juana had seldom left her village and missed her familiar surroundings. José and Mateo were equally happy to return home in view of the upcoming fiesta. With the money they made in Qoripampa, they were able to buy for their families, neighbors and friends those special items they could not grow or obtain in their remote village. They would surprise them with bags of cabbage, sweet potatoes, carrots, onions, garlic, apples and corn for the *t'inpu*, the most delicious meal of the entire year. From the corn the women would make *chicha*, the beer that had already intoxicated their Inca ancestors and was still cherished by adults and by the deities receiving it in the form of an offering.

Ica was excited about this adventure to a place where healers, elders and shamans were said to still remember the wisdom of their ancestors. This fiesta should reveal much about the Andean people and their spiritual encounters with the cosmic forces.

She had not given up hope that Ayar would join them, or at least come to say good bye. What had started as a relationship involving work, had turned into friendship. She wanted to leave it at that, but lately her thoughts had frequently turned to him and his absence had become increasingly difficult. She tried to remind herself not to become too dependent on him and his presence while everything went well with her work and with the villagers who had accepted her in their midst. Nor could she completely erase the fear in the back of her mind that, like the man in her previous relationship, Ayar, too, might have a darker side to him. But for now she didn't want negative thoughts to interfere with her excitement in seeking ancient wisdom in a place where oral history was said to be preserved in its purest forms.

José and Mateo had loaded the horses. With an enthusiastic "*Hakuchis* - let's go," Juana set the pace for the journey. Along the way she became more talkative than she had been when Ica met her at the Rodrigues home. Short and slightly plump with several woven skirts around her waist and a heavy poncho against the rain, she walked astonishingly quickly, while talking to herself and to her companions. Ica listened with great interest to the sad and wonderful things that had happened in Juana's high village. She had given birth to five children. Three had survived and were living in Ritipata with their young families and their own small herds of llamas and alpacas. Her other two children were with Pachamama, the revered Earth Mother, and their spirits had soared to the Apus, those sacred mountain peaks. Juana was excited to introduce Ica to her village, her family, her animals and to the great Apus, which were so close and eternally watched over them.

In their late teens, José and Mateo were eager to play their instruments and participate in the songs and dances that would last throughout eight days and nights. Both were humming the ancient melody that was to accompany the entire fiesta.

As the group advanced, the path became steeper and soon disappeared in a field of newly accumulated debris. Much of the soil was waterlogged and ready to slide off the steep slopes. Ica's three travel companions did not seem worried by these conditions which occurred every year between October and April. The remaining months of the year were dry, but then the cold was almost insupportable.

The group approached the Puka Mayu, the Red River, which had turned into a raging stream. The water in the normally shallow crossing had become deep and turbulent. The horses refused to cross here and at several equally dangerous places further upstream. At one point a narrow bridge still spanned the river, but it no longer looked sturdy enough to hold the horses. Ica and her companions had no choice but to take the high route to Ritipata on a zigzag path along the steep side of Mount Chakata, by which they could eventually reach their destination without crossing the thundering torrent. But the journey would be longer and the path steeper. Juana felt what lay ahead for them was as good a reason as any to call for a picnic.

She offered cooked potatoes from her woven bag, while the boys distributed some of the bread they had bought, and Ica shared *tumbos*, *tunas* and *capulí*, delicious fruits that grew along the valleys during the rainy season. While eating quietly, everyone looked at the mountains above. In their rocky peaks Juana and the boys recognized the shapes of a petrified condor, a sleeping llama, a rabbit-like *viscacha* and a running puma. The local people believed that these rocky outcrops were as alive as Mother Earth, who always received the first few drops of any drink. Ica enjoyed the stories her companions told about these powerful relics within the landscape, some of which were believed fierce, others benevolent. Finally Juana cautioned that it was time to continue on their way to get home before dark.

The group advanced slowly as the path became more precipitous. Ica felt uneasy crossing the piles of debris left by fresh avalanches of earth and rocks. But José and Mateo did not seem to mind these obstacles, nor did they show signs of fatigue. Only Juana emitted a deep sigh from time to time, but she was happy for every step that brought them closer to their village.

At times the sun appeared between thick cumulus clouds. Soon much darker cloud formations moved across the peaks of the mountain range to the north. The horses stopped at intervals and nervously listened to sounds coming from fresh avalanches that were starting to form. Ica was unaware of these signs nature provided, but the animals seemed to understand them quite well. In turn, her companions knew the behavior of their horses, but in the excitement of the day did not pay attention. Although happy to be part of this adventure, Ica started to wonder about Ayar's warnings and his resistance to joining on this journey. Did he fear the unleashed powers of nature? And why hadn't he come to say goodbye?

But Ayar had sunk into a deep sleep after he had lain awake for many hours. It was almost 7 a.m. when he awoke. Through the window he saw the puddles which the rain had transformed into small lakes during the night. Hoping that the rains had delayed Ica's departure, he hurried to the Rodrigues' home only to find out that the group had already left. At the corner store he met two men who had just come down from the mountains. He inquired and was informed that they had seen a party of four people with two horses in the distance approaching the Chakata mountain range.

"Not good", they said. "People seldom take this route during the rainy season and only when the horses will not cross the river."

Ayar thanked the men in the dripping ponchos. Knowing the danger to which Ica and her companions had exposed themselves, he rushed back to his house, grabbed his emergency bag and a blanket and headed toward Ritipata. The thought that the group might be in trouble would not leave his mind. He wondered why Juana and her companions chose the high route along a treacherous mountain range that had taken so many lives in the past. The idea of losing Ica made him shudder. Since he first saw her in the cemetery on Todos Santos, he had been deeply attracted to her, but had managed to hide his feelings from others and had not admitted them even to himself. Her smile could melt ice fields and left him yearning. But he knew he could never expect her to love him.

He sighed, wishing she was as straight forward about her feelings for him as she was in all other matters. But then again, how honest was he? Was he not trying to hide his feelings and even his background and his ancestors, his very roots? He knew that Ritipata might solve his problem if he was lucky. But it could also put an end to all his hopes.

Hours passed. Ayar had arrived at the point where a narrow path led toward the treacherous Chakata mountain range and where the men in the ponchos had seen the group in the distance. Despite the steep terrain, he accelerated his pace as black clouds began to conceal the sun and it started to rain.

He hurried across the remains of fresh landslides obstructing the path, climbing higher and higher. But he saw no one.

Further uphill he was able to overlook the terrain as lightning brightened the sky. Thunder followed and a rainstorm broke loose. Through the pounding of the rain Ayar heard horses neigh in the distance. The group must be close, he thought, running faster with the rain beating his face. The horses neighed again, loud and nervous as he reached a bend in the path clustered with the debris of a fresh rock fall that had recently plunged down the mountainside. He climbed across it and saw Juana, José and Mateo in the distance, with Ica trailing behind.

Suddenly the horses reared up, desperate to turn around, but their human companions obstructed the narrow path that was cut into sheer rock. Ayar saw the earth begin to move on the steep hill, well above the group, first sluggishly, then faster.

"*Loqlla!*", he shouted. "Stop! A landslide!   Turn back?" He threw the heavy blanket he had carried with him under an overhanging rock and raced uphill.   Now the group was almost immediately below the moving earth with Ica still trailing behind.

"Turn back!" he shouted at the top of his voice. "A landslide!"

 Ica heard him. She stopped walking and looked up the hill. "*Lloqlla!*" she called out to her companions who were passing alongside a wall of rock that obstructed their view of the hill above them where the earth was moving.

"Come back immediately, all of you!" Ayar's voice sounded furious. He threw his bag on the ground and rushed forward, grabbing Ica by the arm, pulling her back down the path at high speed. The horses neighed in fear. Then their cries were overcome by the thundering landslide that tumbled across the cliff into the abominable depth of Yawar Q'asa, the Gorge of Blood, carrying the people and horses with them.

Ayar held Ica's hand as they raced down the path, pursued by mud and rocks. She tripped and lost her balance. Sliding toward the edge of the precipice, she reached for bushes and *ichu* grass. Ayar threw himself on the ground, grabbing her arm as she slid further toward the abyss. The mudflow that had caught up with them, transformed itself into an unstable platform that flowed along the path and over the edge of the cliff with both caught in it.

"Save yourself, Ayar. Let me go!" Ica cried.

Ayar spotted an elongated rock that protruded from the side of the path. He grabbed it with one hand, holding on to Ica with the other. Inch by inch he pulled himself closer to the rock. He felt Ica's strength failing and with a powerful movement lifted her back onto the path and on her feet.

Holding on to one another they slid down the muddy path, finally coming to a stop at a rock outcrop with an overhang. Within the outcrop they found a small cave. Exhausted they entered, moved toward a platform of stone, and collapsed upon it. "*Gracias*," Ica whispered, "*Gracias*."

"Thank you for being alive," Ayar answered with a smile of relief. Soaking wet, plastered with mud, cold, exhausted, and shivering, Ayar knew that Ica required quick treatment against shock and hypothermia. But the emergency bag with his medicine, thermos and dry clothes had been taken by the deadly flow of mud and stones.

There was no way he could start a fire for warmth, or offer a hot drink. Then he remembered the blanket. He ran out of the cave and down the path and there it was, still dry under the small rocky shelter where he had left it.

Rushing back to the cave he urged Ica to take off her wet clothes and wrap herself into the blanket. He quickly spread a pile of dry grass that lay in the corner of the cave across a platform of stone, placed the blanket on top, and went outside. Being used to high altitude and harsh weather conditions, he remained less affected by the ordeal.

Within minutes he returned. Ica's wet, muddy clothes lay in a pile on the cave floor. She had wrapped the blanket around her and lay on the thin mattress of grass atop the large flat stone. Her skin was pale and cold, her breathing was shallow and her pulse was faint. She shivered and her body was unable to warm itself.

"Sorry, Ica, there's no other way," Ayar said in an apologetic tone of voice, as he threw off his outer clothes and slipped into the blanket with her. Pressing her shaking body against his, he hoped that his body heat would give her back the temperature she needed to stay alive. He wrapped part of the blanket around her head and neck to retain as much body heat as possible and rubbed her cold limbs.

In a faint voice Ica asked for Juana, José and Mateo.

"They are fine," Ayar answered, kissing her forehead. He knew that she had to stay awake until her body temperature had returned to normal and she was beyond danger. To distract her, he told amusing stories about the comic side of the Andean world. Eventually they both fell asleep.

When the dim light of the early morning entered the rock shelter, Ayar looked at Ica resting peacefully in his arms. Her hair that matched the color of the yellow *ichu* grass of the dry season, lay across her forehead and partially covered her attractive features. He was seized by a feeling of love of a kind he had never experienced before. He wanted to embrace her with all his passion and tell her how much he loved her. But he knew that this was not the right time. Cautiously he slipped out of the blanket and stepped outside, greeting the warming rays of the sun. He put on his trousers and placed the rest of their clothes on the branches of nearby bushes to dry. Below him he saw the precipitous slopes of Yawar Q'asa, the Gorge of Blood, which had taken its toll of travelers throughout the decades and where he and Ica would be resting now close to their travel companions if luck had not been on their side.

Ica awoke. Exhausted but relieved, she greeted Ayar with an enticing smile, putting her arms around his neck as he bent down to kiss her forehead.

"You are extraordinary," she whispered. "How on earth did you keep from slipping down the cliff?"

"Magic," Ayar responded with a triumphant expression in his dark eyes.

Then her face took on a more serious expression. "We must see how Juana, José, and Mateo are doing. What if they did not find a shelter?"

"We will look for them," Ayar interrupted, still not ready to release the truth that could put her back into a state of shock. He stepped out to bring her the rain water that had collected in a hollowed out stone by the path.

"You are amazing," Ica gasped from within her blanket. The water tasted good and so did the grains of *quinua* and amaranth he took from his pocket, soaking wet from last night's rain.

Ayar stepped out, allowing Ica to put on her clothes which he had brought back still slightly moist and muddy. They walked uphill. But they did not get far. The path above the shelter was too slippery to advance. Higher up it was obstructed by piles of mud and rock. The whole area looked unstable and ready to move again.

Ayar turned to Ica, "We must go back on the same path that took us up here yesterday."

She wanted to contradict, but he gently put his hand over her mouth. Hesitating for a moment, he uttered with sadness, "I must confess something ..... I could not tell you yesterday ..... Your travel companions........" He hesitated again, gazing into the gorge.

"Do you mean ...?" Ica asked, grasping his arm in despair.

Ayar held her tight. "I could not tell you yesterday, you were in shock."

Ica took a step back. "We should have looked for them right away," she objected in an anxious tone of voice.

He pointed to the gorge below the steep precipice. "No one could survive this, but we must look for remains in case the avalanche has left a trace."

Ica began to cry. She remembered how exuberant her friends were at the prospect of returning home for the greatest fiesta of the year, when the whole village would come together celebrating in solidarity.

Holding on to one another they silently walked downhill on the waterlogged path, trying not to slide sideways toward the menacing gorge. Ica's sobbing was subdued by the squeaking sounds of their wet and muddy shoes that released drops of water with every step.

"Look," Ayar sighed as they reached the bottom of the gorge. "Look at this."

They scanned the masses of fresh debris that had thundered from the heights the previous night. There were no signs of people, animals or belongings.

Ayar looked at Ica, wondering whether she should return home after last night's terrifying experience.

"Can you walk all the way to Ritipata?" he asked. "It will take many hours."

Ica nodded silently, looking at the deadly site with tears in her eyes.

He, too, knew that there was no alternative. They had to keep going to bring the sad news to the families of the deceased.

Overwhelmed by the tragedy of her companions, Ica continued to cry as they climbed up the path, and then carefully crossed a narrow bridge made of branches, rocks and grass that was still standing and brought them safely to the other side of the river. Ayar was filled with sadness as well. Yet, hoping to help her cope more easily, he explained death to her the way his people saw it.

"Juana and the boys now rest safely in the womb of Pachamama, our Earth Mother. She gives us life, nurtures us throughout our existence and takes us back when our time has come." Hugging Ica with tenderness, he continued, "While our bodies rest with her, our spirits soar to the sacred Apus, the mountain gods, which are Pachamama's highest peaks. There the condors wait. They carry our spirits to a different dimension of existence. Then eventually we return to this earth for yet another experience."

He looked at Ica with love. "We are all caught in this eternal cycle of life and death. Death will come eventually to all of us, but let's think of life now."

A faint smile crossed her face as she reached for his hand. "Thank you, Ayar. I think I understand."

They arrived at a site with ancient ruins that caught Ica's attention. The remains of houses, towers and plazas were partially hidden by underbrush. The aroma of herbs was strong and calming.

"The Wari people, our ancestors who preceded the Incas lived and worked here," Ayar explained. "Look at the stone masonry! It's exquisite, different from that of the Incas, but equally pleasing." He touched the walls. "They used smaller stones than the Incas. Yet, they too have lasted for centuries."

Ica walked to the irrigation canals. "How could people build so well in such precipitous places," she wondered. In awe she pointed to the ruins. "This must have been a small town with differently shaped buildings – square, rectangular and round. It's amazing. And the place must have been provided with water all year round."

"Eventually the Wari were conquered by the Incas who added their own structures," Ayar explained. "We will see those higher up."

Fascinated by the enigmatic relics in stone, they talked about the civilizations that had preceded today's society. Then they arrived at a site where terraces wound up the hills. Most of them were in decay and overgrown by vegetation. They noticed the remains of a network of irrigation canals not far from the terraces. Through the vegetation they saw large polished stones strewn across wide level areas, reminiscent of plazas. An imposing gate rose above the shrubs and trees, perfectly constructed and relatively intact.

"This is what the Incas left us," Ayar said in a proud tone of voice.

"It's amazing," Ica uttered. "Your ancestors were amazing."

"You will see more of what they left behind, higher up, closer to the mountain peaks," he said, content to see her enthusiasm return.

They sat down on one of the pink stones, polished to a luster.

"Was this one of the summer residences of an Inca emperor?" Ica wondered.

"Perhaps. Or it belonged to one of the Qoyas, the empresses," Ayar responded. "The Qoyas had their own lands and properties. They also ruled and were as important as the Inca emperors. Our elders have learned from oral accounts that the Qoyas were often remembered with greater appreciation than the Inca emperors themselves."

"That's extraordinary!" Ica exclaimed laughing. "Why has so much changed?"

"Things have changed little in places such as Ritipata," Ayar asserted. "You will see. There the women still make most decisions, either together with their husbands or alone. Just as Pachamama is honored every day, the females of our species have been held in high esteem." Looking fondly at Ica, he added, "After all, it's the female essence that counts."

"I'm glad you recognize this," she responded teasingly.

She was overwhelmed by the beauty of the landscape she viewed from her polished throne of stone. The silence of this pristine place was interrupted only by the murmuring of the river as it moved through its overflowing bed in the gorge below. The rivulets that joined the river's course from various directions added their own sounds as did the chirping birds in trees and bushes, and the insects humming their tunes. In the distance several slim waterfalls sparkled like silver threads against the sheer rocks from which they tumbled. Snow-capped peaks lined the horizon, contrasting with the blue sky of summer.

Spellbound by this other worldly setting, Ica began to daydream, imagining what those people were like before the conquerors destroyed their society. As she scanned the landscape thinking of times long gone, she noticed that Ayar also seemed to daydream as he looked far into the distance. Seated on a stone, finely polished by his ancestors, he had an air of royalty about him. His high cheek bones, slightly aquiline nose, his intelligent and sophisticated facial expression and his athletic stature made him, in Ica's mind, look like an ancient ruler, perhaps the Sapa Inca, the great ruler himself. As she admired his profile, he turned and their eyes met. He smiled at her with those dark eyes that were sometimes kind, and then serious, teasing or mischievous, but always full of mystery.

Not admitting what she was daydreaming about, she said in a nonchalant way, "Not a bad place to build a palace. I think I could stay here forever."

"So could I," Ayar responded laughing. "But night will fall soon and Ritipata is not yet in sight."

They drank water from one of the nearby springs and tasted the *qochayuyu*, the algae washed down by rivulets from a high mountain lake. Ica grimaced given its unfamiliar taste, but she chewed and swallowed all of it, following Ayar's advice about the nutritional value of this sacred plant.

"It will be offered during fiestas," he said. "You will get to like it."

Refreshed and energized, they advanced at a faster pace toward their destination, close to the permanent snow. Llamas and alpacas now appeared from all directions. They lifted their heads, looking at the newcomers in a curious and seemingly arrogant way. Protective of their newborns, they let no one come close.

Ayar and Ica had thus far not met anyone on their way. As dusk began to lay a grayish veil across the landscape, they arrived on the outskirts of Ritipata. A few local people crossed their way. They greeted Ayar with great respect, while welcoming Ica to their village. Why do people know him, she asked herself.

Then her thoughts suddenly plunged back to the terrible tragedy of her companions. For part of the ascent they both managed to keep the terrifying experience at bay, captivated by the enigmas of the past. Now the tragic memories returned with full force.

They entered the village center that consisted of a small plaza surrounded by one-storey buildings. In the dusk they saw an athletic man walking toward them from one of the adobe houses. Somewhere in his forties, with a dignified face and surprised expression, he greeted the newcomers, welcoming them by touching their shoulders with outstretched arms.

"Ayar," he said. "How good to see you after such a long time." Looking at Ica, he added, "And thanks for bringing this charming young lady. Please stay with me and my family." Pointing to his little house close to the plaza, he said in a slightly apologetic tone of voice, "We still reside in the same place and now we have two young children."

"Thanks so much, *compadre* Julian," Ayar responded. "We accept your offer with pleasure." He introduced Don Julian to Ica, explaining that Julian's combined talents as community leader and healer make him invaluable to the village.

Ica and Ayar were happy with the warm welcome and relieved to remain in the village center after their exhausting ascent. There was no need to continue to the higher regions where the majority of the people lived. This kind of village, made up of dispersed settlements, suited a society of pastoralists, since it gave enough grazing space to each family's herd.

They entered the small earthen home. It consisted of a single room, lit by a lonely candle. An earthen stove in the corner provided warmth and its flames added light to that of the candle. Ica noticed several stools arranged around a low table. At its side she saw a basket with an assortment of pots, plates, dishes and cups. Shelves attached to the adobe walls contained the few necessities the family used in their daily lives. Along the far wall, a mattress lay on a low frame stacked with several blankets and alpaca hides. The smell of burning eucalyptus branches came from the open fire. Ica's face lit up as she noticed small groups of guinea pigs which busied themselves shuffling eucalyptus leaves from one corner of the room to another.

Don Julian introduced Ica to his wife Juanita and their two young daughters, who received their visitors with welcoming smiles. Juanita talked to Ayar like to an old friend. The children remained shy, but were curious about the visitors. Looking at both guests the hostess said laughing, "You arrived right on time. The soup just came to a boil."

They ate silently, giving thanks to the Earth Mother who had provided the treasured potatoes for their meal.

After supper, seeing that Ica could hardly keep her eyes open, Doña Juanita brought alpaca blankets to make the beds for her guests on the floor, close to the fireplace that still emitted some warmth before the cold of the night was to arrive. Ica thanked Juanita in Quechua or *runa simi*, the 'language of the people,' that had been spoken since Inca times and still persisted across the Andean highlands. She had started to learn it in California and knew it well enough to make herself understood. But she was far from mastering this complex language.

After the devastating experience of the previous night, and the long ascent, Ica fell asleep at once. Ayar continued to talk to his hosts who were shocked to hear about the fate of Juana, José, and Mateo. He and Julian decided to leave immediately to bring the sad news to the families of the deceased.

A Secret Revealed

In the pitch dark of night Don Julian and Ayar walked for almost two hours through the precipitous terrain up to where Juana had built a small earthen house many years ago. In the beam of Ayar's flashlight, they found the entrance door and knocked. The dogs were the first to answer with agitated barks. Then the door opened and the visitors were welcomed with a surprised look followed by *imaynallan kashanki*, a warm and enthusiastic welcome. Several members of Juana's extended family had assembled to organize the activities for the upcoming fiesta.

"What brings you here so late in the evening?" Leandra, one of Juana's daughters asked.

"We cannot bring you good news tonight," Don Julian said with sorrow.

Everyone looked at him in surprise.

"All news must be good with the fiesta starting tomorrow," José and Mateo's father said with a smile.

Ayar knew that it was his task to destroy the joy of the evening with the tragic news. He hesitated, then with deep sadness told about the devastating events of the previous night. The family members listened, becoming stiff and motionless, unable to utter a word. Juana's youngest daughter Alicia started to cry quietly. Sobbing she mumbled, "Our mama has joined our papa."

Leandra, her older sister, comforted her and Juana's grandchildren who sat quietly on the floor crying. After some time Leandra said in a shaking voice, "Tomorrow we will honor the spirits of our mama, of José and Mateo, so they will be free to soar to the Apus." She waved her hand toward the east, acknowledging the deities.

José and Mateo's parents had remained silent, frozen in place. Finally, with a hoarse voice, the father addressed the visitors who had brought the sad news.

"Thank you Don Julian. Thank you Dr. Ayar, for telling us where our sons are resting. We will go there to honor Pachamama and the spirits of our sons, so they may rest in peace."

The boys' mother sobbed. She looked through the narrow window into the night whispering, "Apus, you sacred mountains, why did your condors call them so soon? Illapa, mighty god of thunder, why did you bring the heavy rains that moved the earth. Why? Why?" She continued to sob.

Her husband put his arms around her as he said, "We will mourn tonight, and again when the fiesta is over, but after the sun sets tomorrow, we must be happy. If sorrow fills the cosmos during the fiesta, sorrow will rule the coming year."

The adults nodded, knowing only too well that the laws of the universe may not be tampered with. Ayar knew that he had to inform Ica as well, so she, too, would hide her pain during the fiesta.

Ayar and Don Julian took their leave with their hearts aching. They arrived home after midnight.

The next morning after breakfast, Don Julian, Doña Juanita and their two children took their guests to collect special items needed for the rituals that would begin that night. They selected them in accordance with the degree of life force they contained. Juanita led the way to a number of isolated places, close to the permanent snow, to clear springs, to sacred mountain lakes. Special stones, flowers, and crystalline water that had just seeped from the earth, were among the most powerful ritual ingredients. Juanita's seven year old daughter Sabina found a small stone that resembled a condor. She ran to Ica holding the tiny treasure in her outstretched hand.

"This is for you, so luck will be with you always," she said with a gracious smile.

Ayar asked Ica to come with him while the others continued their search for the treasured items. Sitting on a cool stone beside a gurgling spring, he held Ica's hand, looking at her with affection.

"You have been so quiet. I know your sorrow returned last night when we entered this village where your companions once lived."

Ica nodded, remaining silent as Ayar spoke to her, "Their families understood and they mourned when they heard the sad news, but starting tonight and throughout the fiesta they will show happiness."

Ica looked surprised as Ayar explained, "You must know that the fiesta that starts tonight is most important to the people of our villages. Our ancestors taught us that through our thoughts, our feelings, our movements, we all are connected with one another and with everything in the cosmos. Sometimes the energy that moves through the cosmos dissipates, especially now when the rains are heavy. Then we must honor the deities with a fiesta that will replenish the cosmos with all the good energy it needs, energy that heals, that inspires, that gives joy, the energy of love."

Ica nodded.

Ayar continued, "This positive energy which we call *enqa* or *sami*, is the force that is needed to sustain all life. Rocks and many other things, including ourselves, absorb and reflect this energy that connects all and everything. Therefore our thoughts and feelings must be positive, happy, and harmonious."

Then Ayar told about the power of the mind, the power of one's thoughts and feelings that must be expressed in a focused way during the rituals of the night to achieve luck and well being for all. Moving closer to Ica he whispered, "The ancients believed that the combined mental power of tens of thousands of pilgrims who congregate every year on the snow fields of Qoyllur Rit'i is so strong that it can chase away negative energies and allow the constellation of the Pleiades, that had disappeared, to move back into the sky."

Ica looked perplexed. "We must go to Qoyllur Rit'i," she said with deep emotion.

"We will," Ayar answered, holding her hands and pulling her to her feet.

Before dusk they arrived at Juanita's and Julian's home where the children became increasingly excited about the fiesta. Too young to participate in all the rituals and understand the full meaning of the ceremonies, they still indulged in the excitement of it all.

Night fell quickly. After supper family and guests sat down by the fire and the dim light of candles. Juanita brought each person a ceramic bowl, used only in this ceremony, filled with the crystalline water that had been collected from various springs. With gestures denoting a ritual cleansing, everyone dipped their fingers into their bowl. Now purified, Julian took a woven bag with intricate geometric symbols and filled with coca leaves from its secret hiding spot known only to husband and wife.

Coca leaves made the round. These leaves were considered sacred even before the Incas ruled. Ica knew that the vitamins, minerals and calcium they contained were important to the limited diet of the high Andes. Now she learned that they had another significant role as intermediaries between people and the realm of the sacred.

Each person in the circle fashioned coca *k'intus*, small bouquets consisting of three perfect coca leaves, green side up. Ica remembered receiving a *k'intu* from a passenger in the bus the day she arrived in Qoripampa, so she could appease the thunder god. Now she heard the adults whisper their wishes as they held the tiny bouquets toward the east, blowing on each one before placing it in the middle of the room upon a sheet of white paper that rested on a special woven cloth, serving as *mesa*, or ritual table. Among the Apus, which were central to this ritual, the name of the highest in their midst, the mighty 6384 meters tall Ausangate, was addressed most frequently with a *k'intu* and asked for favors. The power of this and other snow-covered mountains with their life-sustaining snow fields had been revered since time immemorial, long before the Incas made their appearance. Ancient songs testified to the close ties between the people and their mountain gods.

"Concentrate on your wishes," Ayar urged Ica in a whisper.

She remembered the advice he had given earlier by the side of the spring, "Our thoughts and feelings flow with the energies of the universe. If emitted in good faith, the cosmic energies return to us, bringing health and happiness. So we must concentrate deeply on everything that is good.

Through our mind our very being is connected with the force that creates and sustains life."

Ica felt as though she were in a trance. The rituals appeared to take place behind a dense layer of smoke. She was over-taken by happiness of a kind she could not explain. She observed as Juanita took the sacred items from the well guarded woven bag. They had been with the family for generations. Sea shells appeared, then gourds which she put on the *mesa*.

Now the items collected on this and previous days, among them special stones and piles of *phallcha* flowers that grow close to the permanent snow, took their special places on the *mesa* close to the old family treasures.

Finally Julian opened the *unkuña*, a special cloth that con-tained the most sacred items, the *enqaychu*. These effigies in stone represent alpacas, llamas, other animals and plants whose *enqa*, or life force, is necessary for the survival of people and animals alike. Only when the vital energy of the *enqaychu* is replenished during the ritual, will the coming year be good. Ica sensed anxiety within the group. She wanted to contribute to the offering and started to place her small stone condor on the *mesa*. But Sabina cautioned to keep it hidden in her pocket.

"It's for you, only for you," she insisted in a whisper.

Ica put it back in her pocket, smiling at the little girl.

Now everyone focused on the white sheet that would soon contain the offering to be burned. Julian added a handful of carnation blossoms to the coca *k'intus* which had been placed there by the group. The dark red carnation blossoms were dedicated to Pachamama, the white ones to the thunder god.

The seeds of the coca plants were added to bring luck. Thin gold- and silver-colored paper and threads of yarns, symbolizing prosperity, were placed beside the seeds. Hoping for many alpacas and llamas, lots of tiny grains of *quinua*, landed on the paper. Sweets, believed to be special treats for the deities, and the pure fat of an alpaca, symbolizing the life force, were carefully added to the offering.

With all the items in place, more coca *k'intus* were offered to the deities and to the *enqaychu* which were believed to communicate directly with the gods who endowed them with renewed life force.

Juanita opened a ceramic container in the form of a large vase. It was full of *chicha*. She took a cup, filled it and threw the precious liquid to the east in honor of the gods. Then all adults spilled drops of the sacred drink on the floor, dedicating it specifically to Pachamama. Using thumb and forefinger, they sprinkled it into the air in honor of the Apus, the thunder god, and all the deities in the cosmos which affected their lives. The four corners of the *mesa* and the *enqaychu* received frequent blessings as they were showered with *chicha*.

Ica was puzzled. She knew these items had strong symbolic significance, if only she could understand the whole story they told. Each of the items seemed to represent a different element, an ecological zone, or time period. Together they represented the duality of forces – old and new, high and low, life and death. Coming from different ecological zones and the four cardinal directions, she knew they would reveal something about Tawantinsuyu, the four regions of the Inca Empire.

After midnight the offering on the white sheet of paper was wrapped and burned outdoors in a cave-like depression in the animals' sacred corral. From there the smoke rose to the heights of the mountains, bringing thanks to the gods and appeasing them, so they would help protect people and animals for yet another cycle of seasons. Ica was relieved that her ignorance had apparently not upset the gods, or else the offering could not have released the smoke for the deities. She felt a tremendous desire to understand what lay behind the symbolic complexity of the rituals. But she knew, it might take her a lifetime to gain insight into the ideology represented in those ancient ritual practices.

With the deities content, people relaxed. But the cosmic forces were not yet fully satisfied and would receive more offerings, libations, music and dance over the next eight days.

The children were fast asleep on their alpaca furs as Julian began to play a pentatonic tune. He then handed his flute to Ayar, who also played the same ancient melody that predated their Inca ancestors. They drank more *chicha*, the nutritious beer that Juanita had made from the corn for which she had bartered in the valley.

Don Julian faced Ayar across the circle where everyone sat on woven blankets spread upon the floor. In a nostalgic tone of voice he addressed Ayar, "We are very grateful to your ancestors."

Juanita nodded her head.

Then Julian began to reveal what had happened long ago, when he himself had been a young lad, strong, healthy and daring. But one day he was attacked by a disease that started to consume his life force. He looked at Ayar as he explained, "At the brink of my death your father came to see me. He visited me every day to call my soul back from the journey it had begun to take to the world beyond."

Looking at Ica, Julian confided, "Ayar's father gave me potent brews he made from a variety of herbs. He appeased the deities and called the spirits of our ancestors. I survived, I got married and here we are with two children." He smiled at Juanita with great satisfaction.

She added with a deep sigh, "We owe so much to your family, Ayar, so much."

"Did your parents live right here in Ritipata," Ica asked in surprise.

Remaining silent, Ayar stared on the floor, moving coca leaves in a circular motion between his hands.

"Yes," Juanita answered. They lived high up at the foot of Apu Uturunku until ....." She wiped tears from her eyes, unable to disclose more about their deaths. Then she resumed, "We remember them with love as does everyone in this village. They always helped the sick." Looking back at Ica, she continued, "Both were *altomesayoq*, those shamans and healers of the highest order. They were able to cure many local diseases, yet they knew little about the dreadful one which our young people brought from the jungle regions where they went to work during times of hunger."

Julian looked at Ica and continued, "I learned so much from his parents. After they were gone, Ayar lived with us for a few years. He was a great boy. He climbed the highest mountains. He played the flute and drum like no one else. He danced and sang and he followed in the footsteps of his parents. He became a healer."

"Please tell me more," Ica pleaded.

Juanita resumed. "After his only sister, the beautiful Cora, died, Ayar was heartbroken for a long time. No one knew how to cure the terrible disease she had brought from the jungle. We call it *espundia*. Some call it the white leprosy, but it is not leprosy.

"I know," Ica interrupted. "It's leishmaniasis."

"Yes, it was sad," Juanita deplored. "At the end Cora had a hard time breathing and could barely see any more. The face of this beautiful young woman had been eroding. All this, just to help us subsist as the harvests failed on our land and the animals died during times of drought."

Julian took a deep breath as he added, "She also wanted to save money so Ayar, her younger brother, could study medicine as he grew up, so he could help others."

Juanita shook her head in dismay as she recounted, "Cora had been hired for next to nothing washing gold in the jungle. This has also happened to many others who worked there. They returned sick from this green hell as they still do today."

Ayar remained silent, covering his face with his hands.

"He was about fourteen years old when his sister was buried," Juanita disclosed, "And he was determined to learn how to cure this dreadful disease. So he left us to live in the valley."

Ayar had been staring motionless on the floor, moving the dispersed coca leaves into small piles.

"But we must think about the happy side of life," Julian suggested in a spirited tone of voice. "Please, Ayar, sing for us. Who knows when you will return to visit us again?"

Ayar felt frozen in place. Everything had happened the way he had feared it would. Without meaning harm, his good friends had given him away.

As Julian started to play the flute, Ayar remembered an old legend that reached back to Inca times. It had been a custom then that the most beautiful girls from the four corners of Tawantinsuyu, the Inca Empire, would become Virgins of the Sun. They dedicated their lives to the gods and the Inca nobility. It was dangerous for any commoner to fall in love with a beautiful girl who assumed such a high status. He would arouse the anger of the gods and the Inca emperor himself.

"It will be the song of the thunder god," Ayar decided.

Julian hesitated for an instant. Then he quietly played the haunting melody. Ayar sang the story of a young herder who was in love with a beautiful girl. She was so beautiful that Illapa, the god of thunder and lightning, became jealous. On the day before a great fiesta, the young herder ventured with his flock to the mountain peak Choqilla to pick flowers for his love with which to adorn herself and make wreaths to embellish her animals.

Singing and whistling, his arms full of flowers and his heart full of joy, he began the long descent. He decided that during the fiesta he would dare to ask his beloved to live with him forever, until Pachamama would take them back into her womb, and their spirits would ascend to the lofty peaks of their mountain world. As he passed the black lagoon Yanaqocha, thick clouds formed over the mountain peaks, coming closer at a threatening speed. Lightning flashed through the clouds, followed by a deafening roar. The thunderbolt hit the young herder. He fell to the ground, only to awaken as the sun was setting behind the snow covered peaks.

He bent down to wash his hands and face in the lagoon, but the mirror-like surface of the water did not reflect his former image. The lightning had disfigured him to where he could no longer recognize himself. He was seized by disbelief and terror. He collected the flowers, dispersed by the lightning across the muddy ground. Looking back into the lagoon, he hoped this had been a dream. But the reflection on the water showed the same distorted image. A tremendous longing to run to the valley to hold his beloved struggled with his fear that she would reject him. He hesitated. As his herd had disappeared in the haze of the evening far below in the valley, he climbed uphill toward the snow-covered peaks. He walked until his spirit left his body to continue on its own the journey to the highest peak where the condors waited. There in the realm of his ancestors he was to roam eternally, longing for his beloved to join him.

At the end of the song there was silence. Although Ica had not understood all the words Ayar sang in the Quechua language, she had felt the deep emotion of the singer who, like the unfortunate shepherd, seemed tormented by something she could not understand. She felt the strong magnetism that radiated from his presence, but there was something else, something that was difficult to decipher.

Challenging the Thunder God

Ayar could not sleep that night, worried by his friends' revelation. He looked across the room where he could barely discern Ica's silhouette, as she slept close to the children by the earthen stove that still emitted some warmth. He knew she had discovered earlier that he was known in Ritipata. But that he was actually a product of a society arrested at the initial stages of a long haul to modernity, must have been a shock to her, as it was to other outsiders he had met in his life.

It also dawned on him that in his despair of losing her, he had sung a sad legend at a time when happiness had to reign in the cosmos to assure a good year for everyone. How could he have forgotten that the thoughts and feelings that flow during the fiesta had repercussions for the entire year? He admired Ica for hiding her grief about the death of her travel companions in order to make the fiesta a success. He had asked her to think in positive terms, but then he himself had acted against his own advice and the beliefs of his people and against the laws of the cosmos.

As dawn crept through the narrow windows, he was determined to live up to his promise and to help create a pleasant atmosphere for all. He would be positive throughout the fiesta despite his doubts and fears. He would enjoy everything that was offered and give all he had to make this fiesta a success.

Juanita had started a fire in the earthen stove. Soon the aromatic odor of freshly burned eucalyptus wood permeated the small hut awakening those who still slept. The two little girls helped peel tiny potatoes, as well as *oca* and *ulluku*, other delicious Andean tubers. Isidora, just five years old, brought water from the spring and soon a meal was prepared, as they added a small amount of alpaca meat and garlic. Julian offered a bowl of soup to each person.

"You must eat well," Juanita advised her guests in a cheerful voice. You will have to dance all day and through the night to satisfy Pachamama."

After the meal the dogs and cats eagerly consumed the left over soup, while the guinea pigs emerged from the four corners of the kitchen and gnawed happily on potato peels.

"It's our turn to wash dishes," Ica said laughing as she pulled Ayar to his feet.

"My favorite activity," he responded teasingly. He placed the dirty dishes into a large bowl and they left for the nearest spring.

When they returned to the house they saw Juanita stand by the door with an elderly man. Don Apaza had come by horseback from a far off corner of the village. His wife had broken her arm as she fell into a creek bed. With Julian working on his fields, Juanita borrowed two horses from a neighbor for Ayar and Ica and off they went with Don Apaza, taking along the plaster Juanita provided to set the woman's arm.

The elderly couple lived still higher, where the mountain sides were barren and the llamas had to travel far to get sufficient nutrition. Yet these people loved their mountain wilderness and did not mind that they only occasionally met with other villagers.

The horses galloped up the hills and within less than an hour the group arrived at Don Apaza's place. His wife was happy to see them come so fast. When Ayar was done setting her broken limb, she complimented him on his expertise.

"I'm sure you learned this from your parents," she said with a smile. "We still miss them so much." Looking at Ica, she added, "They were powerful healers, very, very powerful."

She thanked the doctors profusely for their much appreciated help. They, in turn, wished her a speedy recovery. With gratitude they accepted her gift of a bag of delicious freeze-dried *moraya* potatoes, and off they went.

The horses seemed to enjoy the outing as much as their riders. Ica loved galloping through a landscape where the mountain sides took on different shades of red, brown, yellow and purple, depending on the minerals in the soil and the way the sun touched them. With Ayar by her side she raced along the line of the permanent snow and descended into gorges where bushes and small trees could find enough earth to grow. Both wanted to ride to distant places in the refreshing wind that blew from the mountain peaks. But it was time to return to Ritipata to join in the young villagers' dances.

Back at their friends' home, Juanita showed Ica a splendid woven outfit of many colors with intricate geometric symbols woven into the cloth. "Please wear it during the fiesta. I wove it myself," she said smiling with pride. She handed Ayar a festive poncho with different but equally intriguing Inca symbols, her wedding gift for Julian.

They looked exquisite, Ayar in the poncho, a woven cap with earflaps, called *ch'ullu*, traditional black woven pants and a belt of fine wool in a myriad of colors arranged around his waist. He smiled at Ica who proudly wore her colorful garb consisting of several woven black skirts with patterns along the hem, a blouse and jacket, a flat hat, and a finely woven *lliklla*, the kind of shawl that had also been worn by Inca queens.

Soon the mountains resonated with the joyful laughter and animated calls of people in a festive mood. Proudly they walked to the dance atop Puka Orqo, the Red Peak. They greeted one another with elegant gestures and well chosen words. Ayar was at the center of attention. He had not been forgotten despite his years of absence. Ica received a warm welcome and people thanked her for coming from so far to join in their celebrations.

The pentatonic music from ancient times, the melodies of *huaynos* and *haravis* and dances that had hardly changed in hundreds of years, created an atmosphere that resonated of another world remote in space and time. The people moved and spoke with a very special elegance which Ica had never seen in the valley.

Enchanted by this gathering, intoxicated by the music, by the rhythmic movements of the crowd, and a feeling of love and understanding, Ica and Ayar danced throughout the evening and into the night. On each of the next six days and nights the young people danced in different regions of their mountain world. Then they visited their elders in their small houses dispersed throughout the countryside, wishing them health, happiness, luck and prosperity.

On the seventh day of the fiesta the dances were held right by the snow-covered Apu Illapa, the Thunder Mountain. It was well known that the thunder god had selected this region in which to play his wildest games, by tormenting his inhabitants and the dancers who dared to confront him with a defiant show of courage. And courage was exactly what the young people wanted to display as they tried to impress the opposite sex in the hope of finding a partner for life. In a world so full of challenges, courage was a much esteemed characteristic of both males and females. This was so when the Incas roamed the high mountains and it had not changed in this remote community.

In the afternoon Ayar and Ica arrived at the dancing grounds, close to Apu Illapa's line of permanent snow. They were greeted by elders standing in a circle around an altar of stone. Behind them, just above the snow-covered peaks, a rainbow spanned the sky in an arch of splendid colors.

"This is magnificent," Ica marveled.

But for her companions, this phenomenon of nature had different, more somber connotations. It spelled danger, an omen that could not be ignored. But on this occasion, no one would leave this sacred site where nature presented itself in spectacular, yet dangerous ways.

Dancers from different sectors of the dispersed community greeted one another with great respect and began to dance to the sounds of flutes. Haunting echoes returned from the surrounding peaks. The monotonous tunes of this celebration had endured for centuries, perhaps millennia. Soon they mixed with the laughter of the dancers who moved in honor of the earth and the mountains that fed and protected them and provided the life-sustaining water. Yet, these deities displayed dual personalities as they were also known to destroy the very grounds they protected by bringing earthquakes, landslides, torrents and hail stones, playing havoc upon its inhabitants.

Ritipata's elders stood around the central altar, a large and carefully sculptured rectangular stone. They offered coca leaves and the first drops of each drink to appease the deities, while the young dancers stamped the earth, eager to engage in a show of courage. To the rhythm of the music the first couple danced toward a wall of sheer rock that plunged into a deep crevasse. On the other side a platform atop an equally steep rocky cliff awaited the dancer who dared to jump across the opening which was as wide as a man's body with outstretched arms.

As the first couple arrived at the rock face, the young man left his partner and leapt across the wide fissure. He landed safely on the other side and jumped back, unharmed. Lightning began to flash across the sky followed by a thunderclap. Every time a young man or woman jumped and returned safely, the crowd of dancers emitted sighs of relief. One young man slipped as he landed back on the edge of the dance area. He managed to pull himself to safety. Ica shuddered. With dusk starting to obscure the landscape, most couples stopped this dangerous game. Only the most skillful dared to jump in the near dark.

The music resumed. Ayar danced with Ica closer to the abyss.

"No," she whispered. "Please don't."

As lightning zigzagged across the sky, he freed himself from her embrace and jumped across the yawning fissure. Like an acrobat he returned with a vigorous leap, accompanied by the sound of thunder. He looked splendid, illuminated by a flash of lightning high above the sheer rock faces. But Ica could not enjoy this breathtaking image while her heart pounded with fear.

Ayar's leap ended the contest. Rain mixed with snow began to fall. A few couples moved to the altar of stone to announce to the gods their decision to remain together for life. An elder responded by blowing across a bouquet of three coca leaves asking the blessings of the gods. Other couples danced into the distance to be with the one they loved, alone among the mountain peaks on top of the world.

After midnight Ayar and Ica took leave from the elders and their age mates. They had promised Juanita and family to spend the next day with them before they had to descend to the valley. To save time, they decided to take a shortcut by climbing across the edge of Apu Illapa's glacier.

They advanced slowly on the icy terrain. Sometimes they slipped, clinging to one another while joking about their adventure in the darkness. Suddenly the wind picked up and they hurried toward firmer ground. A storm erupted. Lightning brightened the sky and hail stones, some as large as chicken eggs, pounded the ground. The roar of thunder came closer.

A large hail stone hit Ica on the head. She fell to the ground but managed to sit up. Ayar threw off his poncho. He folded his vest to cushion his head against the rocky wall. Then he placed one end of his poncho at the back of his head which he pressed against the rock behind him to keep it from slipping. Grasping the other two ends of his poncho, he stretched out his arms, producing a makeshift tent that reduced the impact of the hailstones while protecting both of them. Ica helped holding up the 'tent' when Ayar needed to relax his arms.

Within minutes the hailstorm was over. The path had turned white.

"We are on our way," Ayar said, smiling with confidence, as he shook the hailstones off his poncho throwing it around his shoulders. "It never fails," he grumbled with some humor,

"Up here the weather god torments visitors by playing tricks on them."

"You are ingenious," Ica responded, kissing his cheek. "Your 'tent' saved us."

Ayar touched her head where a bump had appeared. With a smile he reassured her, "It will soon vanish. In the meantime it does not make you less beautiful."

"That's the least of my worries," Ica responded laughing and getting to her feet.

"We'd better pass the rest of the night in the first house we find," Ayar cautioned. "Hail storms at this altitude can be even more ferocious."

Ica nodded in agreement. Her head still hurt from the blow of the giant hailstone and her hands were frozen stiff, but she did not complain.

Holding hands, they hurried downhill. Another storm was approaching rapidly.

"We must go faster," Ayar urged, trying not to slip on the blanket of hailstones that covered the ground. He pointed down the slope to a little house half concealed by a huge boulder that appeared as lightning flashed across the sky. They approached, but saw no light shining through the tiny windows.

"The inhabitants must be sleeping," Ica whispered as they arrived at the door.

"It's alright to awaken people during the fiesta. It is our custom to bring good wishes to everyone," Ayar insisted.

More hailstones pounded from the sky. Ayar knocked on the door. An old man, looking sleepy, but with a welcoming smile, opened the door while his wife lit a candle.

"*Allillanchu hamushani,*" both exclaimed simultaneously, welcoming the visitors into their house.

"Come in quickly, a big one is about to break loose," the old man urged, pointing to the sky. "It never stops at this time of year."

"Sorry, we woke you in the middle of the night," Ica said in an apologetic tone of voice.

"Do not worry. We are glad you arrived in time. This one could be deadly," the old lady muttered as hailstones began to pound on the roof and the ground, resonating from the boulders around the house, creating a cacophony of deafening sounds.

She introduced herself as Doña Willka and her husband as Don Paukar. Then she offered coca leaves to the guests and blew across a *k'intu* in honor of the thunder god and the Apus, protectors of their cherished llamas and alpacas. She asked them to spare their animals' lives, especially the young ones, born two months ago and still so vulnerable. Ayar, Ica and Don Paukar followed her example as they, too, joined in appeasing the thunder god.

Turning to the visitors the old lady explained, "Adult animals shelter their young from the hail, from foxes, pumas and condors and from the ferocious winds, but only the gods decide which will survive."

After the storm had subsided, the old couple rushed to the corral. They returned quickly with a relieved look on their faces.

"All of them live, all forty-two of our animals," they reported.

"You count fast," Ica said surprised.

"No need to count," Doña Willka affirmed. "We see at a glance if something is unusual."

Ica threw a questioning look at Ayar.

"Numbers and amounts are perceived differently up here," he explained. "These people do not need to count their animals, nor the threads they weave into cloth, nor the stars of the constellations in the sky. They see at a glance if all are there."

"This sounds like magic," Ica said puzzled.

"I'll explain it sometime," Ayar responded, equally relieved that no damage was done to the animals which were both loved by their owners and needed for their survival.

"Have a cup of hot tea," Doña Willka interrupted, as she poured boiling water over *phallcha* blossoms she had placed into large cups that sat on the earthen floor. "Warm yourselves, and then tell us about the dances where you challenged Qhaqya or Illapa as our Incas called the thunder god. Tell us," she whispered with a grin on her face. "Did anyone fall in love, as we did so long ago?" She smiled at her husband of many years.

"We did." Don Paukar confirmed. "Every year during the fiesta we went to the dances at night. We proved to the gods, to the dead and the living that we were brave, withstanding the ferocious forces of the rainy season."

"Yes, we had a good time, a really good time," Doña Willka resumed. "And our days are still good, although we can no longer go to the dances." Holding her husband's hand, she continued, "Now we are grateful to still be alive and live here together." They looked at one another with an expression that confirmed that for them love is forever. Ica looked around the small one-room adobe hut, void of anything but the bare essentials. How satisfying it must be to be grateful for what is truly important in life, she thought.

Doña Willka brought alpaca furs to sleep on and to use as covers. "Stay here until daybreak," she suggested. "You have had enough surprises tonight. *Allin tuta*," good night, she wished her guests as she blew out the candle. Don Paukar had already fallen asleep.

Early in the morning they ate a hot potato soup. Ica and Ayar thanked their gracious hosts with a big hug and many good wishes for the year to come. They walked rapidly, eager to spend the day with their friends as they had promised.

Julian, Juanita and their two daughters waited nervously in front of their home. The moment their visitors appeared in the distance, the children ran to meet them, hugging them and holding their hands while walking together to the house.

"It's a dangerous time of year," Julian said with concern, as they arrived at the door. "Lightning has struck many in the past who went to Apu Illapa."

"We are glad you are home," Juanita affirmed, beaming with joy. They hugged and led their visitors into their little house.

Sabina and her younger sister Isidora offered their guests boiled potatoes and corn bartered in the valley. They also gave them *ch'arki*, dried alpaca meat, a delicacy reserved for fiestas. With the meal over, the children showed their guests the progress they had made in weaving small belts. Five year old Isidora was still struggling with the many colored threads, not yet able to construct any complex figures. Sabina was quite well versed in the activity and ready to view the threads at a glance, without having to count them one by one.

"That's what I meant at Doña Willka and Don Paukar's place when they recognized at a glance that all their animals were present," Ayar said. "And now you see the weavers work on intricate patterns without counting the threads one by one. These people master mathematics in a surprising way."

Juanita explained, "The children learn ancient designs early on and soon they know how to weave complex geometric patterns that appear clearly on both sides of a woven cloth."

"What amazing talents are born here," Ica said, looking puzzled.

The adults sat down to admire the children's weaving skills when a neighbor knocked on the door.

"Don Julian," he called out, "Please come quickly. Don Mamani up on Mount Yana Orqo has a high fever and a stomach ache. He has been coughing for hours."

"I will come along," Ayar said, "Do you have *huaman lipa* against cough?"

"You should also take *pirca* against inflammation," Ica advised.

Taking her husband's bag from the corner, Juanita put in the herbs they suggested. She added a bottle with boiled water and *muña* plants to disinfect.

"I'm glad you are coming, Ayar," Julian said as he thanked Juanita for handing him the bag and off they went with the neighbor.

"We are almost out of medicine," Juanita disclosed. Looking at Ica and her daughters, she suggested, "Let's go to the meadows to collect herbs. Many people fall ill in the rainy season, whole neighborhoods can become infected in no time." She gave each a basket and they left for the higher meadows.

When they reached the area where medicinal plants were abundant, Juanita was surprised by Ica's extensive knowledge of Andean herbs. Yet, some of the plants they found were new to her and she listened with great interest to Juanita explaining their healing powers. Sabina and Isidora were proud to show Ica rare medicinal plants that grow only at high altitude. Ica put some of them aside to study them in Qoripampa.

With their baskets filled and dusk approaching, the herb collectors arrived home. The children spread the plants on wooden shelves to dry while Juanita and Ica prepared supper. As soon as the potato soup was ready, the children ate and went to sleep in the corner of the room. Much later, Ayar and Julian arrived. They looked tired but hopeful. Don Mamani's fever had gone down and he had stopped coughing. But he still had a severe headache and his muscles were sore. He slept in a small hut, attached to his adobe home, so he would not infect other family members, should the illness be contagious.

"I will look after him until his health has returned, "Julian insisted.

"Tonight is Kacharpari, the end of the fiesta," Juanita sighed as everyone prepared to go to sleep.

A Magic Night in Rimaq Mach'ay

The next morning everyone rose early to have some time together before they had to part.

"What a fiesta," Ayar said in a nostalgic tone of voice. "Thank you so much, my friends, for your gracious invitation."

Looking at her hosts, Ica nodded with a broad smile, "It was marvelous, so different, so engaging."

"Stay a few more days," Juanita pleaded. "We are sad to see you leave."

"We cannot stay any longer," Ica responded. "But we will return. This is a different world, I love it and I learn so much from you."

"You bring us exciting news as well," Juanita added in an enthusiastic tone of voice. "You tell us of things we should know. You must teach us more about treating disease as it's done in your country. We know how to cure some ailments and we do it well, but there are others that kill before our remedies can take effect." She wiped tears from her eyes as she continued, "We lost three of our children."

"We will build a small hospital in the valley. I won't return to my country until it is done," Ica responded with conviction. "We will exchange more information about traditional and modern medicine and we will get to know the fevers that ravage your people. We must work together."

The two women looked at one another confirming their common goal.

The next morning Juanita and Julian prepared food for their guests to take on their way back to the valley. They hugged them good-bye, only releasing them after they promised to return soon. The children accompanied their new friends across the creek. Their parents waved until Ica and Ayar had disappeared in the distance.

After a long silence, Ica looked back at Ritipata. "The fiesta is over," she said. "I wonder whether the people are still as happy and positive as they were all these days when so much depended on the way they felt and acted."

"Are *you* still as happy as you seemed all these days," Ayar asked with a tinge of nervousness in his voice. "Or do you now see this place in a different light?"

"I see material poverty and a sense of despair when young children die....," Ica started to say, when Ayar interrupted her.

"I feared you would take an objective look and speak your mind now that the fiesta is over. I had hoped, but I also knew..."

"What did you know?" Ica broke into his sentence with a teasing tone of voice. "Do you want to say that you can read people's minds, not only cure their bodies, Dr. Ayar?"

He shrugged his shoulders. Ica held on to his arm and looked into his eyes.

"People own little and they fear the diseases they cannot cure. But otherwise this place is amazing." Looking back at Ritipata she disclosed, "I found something here I thought no longer existed, or perhaps has not yet developed elsewhere."

"Hm," Ayar reflected, not sure what to think of Ica's views of a society so different from her own and appearing so backward on the surface.

She surveyed the splendid landscape caressed by the sun. Green hills graded into snow-covered peaks which reached for the deep blue sky. Only a few white clouds were left clinging to the high mountain peaks.

"What is it, Ica, tell me," Ayar insisted.

She stopped walking and looked at him. "This society is intact."

"What exactly do you mean?" Ayar's curiosity was aroused.

"I mean that in this village people behave in a more respectful and compassionate way toward one another than in any other place I've been. They seem to care and I see true kindness and generosity."

Ayar looked puzzled. "Don't you mind the lack of comfort, or, as some say, the stone-age way of life?" He turned to face her. "Could *you* live here?"

She hesitated, then admitted with a smile, "I think I need a little more comfort. I guess I'm spoiled. But that's all that's missing, just some things that make life easier. In every other way this society has achieved what is most important – dignity." She looked into the distance and said with a sigh, "It hurts to think of the greed and hostilities one finds in so many parts of the 'civilized' world." Then turning to Ayar, "You must be proud to be a member of this village."

He looked surprised, "You have a unique way of looking at things."

"This may be so," Ica maintained, "And I'm proud that your people have accepted me the way I am."

Ayar reflected. "I am proud of my heritage and so are others in my village. But for centuries we have been called primitive, ignorant and worse and the stereotype clings. Life is difficult for the native people of the high Andes, and few can realize their potential. If they want to make it in mainstream society, they must put aside their heritage and culture. To be accepted they must above all obtain the modern technology that sets them apart."

"And we will," Ica said, flashing a radiant smile. "As soon as we arrive in Qoripampa, we will start to build our hospital. Everyone needs it, whether they live in the valley or the high mountains.

They arrived at the southern slope of the Condornuna mountain range where medicinal plants abounded. They filled their woven bags with the precious herbs.

"Look, Ica," Ayar said with joy as he discovered herbs that in combination with others could cure the cutaneous form of leishmaniasis. "But no plant has been found that will prevent or heal the mucocutaneous type, the terrible *espundia*," he uttered with concern. "One must be hiding somewhere, perhaps in the jungle."

"We will find it," Ica said, "We'll have so much time together. I'm in no hurry to leave."

A sudden wind chased cumulus clouds across the sky and it began to rain. Ica followed Ayar who hurried toward a rock shelter to prevent the plants from getting wet.

"It will rain for quite some time. We'll not make it to Qoripampa before night falls," he warned. "Besides," he added with a fond expression in his eyes, "The time up here has been too good to end so soon."

"And so wet," Ica added laughing.

The place that granted them refuge from the rain looked from the outside like a simple rock shelter. Yet, as they entered, they heard a murmur that turned into a roaring sound, loud and eerie. Once inside, the sound was gone.

"What is this?" Ica inquired with a puzzled expression on her face.

"This is Rimaq Mach'ay, the cave that speaks," Ayar explained. "It is magic," he added in a teasing tone of voice, "You will see."

"I need to know now," Ica demanded with increased curiosity as she entered and left the cave several times to observe the perplexing phenomenon.

"Look," Ayar said, pointing to the overhanging curved rock above the entrance, "This formation catches the roaring sound of the river in the gorge below us and releases it at the entrance."

"I see," Ica replied. "But it still sounds like magic."

The cave was carved into bizarre, irregular, yet pleasing shapes with a large polished table of stone sitting in its middle. Ica knew that this had been used as an altar where ceremonies took place. Ayar noted that it must have been occupied long ago as the stones and elongated altars carved from bedrock and worked into smooth surfaces testified.

"This is the work of our Inca ancestors," he said with pride. Pointing to the stone walls with ochre imprints of hands reaching for the sky, engravings of double-headed snakes, and other enigmatic shapes, he maintained that these specific symbols could even be older.

"We are in a place that is both sacred and magic," Ica murmured in a devout tone of voice.

"It is," Ayar affirmed, looking at her with affection. He reached for his bag and placed the food and drink their friends had given them on the altar of stone.

"A meal for royalty!" Ica exclaimed, pointing to the potatoes, corn, and *qochayuyu*, the nutritious algae from mountain lakes for which she had now found a taste. There was fresh water in a gourd and even a small bottle of *chicha* left over from the fiesta. Ica poured the precious drink into two small cups and handed one to Ayar.

With respect they sprinkled a few drops on the ground for Pachamama and some in the direction of the mountain peaks in honor of their protective powers. Several drops landed on the walls of the cave, the womb of Pachamama, and also on a spot that looked like an entryway into the mysteries of the mountain. Then they toasted each other.

"To us," Ayar pronounced solemnly, his eyes filled with the joy of someone who had just conquered the universe.

"And to our common goals," Ica added. "Tonight I want to hear about your life, from its glorious beginnings in Ritipata to Todos Santos, when I first fell in love with you."

"I will tell you everything you want to know, *sonqochallay*, the love of my life," Ayar promised. "And I need to discover what made *you* what you are, the biggest puzzle of all."

He looked at her with a radiant smile. She spread a woven blanket on a large polished stone. Nibbling at the meal their friends had packed for them, they leaned comfortably against the wall, while the drizzling rain provided a relaxing background.

Ayar was overwhelmed by happiness, knowing that Ica's love for him and for his people went deep, that her sentiments did not simply gloss over the surface of a society or the poverty of a human being. He felt some remorse about his own sentiments which had ruled him for so long. He knew he had to confess.

Holding her hands, he spoke softly. "Ica, I'm sorry I acted so irrationally. I am sorry I did not want to accompany you to Ritipata. I did not want you to find out about my roots. I was afraid that .... I must tell you, Ica, I must be honest, in case you might fall in love with me."

"Just in case," she said laughing. "I know you are more perceptive than that, and I forgive you. When it comes to irrational behavior, I can tell you that I have done so many things that were considered unacceptable by individuals and institutions, it would fill an evening. And some say the fact that I did not regret anything, made things even worse and earned me the reputation of a rebel." Looking into his eyes she continued, "As soon as you hear about my life, you may not want to forgive me and perhaps you will be ashamed to be seen with me."

"It cannot be so bad," Ayar said laughing. "But I can hardly wait to hear. Please tell me!"

"Remember when I told you that I promised my parents I would study botany right after school? Well, I didn't. The images of my parents dying in the jungle were still too vivid. I decided to study zoology. The first year went alright. I got good grades and started second year. But this was a fatal one. We were supposed to experiment on more than 600 frogs and turtles in the lab. Their central nervous system was to be paralyzed, which is supposed to make them insensitive for experimental purposes. Our lab instructor told us that this was difficult to achieve and many animals would end up still conscious and suffering." Ica shook her head and sighed, "All that, so students could see for themselves that adrenalin speeds up the heart rate when dripped on an animal's open heart, while acetylcholine slows it down."

Somewhat agitated she continued, "When I heard about this ludicrous assignment I refused to participate and convinced many of my classmates. Then I went to see my professors and complained about these horrible experiments, for repeating the same cruelty for the 10,000th time instead of showing a film year after year in all universities. But these professors would not listen to a nineteen year old.

"This has always been done, they said in an attempt to defend themselves. So, hundreds of animals were to be sacrificed. Can you imagine?"

Ayar shook his head, pain written on his face.

Ica continued. "The day the experiments took place, I stayed home. As I lay in bed, I felt ashamed to be such a coward, to let these animals suffer while I turned my back on them. So I rushed to the university. Since my talks had not helped, I went straight to the lab, turned on the hose and sprayed the whole bunch of them, the profs and the students who attended, with icy cold water on an icy winter day. You can imagine how quickly they stopped torturing the frogs and turtles and how quickly I was thrown out of the institution!"

"You are wonderful," Ayar said laughing. "Tell me more."

"Well, I worked on Plant Biology for a while at another university. But when I had to take a required course in medical research, I found out that animal experiments were again on the forefront. Even more animals were used in naive attempts to prove that medicine that works on animals will affect people in the same way." The expression on her face became more painful as she stammered, "One day I saw the worst.... A man I trusted operated on live, fully conscious animals in a lab closed to the public. It was horrible." She sobbed with her hands across her face.

Ayar put his arms around her, kissing her forehead. "I know what you mean; it's one of humanity's darkest sins."

Ica nodded, remaining silent. Then with a tinge of relief crossing her face, she said, "I left university and joined several animal protection groups. I engaged in demonstrations with my friends who agreed that animals are as important a part of nature as we are and have the same right for a decent life. We protested peacefully, but obviously were too loud, appeared too often on the scene, and never gave in. So we ended up in jail, several times for several days in a row."

Ayar looked at her with admiration. "Well done," he said. "I guess I was lucky to study in a poor country where animals were too expensive to be used for such purposes."

"I envy you," Ica admitted. "I could have saved myself a lot of trouble had I come here earlier."

"I'm glad you came," Ayar whispered, squeezing her hand. "Please tell me more."

Ica went on. "Finally I was able to continue my studies with a remarkable botanist. My parents had previously worked with him, so he was prepared to take a chance with me. Over the next six years I received two degrees and did field research in Indonesia. I loved it and was well on my way to keep the promise I made as a child.

"How proud your parents would have been to witness the breakthrough you made in herbal treatment," Ayar said in admiration.

"How do you know?" Ica asked astonished.

"I read about it in a botanical journal and so did Don Rodrigues who was eager to bring you here." Pulling her close he added, "I'm so glad you came."

"I'm glad I'm here," Ica said, "and I can hardly wait to learn more about the medicinal plants of South America where my parents spent so much time with me in tow. They knew the jungle and the coast so well." Looking at Ayar with a twinkle in her eyes she added, "By the way, it seems I was conceived on Peru's dry coast in the little town of Ica where my parents worked at conserving their medicinal plants almost thirty one years ago."

Ayar smiled, "I have sometimes wondered."

As the cold of the night entered the cave, they pulled the blanket up to their chins and huddled closer together. Ayar looked at Ica with love. "We are following the same path, we have the same concerns, we strive for the same goals, we are ...we are made for one another."

"I'm glad you finally realize it," Ica responded with a smile. "I knew it soon after we met, despite the look you gave me which was not so kind."

"You looked too ravishing for me to bear," he confessed. "And your attempts to get used to this place were so charming that I could not get you out of my mind." He sighed. "I never believed you would return my feelings, so I pretended not to care... for a while... then I succumbed, as you know only too well."

"We are a comical couple," Ica laughed, squeezing his hand.

The night was magic. They laughed as they turned to funny events that had occurred in their lives. Ica never saw Ayar so relaxed and carefree, which gave more glow to his already irresistibly handsome features. He felt intoxicated by Ica's charm and the way she described to him her wishes for their future together.

"It seems I have known you for a long time. You have always been in my dreams and now they have become reality," he said, guiding her face closer to his, kissing her with all the love and passion he had felt for her all along, but had not dared to admit.

She caressed his muscular body, feeling a fire that consumed her very being.

"Ica, you are everything for me, my love for you will burn eternally," he whispered as their bodies became one, lost in the magic of love, and their spirits united, soaring to the highest peaks of their mountainous world.

Too excited about their plans for a future together, Ica and Ayar had scarcely slept. Yet, they were full of energy when the first rays of the sun penetrated the cave revealing more clearly its fine surfaces. Small steps led to elevated planes which appeared to be seats and altars. One of the carved and finely polished altars was suggestive of an astronomical instrument. The rays of the penetrating sun drew a line across its center.

"What did your ancestors mean with these intricate carvings," Ica asked in wonder.

"We do not know, it's an enigma," Ayar replied, his gaze fixed on her as though nothing on earth mattered but her presence.

"We may find out," she whispered, looking at him teasingly, "I have even started to decipher the greatest puzzle of all.

"I'm glad you did," Ayar said, his dark eyes caressing her face.

She hugged him, whispering, "Can you imagine how frustrating it has been to be in love with an enigma?"

"Or with a woman who may someday leave," he responded in a more serious tone.

"Never, unless....," Ica started to say, but Ayar interrupted her.

"I will always love you, always." He kissed her with the desire to make this moment last a lifetime.

Two birds flew into the cave, chirping and ready to land on Ayar's bag. At the sight of the unexpected inhabitants, they diverted their flight through a small opening above one of the rectangular altars.

"I forgot we are not alone in this world," Ica whispered. "The birds have come to claim their resting place."

He laughed, caressing her slim body. "I wish we would never have to leave."

"We may soon have a search party looking for us," Ica replied. "The Rodrigues family must be worried." If they only knew, she thought. With a laugh she added, "Perhaps the whole village is talking already."

"What beautiful gossip," Ayar joked.

Ica tried to return to reality. "We must keep this a secret. Once it is known, it will affect our work with the villagers, the hospital ..."

"Yes," Ayar interrupted. "We must present a cool front for the sake of our work until the hospital is built. But then," he hugged her passionately, kissing her eyes. "Then we can tell the world what the gods know already."

They reflected in silence on the love and freedom they had just enjoyed.

"There will be many lonely nights," Ayar sighed.

"They will not be so lonely if we carry one another in our minds," Ica responded. "And we will be working side by side every day," she added with a smile.

Ayar reached for her hands, holding them tight. "Your friendship has given me strength from the beginning. Your love gives me life. You are everything I need to exist, to be happy and reach beyond the stars." With his eyes remaining immersed in hers, he whispered, "Wherever we are, we will never again be alone."

The breakfast that consisted of left over edibles from the fiesta, packed by Juanita for the journey, tasted delicious as it was served on an ancient altar of stone. They left a few crumbs for the birds.

As they set out, the sun had just started its journey across a blue sky. Only a few white clouds clung to the mountain tops. The air was warm and fresh. Wildflowers and herbs, still damp from last night's rain, emitted an intoxicating odor which was dispersed by the gentle morning breeze. The lovers watched two condors far off in the distance, sailing through the air. Their wings seemed to touch as they drew perfect circles in the sky.

Ayar looked at Ica with a smile. "*Sonqochallay*, always remember the ancient legend that tells about the spirits of lovers which, when their time has come to depart the earth, fly up to where the birds of the mountain gods circle their peaks. Imagine, we will roam together forever when the condors call us and we never have to part again."

A Hospital - Dream or Reality

The descent was easy. Light footed they jumped across rocks and rivulets, holding hands, laughing and embracing. Hours passed. Their hearts danced with the wind and the birds and their love carried them along as they stopped from time to time to collect the medicinal plants that grew at this high altitude. In rivulets, washed down from mountain lakes, they found more *qochayuyu* and *llulluch'a*, the highly nutritious algae which Ica put into her bag.

"The Rodrigues family will love this delicacy," she said in anticipation of giving them a highly prized gift.

"Look," Ayar said, holding up a small mushroom. "This is the delicious *Agaricus campestris* that grows very quickly following a lightning storm. Our people love these mushrooms and they can even be sold to restaurants in the valley." In a serious tone he continued, "But one must take care, there is a similar looking variety that's very poisonous. People get sick and can even die if they ingest the poisonous twin of this delicious one. The difference is in the texture of the mushroom."

"I had better stick to medicinal plants," Ica said laughing. "I'm far from being an expert on mushrooms."

They continued collecting through the meadows.

"Ica," Ayar called out, as he found spiny *roq'a* plants growing close to the earth along a steep slope. He picked one of the small, round, orange-colored fruits, explaining, "We call this plant *tuna de la altura*. It belongs to the genus *Opuntia*. The fruits do not taste bad, and they also have medicinal properties." They picked many to take back with them.

Ica admired the bromeliads which also grew along the same slopes. "I like these plants the villagers call *qayara*, and the llamas, alpacas, donkeys and guinea pigs eat them whenever they get a chance." Turning to Ayar she asked, "Do you know what else they are used for?"

"The roots of this plant which belongs to the genus *Puya* are used for firewood, and *qayara* is good for something else." He searched through the spiny plants and broke one of the stems. Coming closer to Ica, he cracked the stem open and pulled out a fat, white larva. "Some healers say these larvae can cure pneumonia and tuberculosis when eaten." Holding it close to Ica's face, he asked with a mischievous grin, "Do you want to taste one?"

"Yuk," she said laughing and taking a few steps back. "I'd rather make tea from the *phallcha* blossoms, which are used to treat the same diseases. We've collected enough of them to last for a long time."

"This mountain provides much for its inhabitants," Ayar said with contentment.

"Yes," Ica responded, "and look at this." She pointed to a place full of plants, locally referred to as *huamanlipa*. "*Saxifraga magellánica* works very well against bronchitis and tuberculosis. Let's take some along for our patients." She asked Ayar to take her scarf from his bag to wrap up the plants since their other bags were full. The scarf was not there. It had been left in the cave.

"We will return soon," Ayar assured her. "Until then it will be safe in our secret *huaca*, our magic place of love." He put a string around the plants and carried them over his shoulders.

Ica smiled, ready to embrace him, but pulled back as several villagers appeared in the distance. Qoripampa was close and people were returning home from working their fields.

The villagers joined them on their way telling them the news that had spread throughout the community two days ago. Bishop Drugán had passed through Qoripampa with his entourage to inspect the land on the outskirts of the village that had been donated to the church several decades ago. Since the village had only a small church, he and his colleagues had decided that this land was the perfect location on which to build a larger church.

"The piece of land known as 'Hampi Pampa!" Ayar exclaimed with distress. "It was promised us long ago to build a hospital."

As they arrived in Qoripampa, they were greeted by the community president and council, by Don Rodrigues, and many elders who had assembled on the Medicine Place or Hampi Pampa in the Quechua language.

"You are back safely," Don Rodrigues said with a relieved expression on his face. "We heard the sad news and prayed for the souls of Juana, José and Mateo. We are glad you were spared. Please join us and help solve our problem."

"We just heard," Ayar responded.

The community president explained, "Funds will arrive from a religious organization in Europe which sponsors the building of churches. Qoripampa has been selected as one of the sites." Turning to Ica, he continued, "Twenty-five years ago promises were made by the archbishop that the land we are standing on would be given to the community. At that time hundreds of people had died in an epidemic and the entire population decided that a hospital must be built. For a quarter of a century the villagers have tried to get title to the land, but it has never been turned over."

"It has been our dream to build a hospital and this dream must not vanish now," Ayar stated in a firm tone of voice.

"We will never give in .....Never!" Don Rodrigues exclaimed, his eyes flashing.

Representatives from surrounding villages arrived to attend a general meeting that had been set the previous day to discuss the steps to be taken in securing the land for a hospital. Everyone present agreed that quick action was needed. It was decided that a written petition should be submitted to the church authorities concerning the land and the need for a hospital that would serve Qoripampa and all other communities within the district.

Ayar discussed his plans for the hospital which needed a consulting room, an operating room, twelve bedrooms, four rooms in which to quarantine people with contagious diseases, a laboratory and a pharmacy. The waiting room was also to be used as a place where health promoters and the public at large could be instructed on first aid, family planning, preventive medicine, hygiene and common diseases. More rooms could be added at a later date as funds became available.

"We also need a facility for the increasing number of leishmaniasis patients who return to our villages," Ayar asserted. "As most of you know, these migrant workers live under abominable conditions in the jungle regions where they work and many contract *espundia*.

Don Rodrigues agreed, "We have no facilities to treat or even accommodate these patients and must send them to the capital where few can receive adequate treatment."

Francisca had joined the group. "We must finally come to grips with *espundia*. For centuries people have suffered from it. This terrible disease that affects mainly the poor is on the rise. We all know, whenever harvests are bad, people cannot survive and therefore must leave for the jungle to log or wash gold." With anger written on her pretty face she continued, "They are exploited, and many return deadly ill."

"It's a shame," Ica interjected. "The Mochica people on Peru's north coast, who depicted the victims of leishmaniasis on their pottery over 1500 years ago, may have done more to prevent and cure the disease than we do today. What a disgrace for the 'civilization' we've created."

Murmurs of agreement came from the crowd.

"We need to find a treatment that is within the reach of everyone," Ayar explained. Looking at Ica, he added, "We must start right away. We must build a hospital and a lab and we need the land now."

Two days later in the general assembly of villagers it was decided that Ayar, Ica, Don Rodrigues, the community president, and representatives from other villages of the district were to take a trip to the capital to meet with bishop Drugán who, during open house, was said to listen to people's problems and give advice.

The group that was to travel to the city of Qosqo decided to put the proposal for the hospital in writing. They worked until late at night. Before sunrise Don Rodrigues arrived in his truck to take the party to the city.

After many hours along a narrow earthen road, Ica noticed a large wall of worked stone that dominated the landscape to the left. She wondered whether this had been the gateway to the capital of the once great Inca Empire. Ancient irrigation canals testified to the agricultural history of the region.

Passing this site, Don Rodrigues pointed to the right of the road where ruins were nestled along the hillside. "This is Pikillaqta," he explained, "A city of the once powerful Wari civilization that predated the Incas." He stopped the car.

"We are early. Let's have a look," Ayar suggested. All passengers were happy to stretch their legs. Ica who had been half asleep in her seat, jumped out into the morning breeze. The group approached the ancient town. From a hillside they were able to overlook the Wari city with its well designed network of roads. Some of them were lined by stone walls. Most of the ancient houses had crumbled, leaving remains at various stages of decay. Although the stone work was different from that of the Incas, it was equally pleasing. Row after row of standing walls of former houses, with streets and open spaces, lined with bushes and trees, came into view. In the southern part of the city the thick, high walls that remained standing, suggested that they had supported two floors. These walls had resisted many earthquakes of major magnitudes.

The stones the Wari used were smaller than those of the Incas and not polished in the same way. They were of many colors, ranging from pink to white to purple. The way they were fitted together gave the impression of undulating waves moving across the landscape. The place felt calm and serene. An invigorating breeze dispersed the strong aroma of herbs, flowers and blossoms throughout this enigmatic city. Ica took a deep breath and imagined how this enticing odor had already enchanted the inhabitants of this once blooming city. Bees hummed in the heat of the sun. Birds chirped merrily.

The group approached an underground chamber with delicate pictures drawn on its walls. The colors had partially faded after centuries of being hidden below the earth.

"What a place," Ica sighed.

"The Wari were a powerful society," Ayar explained. "They left remains of their culture throughout this land. Remember when we saw their ruins on our way to Ritipata?" With a confident smile he said, "I'll show you more of their accomplishments high up on Huaman Orqo when we return to Qoripampa."

Hidden by high walls made by the ancient builders, he looked at Ica who stood in awe, overwhelmed by this dazzling site.

Don Rodrigues called from afar. It was time for them to continue on their way. The capital was still an hour's drive away.

They passed along fertile fields and then arrived on the outskirts of Qosqo, where the traffic became more congested. Endless rows of small stores and workshops, some in a state of neglect, lined the main street leading to town.

The traffic came to a standstill by a bustling market. Ica marveled at the many different products people pushed in wheelbarrows through the narrow lanes of the market. Peasants hurried through the crowd, bent under loads of produce from their fields and meadows. *"Comprame,"* the vendors called out, asking by-passers to buy from them. Customers who found what they wanted, bargained for the lowest price.

"Look," Ica called out as she noticed one of the vendors running after a boy who had stolen edibles from his stall. The man pushed his way through bystanders, then stumbled over two dogs playing between stalls. His swearing was partially suffocated by the loud Andean music that blared from an old radio. As the boy disappeared in the crowd, the vendor took time to brush the dust off his pants and returned to his stall with an angry face.

"Many hungry children live here," Ayar said with a frown. The other passengers nodded.

The traffic moved again. The Qorikancha, the famous temple of the sun, came in sight. "This is where the Incas kept many of their most precious items and also displayed the most significant symbols of their empire," Ayar explained.

"The treasures disappeared and this sacred temple was converted into a church shortly after the arrival of the conquerors," the community president added from the back of the truck.

"Luckily many Inca walls are still standing," Ica said with a sigh. "Your ancestors were such perfectionists."

The truck now entered the center of town with its enormous plaza, the sacred Hawkaypata. Many of the surrounding colonial houses with their distinctive carved wooden balconies rested on Inca stone foundations. Two large churches dominated the plaza contrasting with small gift stores and restaurants behind covered esplanades. Vendors of art objects, fruit and other items sat on stone floors under the roofs ready to sell their goods.

Don Rodrigues parked his truck. The group stepped into the center of the plaza where native *Polylepis* trees provided shade for people relaxing on benches beside well kept hedges and colorful flowerbeds. Water gurgled softly from a fountain in the middle of the plaza.

"This place used to bustle with visitors from around the world," Don Rodrigues explained. In a whisper he added, "Not many foreigners come here these days because of the terrorists. Looking at Ica, he added, "You are quite courageous."

"I feel safe with all of you around me," Ica responded, admiring the hill sides surrounding the city. "But it troubles me that so many people must suffer injustices. So many are losing their lives. I know that a philosophy professor from Ayacucho started the Shining Path movement several years ago and it keeps going." She sighed. "How many more must suffer at the hands of culprits? No one knows who they are or what they are fighting for."

"It's a catastrophe," Ayar responded. "But for now let's explore this great plaza on which we stand and which used to be even bigger in ancient times. Here our ancestors performed important ceremonies until the conquerors arrived in 1534."

"I know," Ica interrupted. "I've read that it was here where Tupac Amaru II, a nobleman and merchant of Inca descent and his family were killed by the conquerors for having led a peaceful demonstration against the exploitation of the native people." She shook her head. "The whole thing turned into the bloodiest confrontation ever to occur in the Americas." In a hoarse voice she continued, "Right here, Tupac Amaru II was pulled in the four directions of Tawantinsuyu, the Inca Empire, by four horses attached to his arms and legs. But his body resisted. So they hanged him." She took a deep breath, "Why does a beautiful place like this attract such evil forces?"

"It's human greed, the desire to gain power over others," Ayar responded. "These people had not learned to respect all life, to connect with the positive energies that surround us and provide us with love and compassion."

The others nodded silently, saddened by the memory of the destruction of a once great empire.

Don Rodrigues looked at his watch. "The archbishop's palace should be open by now. We must hurry."

They left the truck parked by the plaza and hurried along narrow streets bordered by the finest Inca walls. The building they looked for was located in an enclosure of beautifully carved and masterfully assembled stone masonry. It was surrounded by cobblestone streets and walls made of enormous stones perfectly fitted together. Ica marveled at the skill of the talented people who had built this amazing city centuries ago.

An elderly couple in their traditional clothing, he with a worn poncho and she with several skirts tied around her waist, were already waiting in front of the entrance. Soon they were called in, only to emerge a few minutes later, looking sadder than when they entered. Obviously they had not been helped.

The group from Qoripampa was next. Bishop Drugán, a heavy set man in his sixties with small piercing black eyes, dressed in a black satin cloak, received them in his elegantly furnished office. He greeted the group formally and allowed them to sit down on the intricately carved wooden chairs around a large table made from polished wood.

Ica scanned the room. One wall was covered by shelves full of old documents. Several closets with closed doors stood along the adjoining wall. Three large oil paintings, in intricately carved wooden frames, hung on one of the other walls. They portrayed the city's most honored saints who peered into the room from a dark background, painted by artists a long time ago. A crystal chandelier hung from the high ceiling above the center of the large table.

After a moment of silence the bishop faced the group. "What brings you here?" he asked, tapping his fingers impatiently on the table.

"A twenty-five year old concern, your Eminence," Don Rodrigues answered. "Qoripampa desperately needs a hospital."

"We have put our concerns in writing, as we have done every year," Ayar added as he placed the proposal on the table in front of the bishop.

"A hospital!" the bishop exclaimed. "A hospital for Qoripampa! Don't we have a project already for your village?"

He glanced through a pile of papers in front of him. "Yes, the project has been approved. The land will be used to build a church. You are lucky, there are funds from abroad.... Construction will start shortly and ....."

"Your Eminence," Ayar interrupted in a determined tone of voice, "The residents of Qoripampa and surrounding villages have all voted for the building of a hospital. We need it desperately. Many people have died in the past for lack of a medical facility." He pushed the proposal closer to the bishop who flipped through the pages, then lifted his eyes looking at the group.

"There are so many petitions from so many villages. We have little land and even less funds."

"All we ask for is to sell us the land, called Hampi Pampa, that had been promised our people for twenty-five years," Ayar said, suppressing his irritation.

"You need patience, young man," the bishop answered hastily.

"Are twenty-five years not enough proof of patience?" Ayar exclaimed.

"Do not raise your voice at me, you ...," the bishop shouted angrily, looking with contempt at Ayar who was dressed in a poncho, woven pants and rubber sandals, typically worn by peasants. "We received money for churches, not for any hospital," the bishop asserted as he threw the pile of papers from the international sponsors onto the table. The top sheet slid across its slippery surface, and came to rest in front of Ica. She recognized the names of foreign charities. Slowly she took pen and paper from her coat pocket and copied the addresses, while the bishop lectured the group on the importance of practicing religion in the villages instead of worrying about health, which God would give them if only they prayed more often.

"We need a hospital and we need it now!" Ayar exclaimed, jumping from his seat in frustration.

"Since when do *Indios* make decisions about matters pertaining to the church?" the bishop shouted, his face red with anger, his fat diamond clad fingers tapping the table.

"You have not kept your promise to sell us the land," Ayar responded. "We are deceived no longer!"

"Get out of here!" the bishop ordered. "The session is over."

"Just one more question, your Eminence," Ica said calmly as the others were leaving. "Have you ever considered that few people can come to your church, because many will have died so young?"

"This is none of your business, young lady," the bishop responded abruptly.

Ica looked him straight in the eyes. "We will see about this," she said and joined the group which had already left the room.

"There is no hope," the community president uttered in a depressed tone of voice. "Things were better when the former bishop was still alive." The others nodded in agreement.

"We *will* get the land and we *will* build a hospital," Ica asserted quietly.

"You are a great optimist," Ayar said with a smile, the bitterness in his voice gone. "How do you suggest we proceed?"

"We must explain the facts to the sponsoring groups. We must tell them about the urgency of our project. We *are* dealing with a life and death situation. We must let them know how many children die in infancy, mothers in childbirth, people who have accidents. There are epidemics and the *espundia* gets worse every year while there is not a single hospital for more than 20,000 residents of this region. I'm sure they will understand."

Don Rodrigues shrugged his shoulders, "Perhaps."

Ayar looked at Ica with a fond smile. "It wouldn't hurt to try, but we must act quickly before they start building the church, which is less than two months away."

Ayar and Ica decided to stay in the city to visit Ayar's *compadres*, his close spiritual kin, and to write letters to the charitable organizations. The rest of the group returned to Qoripampa.

A Glance into the Past

Ayar's *compadres*, Don Pablo and Doña Placida, were pleased to meet Ica and see their favorite godson who had helped them many times when a family member was ill. Both wholeheartedly supported the plan to write for assistance abroad. *Comadre* Placida prepared a delicious meal while *compadre* Pablo got his typewriter ready and provided paper and envelopes. Ica and Ayar wrote to the four sponsoring groups whose addresses she had copied, telling them about the urgently needed hospital for Qoripampa to be built on the land Hampi Pampa.

Don Pablo went to the corner store to make several copies of the letter, their proposal which the bishop had rejected, and a description of Ayar's recent work which was published in a leading medical journal. Ica put the documents into four envelopes and Pablo took them to the post office.

Ica looked exhausted. She and Ayar had slept little during the last few nights.

"Stay with us for a couple of days and get some rest," *comadre* Placida suggested, and, turning to Ayar, "Do show Ica the marvels of our ancestors, they'll make you both forget your troubles for a while."

"Good idea, *comadre*," Ayar agreed, pointing to a steep hillside they could see through the window. "Let's go to the Temple of the Thunder, some call it the House of the Sun up there in Saqsaywaman."

They rested that evening, slept well throughout the night and early the next morning ascended to the ancient monumental complex towering high over the city. The Incas believed it to be the head of a puma whose body stretched through the city below. The animal's tail was represented by a site called Puma Chupan.

As they reached the monument perched against steep hills, they saw enormous walls, labyrinths, thrones, altars, and carved astronomical devices in stone dotting the landscape. Some stones had been carved *in situ*, others had been transported from remote quarries.

From one of the higher lookouts they saw three exquisitely built cyclopean walls which flanked the north side of the Qollcampata hill in a striking zigzag pattern. As they approached the immense walls, Ica stopped, looking in awe at the spectacular site.

"Was this a fortress as the tourist guidebooks often claim?" she asked. "It looks like something much more important."

"You are right," Ayar agreed. "This monument with the three walls provided protection, but it was, above all, a sacred site." Pointing to the zigzag walls, he noted, "If this configuration were primarily for defense, we would see this pattern more frequently, not only here, but elsewhere."

Ica ran her fingers across the carved stones. Some weighed up to 150 tons and all were fitted masterfully together. Not even the frequent earthquakes that had shaken the Andes for centuries had parted the stones. Ica knew that another reason why Inca walls resisted earthquakes was because they were slightly inclined toward the hillside and their builders had carefully shaped the rocks with concave and convex surfaces which fit tightly together without mortar.

Ayar noted that the care with which this monument had been built, also revealed its great importance. "The ancient architects wanted to ensure that this sacred place would last for eternity, so they used huge boulders for its foundation." With sadness written on his face, he added, "The smaller stones of this and other monuments were plundered. They now adorn churches and the houses that once belonged to the conquerors. Their stone walls are often hidden below whitewash."

"What a shame," Ica sighed, looking in the direction where a large statue of Christ dominated one of the hills. "If only Jesus knew what has happened in his name - the conquest, the inquisition, the destruction of a remarkable culture and the near extirpation of an admirable people." Then, with a more peaceful expression on her face she continued, "What's left still reveals much about the ingenuity of the people who lived here."

"Yes," Ayar agreed. "This whole region from here as far as we can see is full of enigmas. As we come to recognize more of the ancient symbols, we get closer to solving the mystery.

"What mystery," Ica inquired with curiosity.

"The mystery of this entire place which the ancients named Saqsaywaman," Ayar responded with an air of pride.

"Let's continue," Ica suggested with a boundless enthusiasm, holding on to him as they walked across the spine of the hill. They passed the remains of two rectangular towers, then stopped at the foundations of a round tower, composed of eight radial sectors.

Ayar pointed to this intriguing structure. "We know something about its function from Garcilaso de la Vega, the son of an Inca princess and a conqueror. He spent his youth in Qosqo and wrote about it after he had moved to Spain. As a child he saw the tower intact and observed that there was a spring that provided much good water for the city below. In fact, some of the conquerors marveled at the Incas because they apparently knew how to make water run uphill."

"That's amazing," Ica uttered.

"And there is much more," Ayar promised.

They wandered along a network of major and minor canals crisscrossing the enormous site. Eventually they came across another zigzag wall of stone leading to an ancient reservoir that used to gather water from springs and rivulets. Filters made of tiny stones served to purify the water before it entered the reservoir.

"This may have been a giant mirror where the Incas contemplated the night sky," Ayar said. "They believed that for everything we find on earth, there is a counterpart in the sky." Walking along the ruins, he explained, "Astronomy was very important to our ancestors, both here and elsewhere in Tawantinsuyu, the Inca Empire. Many of the stones and their alignments which may represent constellations, or point to them, testify to this."

Ica stood in awe as Ayar continued, "Here in this sanctuary you can learn much about Pachacutec Inca Yupanqui, the greatest emperor ever to rule this land." In a whisper he confided, "Just recently an intriguing artifact had been excavated from the cemetery beside this reservoir. It's a pectoral made of jade with the image of a double-headed snake moving in the form of a zigzag line. This same emblem was held sacred by the powerful Inca Pachacutec. It is a metaphor of Illapa, the god of thunder and lightning who became the primary deity of this celebrated emperor."

"How do you know?" Ica wondered.

"Our elders learned these secrets from their ancestors," Ayar responded. "And they transmitted them orally to their descendents since the Incas had no writing system as we know it today. Our archaeologists have also recovered much that had been forgotten."

From a distance they heard the rhythmic sounds of waterfalls splashing into ancient bathtubs made of carved stone. And then, like a metaphor from another world, a mysterious rock outcrop appeared before their eyes with altars, thrones and carved seats where the mummies of the Inca royalty used to be brought to sit during ceremonies. Below this labyrinth of geometrical configurations in stone, there was a burial chamber where ancestor worship had taken place. An upright rock in the shape of a puma rose from the middle of the site.

"Another zigzag line!" Ica exclaimed as they climbed onto the immense rock with its myriad of carvings. "Everything I see reminds me of water and lightning."

"Yes," Ayar responded. "The Incas knew that water was essential to life. It had to be respected, kept clean and used with care. Therefore the deities responsible for water were honored and appeased in many places, and most of all right here on these sacred grounds."

For hours they walked in a circle through the fascinating sites of Saqsaywaman, then climbed onto a cliff where wide carved steps were oriented in such a way as to suggest an astronomical alignment perhaps with a constellation. From here they again had a direct view of the three gigantic zigzag walls within the symbolic configuration of the head of a puma. Ayar seated himself on one of the twelve smooth stone slabs that faced east toward the rising sun. He asked Ica to sit down beside him.

"This is magic," she uttered, filled with emotion.

"And there is more," Ayar said with a radiant smile.

"What else did your ancestors tell you about this place and the secrets it holds?" Ica asked.

Ayar pointed into the distance. "All this was a ceremonial site dedicated to the worship of water. Most revealing are the three giant zigzag walls just across from us."

Ica scanned the enormous monument. "I have read that zigzag lines were sacred in different parts of the world and that bodies of water, waves, rain and lightning have all figured in zigzag symbolism throughout Inca and pre-Inca iconography. Lightning and thunder must have been magic for the ancients and were honored for bringing rain. The thunderbolt was also feared for causing death and destruction."

"Exactly," Ayar responded. "The dual forces displayed by Illapa, the thunder god, gave him immense power over life and death. This deity was revered throughout the Inca Empire."

"Who built this astounding monument?" Ica asked.

Looking across the plaza to the immense walls, Ayar explained, "When the ninth Inca emperor, Pachacutec Inca Yupanqui, came to rule between 1438 and 1471, he expanded the Inca territory far beyond its former limits. He rebuilt and enlarged the capital of Qosqo, and created administrative and religious centers throughout his empire. While he was away to conquer new territories, his wife, the Qoya Anahuarque, ruled from Cuzco. Pachacutec and Anahuarque became the most powerful rulers of Tawantinsuyu. But then a drought brought much devastation. Many people died from hunger, thirst and pestilence. Guaman Poma de Ayala, a historian of Inca descent, wrote that the elders remembered the drought lasting for seven years. Some say it went on for as long as ten years. The great Inca Pachacutec Yupanqui was horrified as he saw the heart of his empire dry up. He and the Qoya prayed to Illapa, the thunder god, and so did people throughout the empire. Illapa was honored and appeased every day in the hope that rain might fall. He became more important than Inti, the sun god.

"What happened?" Ica asked with concern.

Ayar pointed to the giant walls across the immense plaza. "To honor and appease Illapa even more, Inca Pachacutec Yupanqui designed these immense walls in the form of three zigzag lines. They stand for the three ways by which the mighty thunder god expressed his power, in the form of lightning, thunder, and thunder bolt, or Chuquilla, Catuilla, and Intiillapa in the language of the ancients. The monument was built with the help of people from all four corners of the Inca Empire. It was meant to last for eternity." He paused, then continued, "Finally the rains came and people rejoiced. In gratitude, the Inca emperor elevated the thunder god to the prime deity of the pantheon and declared him his alter ego.

Ica nodded as Ayar went on, "As you know, the Incas believed that for everything on earth there was a counterpart in the sky. This suggests that Inca Pachacutec built the immense monument we look at, not only in honor of his alter ego, the thunder god, but also to himself."

Ica pondered, "So the three zigzag walls of this monument bear enduring witness to the greatness and power of Inca Pachacutec Yupanqui, and they reflect his close association with his equally powerful alter ego, the thunder god."

"Yes," Ayar responded, "A close association with an alter ego or guardian spirit is not a thing of the past alone. Still today some South American Indian tribes strongly believe in alter egos. They assert that a shaman even has the ability to change into his alter ego."

"Regardless of whether this is mythology, history or reality, or a bit of each, it's mind boggling," Ica affirmed. Looking at Ayar's tall, athletic body and sophisticated features she wondered whether the mighty Inca Pachacutec Yupanqui could have been more magnificent.

"So we have solved the enigma of Saqsaywaman," Ayar said with a smile.

"Not quite," Ica answered absentmindedly.

"What do you mean," he asked laughing.

"I wonder how you got the last name Yupanqui," she inquired.

"That's another enigma and will have to be solved another day," he said, smiling at her.

"Uma Puma," Ica wondered after a long silence. "Why would this monument be the head of a puma?"

"Well," Ayar reflected. "The symbology is a complex one. We must understand that the puma is in the same mystical group of beings as is the *qoa* cat. These felines are supernatural beings, associated with lightning and hailstones and therefore share in Illapa's powers. That's why Illapa's zigzag line is part of the symbolic head of the puma, while this feline's body reaches down into Qosqo, the city of the Puma. The puma is mythically connected to Illapa, just as Illapa is connected to Inca Pachacutec Yupanqui."

Ica remained silent as Ayar resumed, "The cosmic life force is a vital energy that connects everything in the universe. Even space and time are connected. They constitute a single unit we call space-time that cannot be separated. In our Quechua language or *runa simi*, the word *pacha* stands for both space and time."

"That's interesting," Ica said puzzled." Some quantum physicists say that everything in the universe is connected and made of the same stuff, and that space and time are not separate entities, but form a four-dimensional continuum, they call space-time." She reflected. "Your ancestors were far ahead of modern civilization." Looking at Ayar she added, "There is so much to discover."

He agreed, "And we have our whole lives to do it."

They remained seated as the evening sun set on the smooth carved stones that served the ancients as astronomical device. Too tired to move, happy to be together, and surrounded by the magic of the site, they only began to descend to the city as the stars brightened the sky.

Compadres Placida and Pablo received them with a hug and a hot supper.

"What do you think of our ancestor's monument?" they asked Ica.

"It's marvelous, puzzling, totally fascinating," she said, still overwhelmed by the experience. "Your ancestors built earthquake-proof monuments; they dealt with astronomy, and created the best organized empire the world has known. I admire their respect for nature in all its forms and their reverence for water. They knew that water represents life." In a more somber tone she added, "I can never forgive the conquerors who destroyed so much and imposed a feeling of shame on the native people because of their beliefs. Looking at her hosts, she added, "What we have seen in Saqsaywaman shows that your ancestors combined a practical mind with a complex religious ideology."

This night Ayar and Ica fell into a deep sleep. They dreamt of their walk through the mysterious past, when the cosmos was perceived without boundaries and all life within it was believed to be connected; when eternity was seen to happen in the moment and to last forever; when space and time, life and death were part of the same cycle, simultaneously divided and united.

A Mysterious Disease

Early in the morning before Ayar and Ica took a bus back to Qoripampa, they bought a variety of materials they needed for their work, mainly containers to hold the different kinds of natural medicines they made and a microscope for their research. In Qoripampa the Rodrigues family welcomed them with a surprise: a small room they had vacated in their house to serve as a work place for their research on leishmaniasis. Don Rodrigues was content that Ayar involved Ica in this important work for which he, himself, has had little time. He moved some equipment and furniture from his own lab to Ayar and Ica's new research facility. Both were happy to be able to work together which would make time pass more quickly as they waited to hear about the land for the hospital.

The next day, before sunrise, Ayar arrived at the Rodrigues' house, ready to begin work. They had just started to organize the small lab, when they heard voices coming from the street. Through the window, they recognized several families huddling around a small restaurant. As they looked down the street they noticed that some neighbors were busy nailing wooden boards across their doors and windows.

"They are afraid," Ayar whispered as he went outside with Ica. "They do this when they hear about a contagious disease."

At closer range they recognized people from Ritipata in their distinctive attire, people who looked weak with feverish eyes.

Victor came running down the street to greet them. "Your friends from Ritipata are asking for you," he said in a quavering voice. "Some have arrived with fever, splitting headaches, stomach aches, nausea and muscle pains. A few have rashes over parts of their bodies." In a whisper he added, "The disease spreads fast. They say that people died only three days after the first symptoms appeared and several have already been buried."

Ica knew that the sick must be quarantined immediately before the disease would spread any further. She saw no alternative but to ask Don Rodrigues and Doña Nilda to let the patients use her room and also the small lab she and Ayar were offered the previous night. The Rodrigues family agreed and immediately helped to reorganize these places to accommodate the sick. With more ill people arriving, they offered two more rooms of their house to the patients. Old grandpa Rodrigues also vacated his room. He moved his blanket and pillow to a shed beside the house. Victor followed his example. Then he was sent to ask the Avaron family whether they could receive patients in their spacious house. They refused.

More people arrived in a state of exhaustion, most of them deadly sick. Ayar led them into the house to check their condition. Those with very high temperatures required immediate attention.

"Victor, I need your help again," Ica urged. "Please ask all our neighbors for blankets and drinking cups."

"*Si mamíta*," Victor responded, running down the street.

Don Rodrigues hurried into the makeshift hospital. He asked Ayar to identify those patients who were able to travel the five hours it would take to get to the hospital in Qosqo. "I will leave right away," he said with worry etched on his face.

Ayar requested that Don Rodrigues bring the equipment to diagnose the disease and find a specialist on contagious diseases who was willing to help.

Don Rodrigues left in his truck with five patients. Forty-two sick people were lying down in various parts of the house.

Doña Nilda, Francisca and grandpa Rodrigues boiled water in several large pots. Ica showed them how to prepare the sugar/salt solution needed to prevent dehydration. Victor came with a friend who helped carry piles of blankets to serve as mattresses and covers. Shortly thereafter eight new patients arrived from Ritipata. Among them was Fernando, the fourteen year old son of the Quispe family who Doña Nilda knew so well. The boy was delirious. His two younger sisters had been buried the previous day. His parents were stranded on the way.

"Many people have died," one of the arriving patients told sobbing. "Some are on the roadside, resting or ... dying. Many are unable to cross the river."

The rooms, the hallway and eventually the whole house of the Rodrigues family filled with patients. Victor continued to run back and forth to collect all the blankets he could. Some local people brought mattresses, cups and drinking water for the sick, then quickly retreated to avoid contact with the mysterious disease.

Could it be typhus, Ayar wondered, a disease with similar symptoms that had struck the region many years ago. But it had not brought death within only a few days as did this epidemic.

Ayar and Ica worked without a break. To keep people alive they had to administer the fluids they needed and keep the fever down. They cleaned up vomit and diarrhea and made sure that their helpers did not come too close, since contact with the sick was dangerous. Only stubborn little Victor refused to obey.

"I'll stay here," he said, in a determined tone of voice and rushed off attending to patients who needed a bucket or a drink of water.

It was almost midnight when Ica finally sat down in a corner to rest. She closed her burning eyes while Ayar and Victor remained awake watching over the patients. Dozing off she suddenly heard the sound of steps and opened her eyes. Immediately she jumped to her feet as she saw Juanita enter the doorway, leaning on her husband who carried their two young daughters. With a faint smile Juanita looked at Ica, then collapsed on the floor.

"Juanita, not you," Ica sighed in despair. She bedded her friend down on a mattress and covered her with a blanket. Francisca placed two more mattresses on the floor for Julian and the children. Ica removed the wet clothes from the shivering little girls, wrapped them in blankets and massaged their exhausted little bodies.

Then everything started to happen at once. Young Fernando talked in a delirium as his fever rose. Ayar fetched a bucket with cold water and rags and hurried to his side to bring his temperature down. Juanita's little girls were thirsty, crying for water. Don Julian had to vomit. No more rags were left, so Ica tore off part of her dress to clean up the mess. With only one blanket left, Victor ran off to look for more in the middle of the night. He soon returned with a pile he could barely carry.

"Thanks, you have been a great help," Ica said faintly. "Now please leave. It's too dangerous here."

Victor responded by immersing some rags into cold water and placed them on Juanita's forehead. Doña Nilda and Francisca brought another bucket with sugar/salt solution and stayed to spoon it into the mouths of the patients.

More sick people arrived early in the morning. Most could barely walk after the long descent from Ritipata through the dead of night. A few courageous villagers used Qoripampa's three stretchers and started to bring the people down who were stranded along the way. There was no more space to accommodate them. The entire Rodrigues house was occupied. Ayar thought about taking the newly arriving patients to the small school building, but reconsidered, given the deadliness of the disease and the difficulty of caring for patients in two locations. So he bedded them down along the walls of the hallway.

Juanita started to vomit. Ica ran to her side to hold her.

"I 'm sorry," she emitted in a faint voice, "so sorry."

"Don't be sorry," Ica answered. "We are friends."

With her eyes half shut, Juanita talked unintelligibly. Julian caressed his wife's head while touching his little girls who were sobbing with pain. Then Juanita gasped faintly. Her head moved sideways with a slight jerk. Ica took her hands, rubbing them. Ayar hurried to her side. Both tried to revive her but without success. Her feverish body gave way to the cold of death.

"No, noooo," Ica cried. She ran out of the house onto a nearby hill and clutched a small eucalyptus tree. Ayar ran after her and held her tight. Her body was shaking; her eyes were full of pain and anger. "I won't take this, I cannot." She freed herself from Ayar's embrace and looked into his eyes, "Tomorrow the land will be ours," she cried out.

"Yes," Ayar said. "And we will build the hospital."

Don Julian lay beside his dead wife with tears in his eyes, too feeble to rise. He stroked his little girls whenever they whimpered. Doña Nilda found Fernando motionless. He had died quietly. She knelt beside the handsome young boy, crying. Others had died as well. Some fell into a coma as the fever rose. Many cried when the pains became intolerable. Ayar, Ica, and their helpers did all they could to put the patients at ease. Some were actually feeling better. But many could not be helped.

The rays of the early morning sun came through the window, touching Ica's face as she continued to give the hydrating solution to the patients and put cold moist rags around their calves and ankles. She looked pale and exhausted. She was barefoot and her dress was torn.

"God, she is so beautiful," Ayar sighed with his eyes clinging to her face for an instant before he continued attending to the sick.

The sound of car engines came closer. Ayar emitted a sigh of relief. Don Rodrigues came through the door, behind him Dr. Dante, a specialist on contagious diseases, followed by several paramedics.

"Thank heaven!" Ica exclaimed. "Thank heaven you are here!"

Ayar and Dr. Dante took blood samples from the patients. Ica gave the sick people the antibiotics which the doctor had brought along. The paramedics distributed masks and plastic gloves to everyone who helped take care of the patients and left several large bottles of disinfectant solution.

Together with some villagers who offered to assist, the paramedics went up the steep path to Ritipata to help bring the stranded people down on the new stretchers brought from the city. In the make-shift hospital the arriving patients took the places of those who had died, after everything they had been in contact with had been changed and disinfected.

Dr. Dante remained three days working between Qoripampa and Ritipata. He agreed with Ayar that this disease seemed related to typhus, but he, too, wondered why so many of the affected had died so fast. "We will have the samples analyzed and hopefully will know soon," the doctor said with a reassuring smile. "I will return as soon as we have the results."

Dr. Dante took some of the sickest people in his ambulance to the city hospital, hoping to find a few free beds in the quarantine section. The paramedics and village helpers continued to bring patients on their stretchers down to Qoripampa. Five days later Dr. Dante returned with the news that this disease was a rare epidemic typhus which had probably been transmitted through the feces of infected lice. But this was not the whole story and did not explain why the disease was so aggressive and patients died so fast.

"Hopefully we will learn more about this epidemic when we get the response from the lab in North America where I have sent the samples," Dr. Dante explained in an encouraging tone. "We must learn how to prevent another outbreak of this terrible disease.

To keep the epidemic from spreading any further, Ayar walked with Dr. Dante and two assistants to Ritipata to make sure the disease had been contained, while Ica and Don

Rodrigues took care of the patients in Qoripampa. All houses were fumigated.

Ayar and Ica were surprised that neither they, nor any of their helpers, had contracted the disease.

"This is no coincidence," grandpa Rodrigues said with conviction. "It's a sign we are meant to continue the struggle to heal the sick and bring justice to our people."

Don Julian, little Sabina and Isidora could not be saved despite Ayar and Ica's desperate efforts. They followed Juanita to the grave, high up close to the eternal snow. Many of the dead from Ritipata could not be buried in the small cemetery of their village and were put to rest outside their high mountain homes, an uneasy situation that added to the tragedy. To restrict any further spreading of the disease, the bodies were buried fast, merely wrapped into clean cloths or woven blankets. The village priest presided over the burials in the valley. In Ritipata a shaman prayed to Pachamama asking her to receive the bodies in her sacred womb, while the Apus were implored to accept the spirits of the dead in the realm of the ancestors.

Three weeks after the epidemic began, most of the survivors had returned to their villages. The disease had taken 152 people, among them whole families, most from Ritipata, some from neighboring villages and a few from Qoripampa.

Now that the danger of contracting the disease seemed to be over, the residents of Qoripampa removed the boards from their doors and windows. Ayar called a general meeting for the next day. The topic was the hospital. The decision made by the villagers of Qoripampa and representatives from villages throughout the district was unanimous. Qoripampa needed a hospital now, not some time in the dim future.

While families were still mourning the deaths of their loved ones, the villagers of Qoripampa prepared to build a small, basic hospital on the land that had been promised them for so long. They decided that the construction would be done in *faena*, the kind of communal labor where at least one member of each family participated. On Sunday morning villagers flocked to the land from all directions with shovels, hoes and measuring tapes. The architectural plan for the hospital, previously drawn by a graduating engineer and former resident of Qoripampa, was brought out. The epidemic had shown all too clearly that the procrastination of careless decision makers was no longer acceptable.

The takeover of the land was no secret affair. It was a happy occasion as the villagers, accompanied by music, flocked to the land to measure and level the site. To build the walls of the hospital, many people brought along adobe blocks they had made for their own homes.

Ayar gave a speech in remembrance of those who had died during the epidemic and on other occasions because of the lack of a facility, of medicine and medical attention. He reminded the villagers of their right to build a hospital for the people of Qoripampa and neighboring communities. The crowd cheered, ready to give their very best.

For the next three weeks, men excavated and collected stones from the vicinity to make a strong foundation. Women cooked at the site where the men worked to assure that no time was lost returning home for meals. The spades and shovels never rested. The villagers of Qoripampa and neighboring communities worked with enthusiasm, accompanied by music. They joked and their sorrows seemed forgotten. Bonds between villages were strengthened and animosities that used to erupt at times were forgotten in view of their common goal. Even the Avarons sent a worker.

As soon as the foundations were laid, the walls sprang up. Families contributed the little cash they had for the supplies they had to buy. Ayar and Ica added what they could from their grant money. The Rodrigues family reached deep into their pockets to cover some of the expenses. People were confident they could raise more money in fundraising activities during fiestas.

Six weeks later in the hot afternoon as the walls were complete and the roof began to take shape, a van stopped by the site. Two police officers and an envoy sent by bishop Drugán stepped out.

"By order of our highest authorities, this work must be stopped immediately," the envoy commanded as Ayar, Don Rodrigues and the community president approached the arriving group. The envoy reported that bishop Drugán had received a letter from the donors in Europe informing him that a foreign church dignitary would arrive in the capital and had asked to visit Qoripampa on his way from Bolivia. The bishop had decided that this visit would be the perfect occasion upon which to officially dedicate this land for the construction of a new church.

Ayar addressed them calmly. "Gentlemen, the community of Qoripampa and the surrounding villages have decided to build a hospital on this site. As you can see, construction is underway. For two and a half decades the church had promised to transfer the land for this purpose. Such a long-standing promise cannot be denied. This is all I have to say."

"Do you realize that you and your people have illegally invaded the property of the church," a red-faced policeman shouted in an agitated tone of voice.

"We do what's right for our people. We consider their health and wellbeing and we work in the name of justice," Ayar responded, holding his head high.

"You disobey my orders! You refuse to stop the construction! You disrespect our highest authorities! You'll pay for this right now!" Redface screamed as he prepared to handcuff Ayar.

At that moment a woman came running toward Ayar. "Help me doctor, please help, my son had an accident, he can barely breathe! Please come!" Before Redface could handcuff Ayar, they hurried off.

Ica stepped forward, planting herself in front of the group. "We have just buried 152 people. Many of these deaths could have been prevented if we had the proper facilities to treat them. We owe this hospital to the living and to the memory of those who died in this epidemic and throughout the decades when this village was neglected and the sick had little chance of survival. This must never happen again."

The assembled villagers murmured in agreement.

Looking at the workers with contempt, the same angry policeman shouted, "You refuse to obey the authorities? This is an embarrassment to bishop Drugán and his eminent visitor who will soon arrive to bless the site where the new church will be erected."

"You will hear from the bishop shortly," the envoy added in a threatening tone of voice.

"These walls have been erected as a refuge for the ill. They will remain. We will never agree to remove them," the community president said with dignity and determination.

"You, too, refuse to obey the law," Redface grunted as he approached the community leader and pushed him to the van where he locked him in the back.

Returning, he shouted, "I'll get this doctor Ayar, the instigator of this lawless endeavor. I'll get him sooner or later."

The other policeman shook his head, somehow troubled by his superior.

"We will be back soon and your doctor had better be here," Redface growled.

While the police scanned the site one more time, Ica ran to the van to tell the community president that she and others would be at the jail the next day, either to keep him company or to get him released. The van took off.

The next day the roof was raised. While the men worked, the women brought food and *chicha* for the inauguration that was to begin in the afternoon.

In the midday heat a black limousine, accompanied by a police car, stopped in front of the new hospital. Bishop Drugán stepped out with two of his colleagues and Monsignor Steiner, the foreign dignitary. They scanned the site. The bishop turned red with anger. With an air of surprise on his face, Monsignor Steiner greeted Ica who had approached and introduced herself.

"Oh, you are Señorita Ica," he said. "We received your letters."

Ica nodded with a smile.

"Now, what is happening here?" the Monsignor resumed. "Some talk about a church, others about a hospital. Please inform me."

"Yes, your Eminence," Ica responded. "But may I first introduce to you the people of Qoripampa and surrounding villages who have put their hearts and labor into this urgent project."

Chairs were brought for the visitors and a welcoming ceremony was hastily put together. *Chicha* and herbal tea were offered. Ica took the old loudspeaker Francisca had fetched from the school and addressed the delegation:

"Esteemed visitors. In the name of our community members and villagers from neighboring communities, I welcome you to the site of our new hospital. Only a few weeks ago during a terrible typhus epidemic we buried 152 people, including entire families. Many of them could have survived if we had a facility to accommodate the sick and prevent the spread of this highly contagious disease. We must never let such a nightmare happen again. So, we did not waste time. We built a hospital on this site which had been promised to the villagers by the church decades ago. God would not forgive further inaction on our part. Soon people can come from the entire region for treatment and instruction. These people have never been able to see a doctor or visit a hospital. Should another epidemic arise, we will soon be equipped to deal with it."

Looking with confidence at Monsignor Steiner, she continued, "With your help, your Eminence, this hospital will soon be ready to accept patients. It must be soon, because at this time of year many of our young people are on their way home from the jungle regions where they must work under abominable conditions to help their families survive. They return weak and sick and often with leishmaniasis, a horrible disease." In a hoarse voice she continued, "Our Dr. Ayar Yupanqui has been working for years to find a cure that the poor can afford. He, too, will have a facility in this hospital to do the work that could end so many tragedies among our people."

Ica gave the loudspeaker to Monsignor Steiner with the words, "Your Eminence, thank you so much for coming to help us. Please speak to our people."

He agreed with a gracious smile.

During Ica's speech bishop Drugán had been sitting in his chair getting angrier by the minute. Ready to jump up at the end of her address, he was now forced to remain seated with a bitter expression on his face. The Monsignor started to talk.

"Villagers of Qoripampa, project leaders and esteemed colleagues. On our way here I was told that this land belonged to the church and had been invaded. Now I see with my own eyes that indeed this has happened. Not only did you take the land, but you went even further and erected a building that looks strong and enduring. You made sure that this land will remain in your hands and be used for your purposes."

Bishop Drugán nodded, smiling with satisfaction.

The Monsignor continued, "People of Qoripampa, you have taken a big step, perhaps too big in front of the law. But you have done the right thing, and I extend to you my sincere congratulations."

The smile on Drugán's face froze into a bitter grimace as the Monsignor resumed: "We all know, God helps those who help themselves. You truly know how to help yourselves with the blessing of our Lord. You, the villagers of Qoripampa and adjacent areas have set a great example for humankind as you work together to help the sick and most desperate and to assure a better future for all your people."

Turning to Ica, he said with a smile, "The letters you sent to us and to the other donor institutions were received with great interest. They were printed in newspapers and the response was overwhelming. Several other organizations were eager to cooperate in your admirable efforts. Thank you for working across international borders during these very difficult times."

Bishop Drugán clenched the armrests of his chair and looked at Ica in disgust.

Approaching Ayar, Monsignor Steiner continued, "And you, young man, seem to fear nothing to assure health and well being for your people. You have achieved much with meager means." He pulled an envelope from his pocket and handed it to Ayar and Ica. Please take this to finish the hospital and supply it with the furniture, instruments and medicines that it needs."

Drugán closed his eyes in bitter defeat, squeezing his thin lips even more tightly together.

Turning to the bishop who had been sitting behind him all along, the Monsignor suggested with enthusiasm, "My esteemed colleague, it seems there is no better time to inaugurate this work of love than now as we are all together." He handed the loudspeaker to bishop Drugán who waved it off with his hands, unwilling to speak. Instead, Father

Tomás, one of the priests who had come from his country parish, addressed the villagers, congratulating them to their admirable efforts and thanking the Monsignor for the great help he had brought to this region.

The inauguration ceremonies began with a speech by Don Rodrigues. Then four villagers dug small holes by the four corners of the hospital. Solemnly they buried offerings of coca leaves for Pachamama, the Earth Mother, asking her to protect this building from earthquakes, floods and fire, so it would never be destroyed. Some drops of *ñawin aqha*, the first glass of *chicha* were poured into each of the holes. More drops were sprinkled toward the east for the deities responsible for the welfare of the people who were to work in this house of health and those who came to be cured. Then the villagers filled the holes with earth and stones and lit a candle at each corner to attract the good spirits.

A young man climbed on the roof to attach a yoke of oxen carved from wood. This symbol of strength would lend endurance to the building. Father Tomás attached a cross to the roof, asking God to protect it at all times.

Among enthusiastic applause, Ayar gave a speech, thanking all those people present for their great dedication to the cause. Ica was chosen to be the *madrina*, the godmother of the hospital.

For the last few days Qoripampa's women had prepared much food and *chicha* for the inauguration. There was music, song and laughter. The Monsignor, the bishop's two colleagues, and the country priests mixed with the villagers, happy to celebrate this important event. Only bishop Drugán remained seated, eating and drinking, with a sullen expression on his face.

"What a wonderful community!" the eminent visitor exclaimed. "Can I meet the village president?"

Everyone remained silent, then Victor stepped forth explaining in a serious tone of voice, "Your Eminence, he is in jail. They took him to the city yesterday, because ..... Because like us he refused to tear down the hospital."

"Tell me more my child," the Monsignor said, putting his hand on Victor's shoulder, guiding him to the side. Shortly thereafter he turned toward the crowd. "It seems that yesterday something has gone wrong," he said. "We need to get to the city and see how your community elder is doing." He thanked the villagers for the friendly welcome he received, for the great inauguration he could be part of, and the good work they had done for their communities. Then he climbed into the waiting vehicle.

Don Rodrigues, Ayar and Ica rode along in the limousine, conversing vividly with the eminent visitor, answering to his interest in health and village life. Bishop Drugán remained silent, brooding in his frustration with the way events had developed.

The Dream comes True

Qoripampa had won its long and difficult battle. With the village president released from prison, the hospital built and ready to be furnished, the villagers were full of hope. The generous donation from abroad proved to be sufficient to pay for the furniture and the medical equipment for the hospital and the lab. Don Rodrigues, Francisca, and Victor, with the aid of many villagers, helped to spread the news to the remotest communities. After several weeks the hospital was equipped with the basics and ready to be staffed by two nurses and one general physician who were provided by the provincial government. Ayar and Ica could now dedicate more time to their research after attending to patients.

To provide the medicinal plants needed to prevent and treat local diseases, the Rodrigues family and other villagers continued to plant herbs in their own gardens and to collect them in the wild in those places where they were still plentiful.

Ayar began to give workshops for villagers on the treatment of the less aggressive cutaneous leishmaniasis. An assortment of specific herbs worked well in healing this condition that manifested itself with ulcers on people's faces, arms and legs. Ayar's research had shown that the wounds should be washed with a solution consisting of *Symphytum oficinale*, a leaf of *Plantago congesta*, two whole *Calendula officialis* plants with stems, leaves and flowers and the white flowers of the malva plant that had been soaked in water for several hours. Ayar stressed that after washing the wounds, they should be dried before an ointment containing the herbs *Apurimacea michelli*, *Harmas*, *Thymus vulgaris L.* and *Calendula officialis* were applied. When these herbs were not available, he suggested that mashed white cabbage leaves could be placed on the wounds like bandages.

Espundia, the much more dangerous mucocutaneous form of leishmaniasis could normally be cured only while in its initial stages by using the imported pharmaceuticals Glucantime and Amphotericin B. These expensive drugs which Ayar was able to buy in small quantities with the funds left over from foreign donations, did, however, have serious side effects. Glucantime caused heart problems, sometimes even cardiac arrest, while kidney problems, convulsions, fever and anemia were linked to Amphotericin B. Pentostam was rarely used and its side effects were also dangerous. Ayar knew that much more research was required to find an affordable treatment with fewer and less serious side effects and that such a remedy would most likely have to be herbal. He was aware that the indigenous population in jungle regions suffered much less from this disease, even though they lived where it was endemic. Some native people seemed to be immune. Ayar often argued that research must be done amidst the natives of the Amazon rain forest because they may hold the secrets we need to know.

To aid in the prevention of leishmaniasis, Ica helped Ayar with a series of workshops advising young people who were about to migrate to the jungle, that they needed to eat well and keep themselves and their surroundings clean. Cleanliness was essential since the sandfly *Lutzomyia*, the vector for the *Leishmania* parasites, laid eggs in places where its larvae could find organic matter, such as household rubbish. Insecticides had proven valuable when sprayed in and around people's living quarters as they helped keep the mosquitoes which caused malaria and *bartonellosis* at bay, as well as sandflies which gave rise to leishmaniasis. But spraying the vast areas where these vectors were found, was impractical.

In their workshops Ayar and Ica repeatedly warned the migrants to protect themselves from sandflies, locally referred to as *manta blanca*, especially in the evening, at night and the early morning hours, roughly between 4 p.m. and 7 a.m. when these insects were most active. Sandflies could also bite when disturbed in their resting places during the day. Ica insisted that people should stay covered during the day and sleep under a mosquito net when spending time in tropical or subtropical regions. But for most seasonal migrants these nets were too expensive as was good food, another precondition for maintaining one's health.

During the next few months Ayar and Ica worked tirelessly preparing herbal remedies and trying to find more effective treatments that would also work faster for their patients. They tried adding different medicinal plants to mixtures that were used to treat the cutaneous form of leishmaniasis, hoping that the added ingredients might produce a more powerful medicine that could also cure *espundia*. Their research did show that when heat was applied at different stages of *espundia*, the advance of the disease could be arrested in some patients for some time. It seemed that *uta*, the cutaneous form of leishmaniasis, could lead to the aggressive *espundia*, but *espundia* also seemed to develop independently. The circumstances under which this would occur were not clear.

Ica sometimes wondered whether the sick man she met in the bus the day she first arrived in Qoripampa would learn about their new facility and come to be treated. The pain and loneliness in his eyes had never left her mind and she wished she had been able to help him in some way. To ensure that all patients were treated to the best of their abilities, she and Ayar worked long hours, knowing that many young villagers, often ill, would soon return from the jungle to help with the harvest in their mountain homes.

With doctor and nurses in place, the hospital running smoothly, and their research lab established, Ica and Ayar were soon to announce their engagement. It became increasingly difficult for them to hide their love. But for now, all their time and energy had to flow into their work. They were happy to be together and see the progress that arose from their mutual efforts.

The villagers were content to see the hospital functioning so well. Yet they remained nervous about the health of their sons and daughters who were soon to return home. In past years many of the young migrant workers returned ill, too weak to work after months of bad nutrition and exhausting labor while logging or washing gold in the jungles of Madre de Dios. With work in the jungle scheduled from dawn until dark, they could not hide from the leishmaniasis-carrying sandflies which emerged at dusk from the infested river margins to feast on any warm body they could find. Sometimes the disease appeared only weeks after a female sandfly had taken her meal. At other times it took years or even decades.

As the harvest season began, the first young migrant workers returned from the steaming jungle and knocked at the door of the hospital. They looked exhausted, some were sick, but all were surprised and happy to find a facility so close to their home villages with a staff that was concerned about their health. Happiness, however, often turned into despair, when the patients learned of the additional toll their exhausting work had taken. Some arrived with tuberculosis, others with anemia, some had the signs of cutaneous leishmaniasis and even *espundia*. Every year there were families who waited in vain for their sons and daughters to return, later learning that they had succumbed to the excruciating work and the heat and diseases of the jungle.

The young people who returned did not speak much of the ordeals they had undergone. One day when Don Rodrigues brought new patients to the hospital, Ica asked him why these young people took such great risks to work in places from where few returned healthy and some never returned.

"It's a sad story," Don Rodrigues responded with a sigh. "Hunger and extreme poverty drives them to risk their lives for their families. These migrations have been going on for a long time. When I was a child I lived in Paucartambo, at the crossroads between the highlands and the jungle. I witnessed how young men and sometimes women from poverty-stricken villages in the Sierra were promised good salaries, a nice place to live and good food, if they signed up to work for a definite time in the jungle, where they would log, wash gold or cook. I saw these people arrive in open trucks in Paucartambo, where the road ended. From there they had to walk two to three days down into the rain forest to their destination." He looked at Ica with pain written on his face, as he continued, "I often heard them sing, 'Bells of Paucartambo, you ring the good bye, I will be going to Kosñipata, not knowing if I'll return.' In this song these young people expressed their doubt that they would return healthy, or return at all, from a journey to an unknown and hostile place."

Don Rodrigues' face became even more somber. "After months and sometimes years of backbreaking work in disease-infested places, those highland people who survived, returned sick with parasites, with severe anemia, with tuberculosis or leishmaniasis. I saw them huddle in the streets of Paucartambo after their ordeal in the jungle and their exhausting ascent across steep forested hills. Few had money left to continue their trip by truck or bus to their villages. Some died in the jungle; others succumbed to hunger or disease on the streets or along the fields of Paucartambo, far from their families. The promises these people had received from their employers were false." Don Rodrigues suppressed his anger as he continued, "Years later a road was extended into the jungle regions where they worked and the journey became a little shorter, but the tragedies continued." Looking at Ica, he confided, "A few young people have always survived the nightmare, some only to find out later that they have *espundia* and would soon walk only by night, covering their disfigured faces with a hood."

Ica sighed, "It happened to Ayar's sister many years ago. It was dreadful for him and her fate drove him to search for a cure and ways to prevent this horrible disease."

Don Rodrigues nodded. "We know the story well. A few years after her death when Ayar was still in his teens, he went to the jungle to experience for himself the exploitation these migrants suffered."

The tragedies described by Don Rodrigues were commonplace in Qoripampa and throughout the region. Ayar and Ica were satisfied that healing the cutaneous form of leishmaniasis was no longer a big problem. They had gained much experience with their natural medicines and the way they administered them. They were especially happy whenever they had been able to successfully heal a person who showed the initial signs of *espundia*, using Glucantime or Amphotericin B, especially when the patient did not suffer the serious side effects of these drugs.

On those days when they managed to treat their patients before sundown and had advanced in their research to where they could take a break, Ayar and Ica climbed to the top of Huaman Orqo from where they had a superb view of Qoripampa and the mountains beyond. They loved to be alone within this spectacular scenery, studded by the ancient remains of once great civilizations. They knew they had found exactly what they needed, one another and their work.

More ill people returned from the jungle and the Qoripampa hospital was soon filled to capacity. Patients from distant villages had to be accommodated in their own communities whenever possible. This meant that local healers and health promoters needed to be taught how to treat patients with cutaneous leishmaniasis. To accomplish this, Ayar decided to spend a few weeks with the healers of Pukamarka, a large village that could be reached in three hours by bus.

As the time came to leave, Ayar gave Ica a big hug. "*Sonqochallay*, you will be in charge of our leishmaniasis patients here. I will return in a few weeks." Looking at the assembled hospital staff, at Don Rodrigues, Francisca and Victor, he said with a smile, "Please continue with your excellent work."

"We will give our best," Ica responded laughing. "But you must take care of yourself. And be prepared for a surprise visit."

In Pukamarka the community president Don Ortiz and his wife Doña Lorenza awaited Ayar at the bus stop. Ayar had previously been called to this village which resembled Qoripampa in many ways, but was twice as large. Doña

Lorenza had arranged for Ayar to stay with them in their small but comfortable home. Ayar knew that drought conditions no longer allowed for good harvests and hunger hovered over the village. Increasingly more young people had to migrate to the jungle to find work and many returned ill. The villagers were grateful that Ayar had offered to train local healers and health promoters from this and neighboring villages in the treatment of cutaneous leishmaniasis and other jungle-related diseases right here in Pukamarka. This permitted patients with the more serious *espundia* to be treated in the hospital of Qoripampa.

The villagers were also hopeful that their problems relating to the extreme scarcity of irrigation water for their fields would soon be solved. An international irrigation project was in the process of being implemented in their village. Old canals were being repaired, new ones were being built, and a large reservoir was under construction above the village. The project was designed to allow more young villagers to remain in the community tending their fields and growing sufficient food for their families to eat as well as to sell on the local market. But for the time being migration was still the only possibility to make some money to help the family survive.

Pukamarka's old health station, unoccupied for some time, had been cleaned. Beds and basic furniture were donated by various local families. Doña Lorenza and several other women of the village were ready to cook meals for the patients.

Ayar started work the next day. The local healers were eager to learn new methods of treating patients with cutaneous leishmaniasis, as well as tuberculosis which was also on the rise, using specific herbal treatments. Ayar himself took on the patients with *espundia*, providing guidance to the locals.

After two weeks he returned to Qoripampa to visit Ica and the hospital staff and to see how the *espundia* patients were coming along with the latest trials. He reported that in a few more weeks Pukamarka's healers would be able to work on their own. Coming closer to Ica, he whispered, "I'm glad that our work goes as well as we can expect both here and in Pukamarka, but I miss you."

The next day they said good bye with a heavy heart as he left on the bus.

The weeks passed quickly as both teams were challenged by an ever increasing number of patients. Meanwhile the inhabitants of Pukamarka began preparations for the inauguration of the irrigation project, another dream come true. With sufficient water during the dry season, people might even be able to bring in two harvests a year.

Don Ortiz and Doña Lorenza had been busy for days making arrangements for the band and the speeches to be given by village authorities and the developers during the inauguration. The village women began to make *chicha* and to prepare a variety of foods to bring to the fiesta. School children rehearsed songs and dances and the poems they would recite at this festivity that was just a few days away.

Ayar called Pukamarka's healers and health promoters for a last meeting. They were satisfied with the progress they had made and felt ready to work on their own with the numerous patients who came for help. As was true for Qoripampa, only those Pukamarka patients who arrived in the health station with very serious illnesses remained there, the other patients received their medication to take with them to their own homes. Three times a week they returned for a checkup.

Ayar was eager to return to Qoripampa to treat the *espundia* patients with Ica and her crew. In the late evening as he observed one last time the newly trained Pukamarka healers treating their patients in the health station, a young teenage boy came running through the door begging him to come to his house where his two younger siblings lay in bed burning with a dangerously high fever. "Please come fast, my mother thinks they may be dying," the boy said. Ayar grabbed his medical bag and ran with the boy up the path to his home close to the reservoir. A few villagers passed them, some recognized him in the dark and greeted him. Out of breath Ayar could only fleetingly return their greetings.

When less than half a kilometer from the reservoir, with Ayar following him, the boy turned right, running across a potato field to a small house lit by a kerosene lamp. Doña Ccanchi, the boy's mother, greeted the doctor nervously with tears in her eyes. She led him straight to a small bedroom where her five year old twin boys tossed feverishly on a mattress on the floor. "They feel hot, so terribly hot," she said in a hoarse voice while placing cool rags on their foreheads. Ayar checked the boys' temperature, and then gave them aspirin and antibiotics which they took after a short struggle and some spilled medicine. He helped putting cool rags around their feet and lower legs to bring down the temperature which at 41 degrees Centigrade was in the high danger range.

"Your boys have a new kind of flu that starts with high fever and usually hits when winter begins," Ayar explained. "It has stricken this region only within the last few years."

Sra. Ccanchi took a deep breath, "I have lost two children to high fevers. I am so afraid," she said. "Please do not leave, Dr. Ayar. Please stay until the danger is over."

"I will stay until the temperature is back to normal," he said in a reassuring tone of voice.

"Please have a bowl of soup," Doña Ccanchi said with a smile. "It's almost midnight, and I know you doctors have little time to spend on meals."

Ayar thanked her for the soup. Then they took turns putting cool rags on the boys' foreheads and lower legs. Their temperature had fallen to 39 degrees Centigrade and they slept calmly. Sra. Ccanchi smiled with relief. "Please stay a little longer, just to make sure my boys are safe."

They started to talk about the reservoir and the benefits it would bring by providing irrigation water during the dry season and also when the rains are late or take a longer break during their rainy cycle.

"Living so close to the reservoir, we were afraid that some day it might break. It's so heavy with water," Doña Ccanchi said, shrugging her shoulders. "But the engineers assured us that this would never happen and we believe them."

"The safety of this reservoir should not be a problem unless an earthquake hits the region," Ayar advised. In a serious tone he warned, "Should it break, you must run up the hill behind your house as fast as you can."

"These earthquakes, they scare the hell out of us," Doña Ccanchi responded. "Is there any place on earth that's safe?"

It was close to two o'clock in the morning when Ayar took the boys' temperature again. "37 degrees Centigrade. Just about normal," he said. "Your boys should sleep through the night and tomorrow you must give each of them one teaspoon of this medicine three times a day until it's gone. If problems arise, call me in the morning before I'll leave for Qoripampa or get one of the healers when I'm gone." He left the antibiotics and aspirin with Doña Ccanchi.

"Thank you so much," she said shaking his hand. I will never forget what you did for us. You saved my boys. Please come back.

"I will come back to Pukamarka from time to time," Ayar said with a smile as he left the house.

After he had taken the shortcut across the potato fields and turned onto the main path to the village center, he heard people singing in a drunken fashion. He saw four men staggering up the path, holding on to one another. One of them approached Ayar, touching his arm and looking into his face.

"Our doctor Ayar, our dear doctor Ayar!" the drunk exclaimed with a lisp. "Please join us for a drink." He chuckled and swayed sideways as he added: "We are known as the four-leafed clovers. You can always find us in the *chicha* bar."

"Thanks for the invitation, but I'd better head home," Ayar said laughing.

Back in the village center he entered the Ortiz house silently, not to awaken his hosts. He fell asleep as soon as his head hit the pillow.

Terror, Flood and Destruction

Ayar was torn from his sleep when he heard people scream-
ing and calling for help. Incoherent speech from anxious
voices came from the street. He caught a few words: flood,
reservoir, death, as he jumped from his bed. Peering out the
window through the mist of the early dawn, he saw women
running in the cold morning air, carrying small children in
their arms. He hastily put on his clothes and hurried outside.
Families were huddling together on the ground, leaning
against houses, some injured and crying. Ayar asked what
had happened. Trembling and in a state of shock several
women exclaimed that giant waves of rushing water had torn
through the upper part of the village taking houses, corrals,
fields and everything in their path. "The noise of the explosion was terrible up there," they said.

"Some people died. Many of those living close to the reservoir were injured," a young man informed. He explained how
the thundering water destroyed many fields and the southern part of the village, but sparing its center. He had helped
bring down several injured people.

"We have lost everything. We have nowhere to go," a woman
lamented.

Ayar ran to the health station while Don Ortiz alerted the
police. More people arrived, some bleeding, others with
broken bones.

As soon as they heard of the tragedy, the village healers
hurried to the station with blankets and everything they
could find to bed patients down on the floor and tend to their
injuries. Doña Lorenza and her neighbors started to cut
clean sheets into strips to be used as bandages.

With no space left in the health station, Doña Lorenza was prepared to take patients with less serious problems into her house. As she arrived there with some injured, a police car pulled up in front of her door.

"Thanks for coming so quickly," she exclaimed. "The new reservoir broke and its flood has caused major destruction. We have fatalities and many injuries. We need your help."

"We must speak with the community president," one of the police officers said in a nervous and hurried tone of voice.

Doña Lorenza called her husband who was getting ready to meet with the members of the village council and the engineers. Greeting the officers, Don Ortiz urged them to go to the hospital in Qoripampa to bring back at least one of the nurses, as well as supplies and medicine.

"We must hurry to see what has happened at the reservoir," one of the policemen said. "Some of our officers are already there trying to determine what has caused this tragedy."

"I'll come along with the two engineers who have designed and supervised the reservoir," Don Ortiz said in a shaky voice. "They are staying close by, right down the road."

The police, soon followed by Don Ortiz and the engineers, hurried uphill, detouring around the areas where the rushing water had torn away the road, houses, fences and canals, leaving mud and debris on its way.

Reaching the still standing walls of the reservoir they recognized, by the way the cement was torn and the stones of the foundation were broken, that the damage was manmade.

"What an explosion!" Don Ortiz uttered, shocked by what he saw.

"We may be dealing with an act of terrorism," the police suggested.

"Terrorism," Don Ortiz repeated, shaking his head with grave concern.   "Are you suggesting that the terrorists have now come to us?"

"What a waste of our efforts," one of the engineers sighed. His colleague nodded, shocked but already beginning to think about the repairs that would be necessary.

"We must try to find the criminals before they can get away," the police urged.

It was decided that some of the policemen would search the area to the north above the reservoir, others would go south. More officers were called to comb the remote parts of Pukamarka's countryside.

"We'll report back to you as soon as we find anything," the officers told Don Ortiz as they hurried on their way.

Don Ortiz and the engineers went to the village center where members of the village council were helping with the injured and those who had lost their homes.

More patients arrived, some in severe condition, carried by their fellow villagers. Ayar urged the police who had returned after an unsuccessful search of the region assigned to them, to drive to Qoripampa to bring back one of the nurses and as many supplies as possible. He also asked them to call ambulances from the city.

Ayar, the village healers, Doña Ortiz and a host of volunteers helped with the sick and injured. A nurse soon arrived from Qoripampa with the supplies requested by Ayar. Several ambulances came from the provincial capital to bring more supplies and take the most seriously injured patients to the city.

A week after the night of destruction, the dead had been buried, the search for the missing had to be stopped, and most patients had been accommodated in the village center. Some were on their way to recovery.

After the police had searched the entire village and surroundings without results, the provincial police chief came to Pukamarka to discover why a search of such effort had not brought any results.   It was decided that more villagers should be questioned about any suspicious act they might have witnessed in the days or nights leading up to the disaster.

Several new policemen came to Pukamarka to replace their colleagues who had been working for days without rest. Three of the newcomers were assigned to work closely with the villagers to discover any possible clues. For several days they had no luck. Not one of the villagers they asked had seen anything that looked suspicious.

Then one of the three new police officers suggested that they visit the *chicha* bar where villagers with time for socializing and drinking met. They sat down beside a group of four middle-aged men.

"Welcome," the four of them called out, each one with a broad grin on his face. "We are the four-leafed clovers." They had obviously been enjoying their *chicha* for some time.

The police began to talk about the disaster that had caused so much damage to the village.

"It's a terrible crime," one of the clovers lamented.

"We live next to it," another of his companions added. "We were lucky that the water rushed around us in the other direction and that it also bypassed the village center. That's why we still can meet here."

"You live up there? Did you notice anything going on that night?" the police wondered.

"Nothing, nothing at all. We had a few drinks. We went home way past midnight and fell into bed," another of the clovers testified. "We hardly even heard the sound of an explosion."

All four nodded

"Did you meet anyone on your way?" the police resumed.

"No one," the same clover added." Who should be about at that time of night except for our doctor Ayar who is always out attending to the sick."

"You saw your doctor the night of the explosion?" the police asked with increased curiosity.

"We bumped into him on the path at night. We invited him for a drink, but he declined. He's not much of a drinker, but he's a good doctor," another clover asserted with a grin.

"Hm," the police said, "that's interesting."

The policemen now decided to enter a small restaurant where they met a few locals, but no one could give them any hint. Finally they ended up in the health station to see whether the injured had noticed anything that could be used as a clue. They arrived just as Doña Ccanchi brought her twin boys to the station. The police held the door open for her so she could enter with her boys.

"Thank you," she said.

"Were you affected by the flood a week ago?" one of the officers asked.

"Thank heaven, me and my three boys escaped the flood," she said. "A wall of water swept our house away and flooded our fields, but we still live." In a whisper she told the police, "We owe it to our doctor that we are still alive. The night of the flood when he came to treat my boys, he told me that we should run up the hill behind our house if the reservoir should ever break, and that's what we did."

"What did he mean, if it should break?"

"We were just thinking of ways it could get destroyed, that's all," she said, shrugging her shoulders.

"What time did he leave your house?" they inquired.

"It was after two o'clock in the morning, when my twins were finally out of danger. I was so glad that he stayed with us for so long."

"What did he do after he left your house?"

"I don't know. I guess he went home. He was so tired," she said. "Now you must excuse me, I must see Dr. Ayar to get more medicine for my boys."

Two days later the police responsible for the inquiries in Pukamarka held a meeting with colleagues from the provincial capital to discuss their findings. The first five officers who testified reported that the villagers had not been aware that anything so disastrous could happen.

The three police who had talked to the four-leafed clovers and to Doña Ccanchi were next. They indicated that Dr. Ayar had been about that night, close to the reservoir, and that he had warned Doña Ccanchi to escape to the hills should the reservoir break. But they cautioned not to jump to conclusions since everyone in town was full of praise for the doctor which would make it odd to tie him to the crime.

The face of one of the policemen, who had just arrived from the provincial capital, got redder as he listened. "You cannot trust that Ayar Yupanqui," he said in a malicious tone of voice, adding, "Some of you may remember that he was the instigator for invading the land of the church in Qoripampa. Isn't such evidence enough to show he's a lawless individual?" He jumped from his chair.

"Calm down." A colleague responded. We all know that Qoripampa needed a hospital more than anything else."

"I will get to the root of the problem," Redface shouted as he left the group and walked to the health station where he met Doña Lorenza.

"I am looking for your doctor," he said without introducing himself.

"He's busy with patients. See for yourself," she said leading him to the adjacent room where Ayar was treating a profusely bleeding man.

"Dr. Yupanqui, we must talk," Redface demanded.

"First my patients, then your questions," Ayar responded as he bandaged the man's wounds and rushed to another patient.

"I'm just kind of interested to know where you were the night before the destruction," Redface insisted.

Doña Lorenza pulled the police man out of the room. "What does all this have to do with finding the criminals?" she said. "Go and look for them. Don't bother our doctor. Can't you see he's busy?"

"Where was he the night of the explosion?" Redface asked, looking at Doña Lorenza with piercing eyes.

"I heard him jump out of bed before dawn when the injured arrived from the hills," she said.

"The reservoir must have been dynamited around 4:00 a.m. Where was he at that time?" he asked, raising his voice.

"Sleeping, of course!" Doña Lorenza exclaimed, frustrated.

"What evidence do you have?" Redface insisted.

"Dr. Ayar works hard and needs to sleep once in a while," she answered with a sarcastic laugh.

At that moment Don Ortiz entered the station with the police chief from the provincial capital. He greeted Doña Lorenza.

"We know what you go through. This is a disaster," the chief said with concern. Looking at Don Ortiz and his wife he added, "My men have searched the entire region from the waterfall in the north to the black lakes in the south. There's not a trace of the terrorists."

"The district is large. There are many hiding spots," the village president informed. "Your men must keep searching."

"We'll do our best. But if these criminals had any brains, they would be long gone," the chief said as he left the house.

Redface followed his boss whispering to him as he climbed into his car.

"Don't jump to conclusions," Don Ortiz overheard the police chief telling Redface, as he drove off.

Hours later, with the injured looked after, Ayar fell asleep on the floor while several healers watched over the patients. In the middle of the night he woke up with Ica leaning over him.

"Thank God you are safe," she said, kissing him on the cheek.

"Of course," he said laughing with his eyes half shut and looking at the patients who were also bedded down on the floor. "I've all these people protecting me." Gazing at Ica, he whispered, "And with you here, what can go wrong?"

"We brought more medicine and supplies," Ica informed. "I can stay for a few days but the nurse must return to Qoripampa to help there."

Throughout the next few days Ayar worked with Ica, the Ortiz family and the healers.

The police reported daily to the village president concerning their progress. The red faced officer stopped by often in the company of another officer from the provincial capital. Ayar remembered well what had happened when Qoripampa's hospital was built. If he had not been asked to hurry to a neighboring village to care for an ill child, he might have ended up in jail. Redface did not forgive Ayar his arrogance in refusing his commands, then or now.

With the criminals still at large, the repair of the reservoir and the reconstruction of the canals were on hold. This situation put increasing pressure on the police. Before returning to the provincial capital, the police chief called a meeting of all the officers who had been working in and around Pukamarka. Every policeman was to report about his latest inquiries.

Redface had his plan. When it was his turn, he reminded his colleagues of Dr. Yupanqui's involvement in the takeover of the church's land in Qoripampa. He reported the way by which the doctor and Señorita Ica had manipulated the situation by alerting the European donors to the importance of the hospital. In Redface's view these facts provided clear evidence that showed that Ayar could not be trusted, that he did not obey the law and that his reputation as a student activist while at the university also spoke against his character as a law abiding man. "And now we have several eye witness reports that Dr. Yupanqui had been in the vicinity of the reservoir the night of the explosion," Redface stated in a harsh tone of voice, looking at his colleagues.

"We know that he was about that night. He did his duty treating his patients," one of the policemen advised.

"He knew about the explosion of the reservoir," Redface asserted. "Why else would he have told that woman with the sick twins that they should run up the hill behind her house as fast as they could should the reservoir break?"

Has anyone else heard about this?" the police chief asked.

The three policemen who met Doña Ccanchi and her twin boys in the health station nodded.

"What is this all about?" The police chief inquired.

"It seems she and the doctor talked about ways of escaping, should the reservoir break," the three policemen answered.

"Hm," the police chief said. "With nothing else to go on, perhaps it will be worthwhile to pursue more closely what happened that night."

Within the next few days, while several officers still combed the countryside, Doña Ccanchi and the four-leafed clover group were questioned more intensively about their encounter with Ayar. They stuck to their stories regarding their conversations with the doctor, always stressing that he was much appreciated and trusted.

Redface, however, made sure that his accusations would spread fast to bring about his desired conclusions to a long and embarrassing search.

A few days later Francisca traveled to Pukamarka where she asked Ica, Ayar and the Ortiz family to meet with her in private. "Things are proceeding without too many problems at the hospital," she informed. "But I have heard disconcerting rumors about ..."

"I can imagine," Don Ortiz interrupted, raising his brows.

Looking at Ayar, Francisca disclosed, "Qoripampa and surrounding villages are shocked about allegations that you should be a suspect in the destruction of the irrigation project. In a low voice she added, "I know that the villagers are behind you. But there are certain powerful authorities who would like to see you punished for your liberal activities. Redface already claims to know who is responsible for destroying the reservoir. "

They remained silent, looking at each other with concern.

Moving closer to Ayar, Don Ortiz whispered, "If the culprits are not found soon, you could end up in jail."

"You will have all the villagers on your side, Ayar. They will fight to the death to protect you," Doña Lorenza added with conviction.

Ica held Ayar's hand, fear showing in her eyes.

"I don't want bloodshed," Ayar responded. "The villagers have gone through enough. They don't need more suffering."

In a subdued tone of voice Francisca disclosed, "But they'll stand up for you. They will fight to their last drop of blood."

"We love you like a son and people need you here and in Qoripampa," Doña Lorenza said with deep emotion. "But it would be better for your safety and that of the villagers, if you were to hide somewhere until those responsible for the crime are found."

"I will be with you, wherever you go," Ica vowed in a determined tone of voice.

Francisca moved closer whispering, "You must hide to avoid bloodshed and you must do it soon."

"I know," Ayar sighed, "But the *espundia* patients need Ica and me, especially now that so many have returned with the disease."

"I've seen her take good care of them. Her success in treating them is remarkable," Francisca noted. "It would be best if she stayed in Qoripampa."

"I agree," Ayar responded, looking at Ica with tenderness. "Above all else, I need you to be safe."

"And I'm sure you both want to know that your work will continue," Don Ortiz added.

Ica and Ayar nodded.

"I must go with you to where you will be hiding," Ica demanded. "I need to know where to find you."

Doña Lorenza put her hand on Ica's shoulder. "He'll return soon. The terrorists cannot be far."

"We must think of a place that's unknown and inaccessible," Don Ortiz suggested, wrinkling his forehead.

"My younger brother Felix knows many secret places," Doña Lorenza revealed. "He travels from the highlands to the jungle and back, several times a year, trading goods."

"Hm," Ica reflected. "How can we get out of the village unnoticed?" A ray of inspiration showed in her eyes as she remembered, "About a week ago the villagers of Qoripampa started to prepare for the pilgrimage to Qoyllur Rit'i, to the glaciers in the Sinakara mountain range. They told me that every year in the dry season, between May and June, when the full moon is in the sky, groups of people from hundreds of villages walk for several days and nights to the glaciers. There they give thanks to the mountain gods and ask for their help in the coming year."

Everyone nodded in agreement as Ica continued. "The villagers of Qoripampa told me that the *ukukus*, the central characters of this pilgrimage, are strong and powerful bear dancers who disguise themselves with face and head masks and long coats of alpaca wool. They act as guardians of order and justice on the long trek and in the sanctuary."

A flash of excitement brightened Ayar's face. "A very good idea. We can disguise ourselves as *ukukus*. No one will recognize us."

With a smile Francisca noted, "For several years Ayar belonged to the brotherhood of the *ukukus*. He knows the glaciers well."

"This could be the safest way out of here," Don Ortiz admitted, taking a deep breath of relief.

Together they began to develop a plan by which the escape could be best achieved.

"Only a few days ago our Pukamarka villagers started to prepare for the pilgrimage," Doña Lorenza recalled. "The tragedy of the reservoir had delayed the preparations."

Don Ortiz interrupted, "Yes, our pilgrims must go to Qoyllur Rit'i this year. They did not make the pilgrimage last year. Some people believe we have had terrorism, floods, sickness and death as a result. We did not do penance and ask for forgiveness from the gods of the snowfields. The pilgrimage must take place this year to avoid more misfortunes."

Leaping from her seat, Doña Lorenza remembered, "Our pilgrims will be off before dawn tomorrow. I must alert Felix, so he is ready to leave in time to guide Ayar from the ice fields to the jungle."

Escape to Qoyllur Rit'i

Ica helped Ayar pack his clothes and the portable parts of his work, so he would not have to be idle while waiting somewhere between the icy mountains and the steaming jungle for the time when he could return. Doña Lorenza came back to the house to report that the pilgrimage did, in fact, start the next day and that her brother Felix had agreed to load Ayar's belongings on his donkeys and accompany him on the steep descent into the rain forest, as soon as the ceremonies in the glacier of Qolqepunku had ended.

"We must inform *caporal* Santiago about our plan. He is the chief of the *ukukus* of the entire province of Quispicanchis," Don Ortiz suggested. He left and headed a short distance down the road where Santiago lived and brought him back to the house.

Upset that Dr. Ayar had been dragged into the terrorist affair, Don Santiago gladly invited Ayar and Ica on the pilgrimage. "Women do not usually disguise as *ukukus*," he said, smiling at Ica. "But since you are taller than most women of the Sierra, no one will notice that you are not a man. Just try to walk less elegantly."

Don Santiago also advised that they should never remove their masks and should always speak in an *ukuku's* high falsetto voice. "This way, everyone within the group may think you are from here, or perhaps are visiting from a neighboring village. No outsider will be able to recognize you." In a whisper he cautioned, "If anyone should find out who you are, we could all be in trouble." He left to fetch two *ukuku* outfits from his house, brought them to Ayar and Ica, then went home to prepare for the pilgrimage.

Immediately they tried on their costumes and accessories. They were unrecognizable in their dark knitted masks that covered their heads and faces, except for the eyes, and their black robes made of shaggy alpaca wool with red trimmings.

"Some pilgrims wear masks and robes of different colors," Francisca explained. "But the dark shades will make it easier for you to hide at night."

As was the custom, both carried a small bottle around their necks that produced whistling sounds when one blew across its surface.

"That's how we *ukukus* ward off sickness," Ayar said with a smile.

Francisca pinned a small doll on the front of their robes. "This is your *wayqe*, your brother, your alter ego," she explained in a serious tone of voice. Moving closer to Ica she reminded her, "You are now an *ukuku* with supernatural powers that allow you to mediate between this world and the world beyond. You must joke with the people you will meet in a high falsetto voice." She demonstrated how this voice from beyond the grave must sound and Ica imitated her without fault.

Don Ortiz gave each *ukuku* a whip. Addressing Ica, he explained, "*Ukukus* incorporate dual forces. They not only joke, but they use these whips to keep order among the crowds during the long pilgrimage and in the sanctuary. There are no police anywhere. The *ukukus* are the keepers of order among tens of thousands of people from many villages."

Don Ortiz and Doña Lorenza looked at their disguised friends with a sense of pride.

"Never forget that you have an important role to fulfill," Don Ortiz disclosed. "Whether the coming year will be a good one depends on you."

Ica emitted a sigh with an uncertain look on her face.

"You will do well," Doña Lorenza said with kindness. "But the ordeal is a difficult one. You must be strong when you engage in rituals on the glacier of Qolqepunku in the bitter cold night."

"Don't worry," Ayar responded with an encouraging smile. "I have done it often enough, and Ica is a fast learner."

"But the crevasses have swallowed many an *ukuku*," Francisca warned.

"The mountain will not swallow us," Ayar answered. "These mountains have healing powers, and they consider us healers as brothers and sisters."

"True," Don Ortiz agreed with new found hope. "It's the escape that still worries me. The police could be back any time now, looking for you, Ayar."

There was a knock at the door. All held their breath. Then Don Felix entered with a grin on his face.

"Thank heaven, brother, it's you," Doña Lorenza said, taking a deep breath.

Greeting everyone cordially, he took Ayar's bags and discussed with him the place and time where they would meet after the night of ceremonies in the glacier. Everyone knew that the meeting had to take place in a remote area, unknown to any pilgrim. Felix took pencil and paper and drew a map of the landmarks that had to be passed to arrive at the spot where they had to meet. He gave it to Ayar and left the house with the same big grin with which he entered.

Before they went to bed, Francisca assured Ayar that together with Don Rodrigues, the doctor and nurses, with Victor, and soon again with Ica, they would take good care of the patients in Qoripampa. They would give special attention to the people afflicted with *espundia*, so the disease would not take too many of them. The Ortiz family also assured Ayar that after the thorough training he had given the healers of Pukamarka, the situation could be managed without him, except for his occasional visits upon his return.

Ayar and Ica tried to get to sleep quickly, knowing there would be little time to rest during the days and nights to come. Before dawn, they ate the hot soup Doña Lorenza had cooked for them, and took the two small containers with food she had prepared for the way. They said good bye, thanking everyone for the help given, and left for the plaza of Pukamarka. They looked like ordinary *ukukus*. *Caporal* Santiago recognized their costumes and welcomed them among his assembled pilgrims.

Doña Lorenza was still standing in the doorway, looking at her disguised friends disappear in the rising dawn, when a police car stopped in front of her house. The red-faced officer jumped out.

"I must see your busy doctor immediately," Redface said in a demanding tone of voice. As the second officer prepared to get out of the car, she noticed handcuffs laying on the seat.

"Our doctor ....he's in the villages," Doña Lorenza informed, pointing in the direction where the rolling hills met the horizon.

"What village," Redface demanded.

"He could be in any village out there. Wherever there are sick people to cure or healers to be instructed, Dr. Ayar is with them," she said, lifting her head high.

"I must know which village he visited first," Redface insisted.

Pointing again to the horizon, she said, "Go in that direction, ask where the sick are and you'll find him. I cannot help you any further. I'm busy enough doing some of his work here, while he visits the villages."

As Redface returned to his car, a police station wagon arrived. The officers exchanged a few words, then Redface pointed in the direction indicated by Doña Lorenza. They drove by the plaza where the pilgrims had assembled.

"Stop here!" Redface shouted at the officers in the other car. "These pilgrims may know exactly where their busy doctor can be found." He stepped out of his car, walked toward the crowd and addressed the chief of the *ukukus*. "Please Sir, would you know where doctor Yupanqui might be found?"

Pointing into the distance Don Santiago proudly announced, "He's away in one of the villages, always working."

"Could he be in one of the villages over there?" Redface inquired, turning toward the far hills as indicated by Doña Ortiz, and in the opposite direction to that in which the pilgrims were about to head.

"Most probably. He always travels widely and visits many villages," Don Santiago explained.

The pilgrims who stood around chief Santiago nodded. "Yes, he often travels far," they murmured in unison.

"Thank you for your assistance," Redface said, looking directly at the chief who was flanked by Ayar and Ica.

Ica turned her head sideways. She feared that Redface could detect her eyes which were lighter than those of the others in the group, and not completely hidden by the woolen mask. But the hurried officer noticed nothing. He returned to his car and together with his fellow policemen drove immediately in the direction where Ayar was said to be.

When they were out of sight, Ayar squeezed Ica's hand. "Well done," he sighed. "It is a good beginning."

With the first rays of the sun brightening the landscape, the large group of forty-two Pukamarka pilgrims walked toward the Sinakara mountain wilderness. The march would take two days and one night. Dancers in their local costumes moved elegantly through the meadows. Among them were the ch'unchu dancers with their colorful costumes and headdresses made of bird feathers. They held palm spears in their hands.

Ayar turned to Ica whispering, "Ch'unchus represent the Indian tribes from the jungles below Apu Qolqepunku. They also represent those mythological beings, believed to be our ancestors, who lived by the light of the moon. This is why there is always a full moon during the pilgrimage to Qoyllur Rit'i."

"I know," Ica responded, "The light of the moon will accompany us."

The ukukus were joking and mock fighting with one another, yet they were eager to keep the whole group in line. Some of the pilgrims carried a cross, others the image of their village saint Asunta, and yet others displayed a variety of paraphernalia, reminiscent of both ancient Andean and Christian beliefs.

"Why this mixture of religious symbols?" Ica asked.

Ayar explained in a whisper that the Spanish conquerors had tried to impose their religion on the Andean people. "Eventually the church had given their consent to some of our people's ancient ceremonies and fiestas," he said, "as long as they were covered by Christian symbols, such as the cross, which disguised their ancient beliefs."

Haunting melodies emanated from the musical instruments, used already before the conquest - flutes, panpipes, large and small drums. Songs about Qoyllur Rit'i, the Star of Snow, filled the air. This pilgrimage had probably been important, even before the Incas ruled the land. Already then the Andean people may have flocked to the ice and snow fields of their mountain gods, honoring and appeasing these deities. In return, they asked them to protect people, animals and crops alike and to provide the healing waters from their glaciers to the people in the valley.

Hours passed. In the heat of the day the group walked across undulating hills and precipitous landscapes in the direction of the Sinakara mountain range, not far from the sacred Apu Ausangate, the highest mountain of southern Peru. As evening approached, the *ukukus* in their thick alpaca robes welcomed the cool breeze which made the ascent less exhausting.

Ayar looked at Ica whispering, "It's good to have this time together."

"If only it would last," she sighed.

"When I return we will always be together, always," Ayar affirmed, hugging her passionately as they walked in the near dark at a distance behind the group with only the moon looking on.

"Tell me about the time when you were with the brother-hood of the Quispicanchis nation. What was it all about?" Ica asked, filled with curiosity.

"It's not easy to explain," Ayar answered. "The beliefs and rituals of Qoyllur Rit'i are deeply embedded in our ideology. It's difficult for outsiders to understand them. This is an ancient Andean festivity. The church participates, but the Christian symbols remain on the surface and do not touch the deeper meaning of this pilgrimage. The rituals have endured for hundreds of years and may well last for hun-dreds more.

"Please explain," Ica pleaded. "After all, I'm now an *ukuku* and should know all about myself and my role in this pil-grimage."

"Alright," Ayar consented, his eyes full of admiration, "You surely are one of the most unique *ukukus* I have ever encoun-tered."

He remained silent for a while as he tried to remember what happened more than fifteen years ago when he had just turned eighteen and was ready to join the brotherhood. Then he spoke, "I was a student of natural medicine con-cerned with the health of our people. It was important that an aspiring healer and medicine man should know about more than just the healing of wounds, broken bones and diseases. So, I had to immerse myself in the realm of the supernatural, to gain access to the cosmic forces that help us heal at a different level. I spent time with our elders, learning about our mythical past and present to understand how spiritual forces contribute to the wellbeing of all life - people, animals and everything born from nature herself." In a whisper he continued, "Tomorrow after we have passed Apu Ausangate, the chief among our mountains, we will enter the Sinakara wilderness where you will see mountain peaks that are very significant for us. They are deeply embedded within the mythology of this land."

"Tell me more," Ica urged.

Looking into the distance, Ayar explained. "The peaks we will visit are deities. Two of them are of great concern to us. The most sacred is Apu Qolqepunku, the Silver Gate. From ancient mythology we know that this Apu watches over the health of our people. As such he is my *wayqe*, my mythological brother."

He was silent for a while, then went on, "Apu Huanacauri, the peak beside Qolqepunku, is another of my mythological brothers. Mythology tells us that one of the four Ayar brothers was converted into a large rock on top of Apu Huanacauri, from where he never returned."

Ica shivered, worried that Ayar, too, might not return. In respect for Andean mythology she said with a forced smile, "You must feel at home among these mythological beings."

Ayar nodded.

Then she continued in a whisper, "I hope the fate of your brothers will not become yours. I hope they will not expect you to remain in their icy world."

"They will not," Ayar said laughing. "But".... looking at her with concern he cautioned, "Be prepared, Ica, we must be strong when we approach Qolqepunku at night in the light of the moon. When we stand on the icy cold snowfields praying for the health of our people, we must not forget that dangers lurk everywhere and it is not rare that the mountain swallows an *ukuku*. The glaciers are full of crevasses and people still believe that our mountain deities require a sacrifice. That's why villagers do not mourn so much when someone does not return from the mountain." He pulled her into his arms as he continued, "Do not worry. Just remember that you must witness the rituals, some of which may shock you. Before leaving we will chop chunks of ice from the body of Qolqepunku. Our fellow pilgrims will carry them down to their villages, so the sick can be cured with the help of the mountain."

"Does this mean that *ukukus* are mythological beings, responsible for healing and for life itself?" Ica inquired.

"Yes," Ayar responded. "We must exert influence on many planes. We must show intelligence and integrity. As metaphors of power and knowledge we must preserve life and order not only in the sanctuary, but also in the cosmos at large."

Ica looked puzzled as Ayar disclosed, "We must confront the spirits of chaos that are strong during times of transition and transformation. In ancient times a new year began in June, after the return of the constellation of the Pleiades. The Pleiades are still called *qolqa*, or store houses, since they influence the agricultural cycle and thus provide us with the food needed to sustain life. If they were not to return to the sky after thirty-seven days of absence, life as we know it could not continue. So, we *ukukus* must show strength of body and mind as we confront the spirits of chaos and thus clear the way for the Pleiades to return to the sky." Holding her hand, he continued, "Our fellow humans expect us to mediate between the past and the present, this world and the underworld, between day and night, order and chaos. They believe in our power to communicate directly with the gods on their behalf."

Ica nodded as Ayar explained, "*Ukuku* means bear in the Quechua language. The spectacled bear of the Andes lives in caves and is therefore associated with both this world and the underworld. It lives between the mountains and the jungle and therefore has dominion over both. As *ukukus* we are metaphors of the bears and we, too, are associated with the twilight as our spirits move between the natural and the supernatural world. But," he paused, "We must watch out that we do not get stuck in the world beyond. We must return to our human society."

Ica sighed.

In a more comforting tone of voice Ayar added, "When the *ukukus* do their task well, they keep the universe in balance and life can proceed healthy and re-energized."

Ica looked worried, "I hope I will be able to fulfill such difficult tasks."

"You will," Ayar responded, squeezing her hand.

The group had almost reached the tree line. Don Santiago suggested that they had advanced far enough to spend a few hours sleeping among the rocks that had collected the heat of the sun throughout the day, giving off their warmth on a cold night at over 4000 meters above sea level.

Ayar and Ica found a cozy spot sheltered by two immense rocks. Sitting down in small groups, everyone offered food to fellow pilgrims and, in return, received similar items, such as potatoes, dried kernels of corn, jerky and dried fruit. They drank water from the clear springs and rivulets that criss-crossed the terrain.

The village band rehearsed the music it was going to play in the sanctuary, while dance groups practiced their choreography. The jungle *ch'unchus* were on the lookout, ready to protect the group from possible dangers. *Ukukus* conversed in their high falsetto voices, joking, mock fighting, and eliciting laughter. Ayar and Ica, remaining fully disguised, participated to everyone's delight.

In their dual roles as tricksters and protectors, *ukukus* are not allowed to sleep once they arrive in the sanctuary. With this in mind, Ayar and Ica bedded down, sheltered by the rocks, lying comfortably on their thick shaggy alpaca robes. They huddled closely together so nothing on earth could separate them, at least not during this precious night.

They looked at the stars and the nearly full moon bathing the landscape in its silvery light. They were close to the sky and felt in heaven. Together and in love, they knew they could overcome whatever life had in store for them. They had already jumped many hurdles and were willing to face more challenges until, eventually, the condors would call their spirits to the mountain peaks. Happy and hopeful they fell asleep.

Another bright day was on its way as the Pukamarka pilgrims continued their journey on the second day of their pilgrimage. Close to Ocongate other groups joined them from all directions, moving toward the sanctuary while singing, playing music and dancing their way up to the heights of Qoyllur Rit'i. Each group brought its special icons, its offerings of music, songs and dances and its hopes for wellbeing and a healthy year for everyone.

In the late afternoon the pilgrims arrived in Mawayani, a small settlement just eight strenuous kilometers from their goal. A cold wind began to blow. Some groups and families pitched their tents on the windswept meadows. With thousands of other pilgrims the Pukamarkans decided to continue on their journey to the sanctuary, tackling the ever steeper inclines.

Night had fallen and the full moon was now shining on their narrow path. Pilgrims stopped from time to time praying by roadside crosses or placing another stone on *apachetas*, sacred cairns that have accepted offerings for a safe and successful journey since time immemorial.

Some pilgrims carried large stones, adding to their already heavy loads of food, pots, pans, sleeping gear or crosses. Some parents carried their children. Ica wondered why people would take such hardship upon themselves at a time when they had to struggle just to survive. These were the most severe economic times in the living memory of the Peruvian people as the Shining Path and other groups roamed through the countryside.

Ayar explained, "The more difficult the ascent, the greater is the sacrifice these people bring to the gods, and the more generous will be the rewards they hope to receive."

The icy wind increased in strength. Away from the hot sun, with their shaggy robes and woolen masks, the *ukukus* were better equipped to deal with the bitter cold than were most pilgrims. Exhausted, but exhilarated, the pilgrims finally saw lights in the distance, coming from an enormous campsite where people cooked and gathered around fires to warm themselves. Some already slept in the tents they brought along or in the open, wrapped in blankets. As the groups approached the sanctuary, they were greeted by a deafening cacophony of sounds that became even louder and more chaotic as they entered the site of Qoyllur Rit'i with its glaciers glowing eerily in the moonlit night. Thousands of people were already present. Each of the hundreds of groups of dancers from different villages moved to its own music, while its musicians tried to outdo the sounds of the surrounding groups. Echoes returned from the rocky walls in the distance, adding to the cacophony of the place.

Spellbound Ica sighed, "This is a different world. I feel as though I'm in a trance."

"This happens when one enters another dimension of reality," Ayar disclosed, equally moved by the dazzling sight.

They stopped in front of the church, at an altitude of 4,900 meters above sea level. Entering through the doorway, they observed masses of people carrying burning candles to a niche at the other end of the church. These pilgrims prayed to the Señor, the Lord of Qoyllur Rit'i which for some represented Jesus, for others the snow-covered Apus. They asked these deities to grant them, a close relative or a friend, good health and prosperity. With everyone so eager to enter the church, it was difficult in the crowd to get to the place where the image of the Lord of Qoyllur Rit'i was said to be imprinted in a rock. Finally they reached this most sacred site where only a few seconds were granted each pilgrim to view the miracle. Then the onlookers were swept out into the icy winter night by the constantly moving flood of people.

"Why a church?" Ica asked. "What does it have to do with this ancient festivity?"

Ayar explained. "In the year 1780 Tupac Amaru II, a descendent of the Inca royalty, and his wife Micaela Bastides, started a rebellion against the injustices the native people had to endure under the conquerors. This rebellion was designed to be peaceful, but turned into the bloodiest revolution ever to occur in the Americas. Tupac Amaru, his wife and family, were killed most cruelly in the middle of Hawkaypata, the central plaza of Qosqo, the Inca capital." Looking at Ica, he said, "You know about this historic event. You talked about it when we stood on the plaza of Qosqo before we went to see the bishop."

Ica nodded. "I know, but how does it relate to Qoyllur Rit'i?"

Ayar continued, "The rebellion of 1780 gave rise to a revival of Inca religion and customs. Since Qoyllur Rit'i was the meeting place for tens of thousands of indigenous people from many parts of the Andes, archbishop Moscoso attempted to control this resurgence and large-scale gathering by placing a Catholic imprint on these pre-conquest rituals. As you can see, he was partially successful."

"Hm," Ica said. "I've heard the story of Mariano Mayta, a little herder boy meeting Jesus who appeared in the form of a white child. They played together in the meadows and became friends."

"That's how the story goes," Ayar affirmed. "It continues telling us that the herd of the little boy's family began to flourish. One day, however, when young Jesus was seen by other villagers, he disappeared forever, leaving the imprint of a cross in the rock. When the herder boy found that his friend was gone, he fell over dead with sorrow and was buried at the foot of the rock. The church was built around this rock, where the miracle is said to have taken place."

"What a sad story," Ica said.

Ayar took her hand. "Let's go to the hills above this campsite, we *ukukus* came to celebrate the Andean cosmos."

Although night had fallen, some people were still sitting within the debris that had accumulated over eons below the glaciers, leaving millions of small stones strewn across the hills. Using these "magic" stones, they traced along the ground whatever their hearts desired – houses, corrals full of llamas and alpacas, cars, airplanes, television sets, and more. At a special rock, named the Virgin of Fatima or the mountain deity Mama Sinakara, located east of the church and believed just as sacred, people deposited pieces of paper, on which they had written the wishes they built from stones, in the hope they would be fulfilled by this female deity.

Ayar glanced at Ica with a smile. "It's heartening to see that people always have hope, no matter how difficult the times."

Ica nodded, gazing at the rocky peaks and the glaciers shining in the full moon. "Yes, that's what keeps us going," she said with a sigh. "Now it helps me more than ever."

As night progressed, the air became still colder. Puddles froze and frost accumulated on the tents. Ayar and Ica joined the Pukamarka dancers, moving to the rhythm of their band, amidst jumbles of sounds coming from hundreds of other bands.

While dancing Ayar noticed a man swinging a bottle over the heads of on-looking pilgrims. He stopped dancing and approached the drunk. Using his whip on the culprit's back in *ukuku* fashion, he grabbed the bottle from him. The drunk's wife came running, apologizing for her husband's misdeed at this most sacred of sites. Ayar ordered the drunk to leave the sanctuary until he was sober.

"You make a wonderful policeman," Ica said teasingly as he rejoined the group for another dance.

Later in the night the *ukukus*, belonging to the brotherhoods of the four nations Quispicanchis, Paucartambo, Paruro and Acomayo, started to organize their activities. *Caporal* Santiago called together the *ukukus* from all villages within the large province of Quispicanchis. One *ukuku* of each group had arrived the previous day to place the village's cross on the ice fields of Apu Qolqepunku. All other *ukukus* had been busy keeping order in the crowded sanctuary, and had been dancing, joking and making others laugh.

From the Ice Fields to the Jungle

At two o'clock in the morning chief Santiago gathered all *ukukus* from his province to begin the ascent to the glacier. They walked in single file in the full moon along a narrow ridge which dropped off steeply on either side. As they advanced toward the ice fields, the music of the many bands throughout the campground gradually became more subdued and finally gave way to a mere murmur.

Having completed the ascent along the dangerous path, the *ukukus* stopped on the glacier, ready to listen to chief Santiago, who took a document from his pocket. He read it, informing the group of the most important events that had happened within the brotherhood throughout the year. He told of the good deeds, the misdeeds and deaths among its members. A few minutes of silence were dedicated in memory of those who had died in the course of the year.

Now the group began the final ascent on the steep slopes of the glacier.

"Ica, give me your hand," Ayar whispered. "If you feel you are slipping, cling to me with all your strength."

"Don't risk your life. If I should slip, let me go," she urged.

"You must hang on," Ayar insisted. "Many pilgrims have been swallowed by the mountain. Crevasses are everywhere, sometimes hidden by the snow."

Despite the danger and the bitter cold, Ica felt a kinship with this mountain and with her fellow climbers whose breath left white shadows in the air as it escaped their woolly masks. This was an image of another world, remote in time and space.

The large group split into subgroups, with members of each village encircling their own cross that had been placed into the ice the previous day. *Caporal* Santiago announced the names of the young *ukukus* to be baptized in the snow. He read the rules which they were to obey throughout their lives and which did not permit improper actions of any kind.

In the immense cold of the night the young men stripped down to their waists and each received three strokes from the whip of an elder. Not one of the initiates made a sound as a few drops of their blood fell in the snow as a sacrifice to the mountain and to Pachamama, the great Earth Mother. Ica could not stand the sight and looked away. Then several older members of the brotherhood came forth. They admitted to excessive drinking on various occasions during the year and asked to be whipped to pay for their sins, to appease the gods, and energize the cosmos.

With the first rays of the sun the *ukukus* fell to their knees. They prayed to the Apus to heal the sick and keep their communities healthy and intact. They vowed to be brave, honest and respectful, and to proceed with kindness and intelligence in all their undertakings.

With unrestrained exuberance the various groups then danced on the glacier, whipping each other's legs to commemorate an ancient dance and to get warm. Using a sharp stone, a knife or small pick, they chopped chunks of ice from the glacier to take with them to the valley.

"Bring these gifts from the Apus to your communities," chief Santiago called out with pride. "This water will heal anyone who drinks it."

With a knife Ayar cut two pieces of ice off the glacier. One for Ica and one for himself and tied them to their backs with rope.

Now all the *ukukus* who had assembled on the glacier, split in two groups. Following the command of chief Santiago, one group lined up in single file and danced in serpentine motions down to the campground. They laughed loudly having successfully passed their ordeal. They were happy that their efforts would make the coming agricultural year a good one, bringing health and well being to the communities and adding more life force to the universe. The other group, equally happy, danced in the direction of Tayankani, as its members started on a journey to the closest town that would last more than twenty hours.

As soon as everyone had moved out of sight, Ayar pulled Ica behind a rock. Holding her hands, he looked at her with love. "Please leave me now and join one of the groups for a safe trip home," he pleaded.

But Ica refused. "I will go with you to where you meet Don Felix," she said in a determined tone of voice. "I can find my way back home from there, I assure you." She put her hand in front of Ayar's mouth as he tried to contradict her. "I will go with you," she repeated as they bent down moving from one rock to another, hiding from anyone who might look back toward the snowfields.

Following their plan, they searched for a pass to the eastern side of the mountain where it jutted steeply into the jungle across several ecological zones. Finally they found the divide between two peaks.

"Look at your mythological brothers!" Ica exclaimed, half in awe, half worried, as they passed between the peaks, those petrified remains of ancient heroes.

"They did not make it back to the valley, but we will," Ayar responded.

Still, both he and Ica could not completely hide their anxiety about the fate held in store for them.

The descent was steep and slippery. To facilitate their journey, they untied the chunks of ice on their backs and offered them to the mountain. Ica put a small piece, that had broken off, into her woven bag. Eventually the permanent snow fields gave way to unstable glacial debris and finally to a grassy meadow.

Ayar took the map from his pocket that Felix had drawn. "We are fine so far and we'll be on time," he said. "Let's rest for a while."

He sat down, pulling Ica into his arms. She felt the warmth of his breath on her forehead. Both were exhausted. Since the magic night in the rock shelter on their return from Ritipata, they have had few moments alone. Now they enjoyed every minute before they had to part and endure loneliness for an unknown period of time.

"We must think pleasant thoughts," Ica proposed, wiping tears from her eyes.

"*Sonqochallay*," Ayar whispered, "Our spirits were united in Rimaq Mach'ay, the speaking cave. They will never be separated, regardless of the distance between us." He hugged her with passion. "You will always be with me."

They talked about their work, about finding an inexpensive method of treating *espundia* which had its roots in the tropical region where Ayar was heading. They knew that native jungle tribes seemed little affected by the disease, and kept wondering whether these indigenous people knew how to prevent the disease, how to cure it at its very onslaught, or whether they were simply immune to it. They hoped that Ayar's time in the jungle would bring them closer to the answers.

"The criminals will be found soon. You will return, and we can be together forever," Ica said, trying to express her feelings in a happier way.

"Yes," Ayar responded with a smile. "They will be found."

Leaning against his shoulder, Ica was about to doze off when they remembered their rendezvous with Don Felix.

"If only we could forget time and space," Ayar wished. "But Don Felix may already be waiting where the paths cross."

"I know," Ica said, as she gave him a small piece of the melting glacial ice she had stuffed into her bag to quench his thirst and give him health.

They continued their descent. The hillside became more lush with every turn. Suddenly they heard a faint voice coming from the distance. They stopped and listened. Then they recognized Don Felix with his two donkeys waving to them from below where the paths crossed. Happy to see him, they accelerated their pace. But they also knew that the time to part was terribly close.

Don Felix greeted them with an encouraging smile. "This is, indeed, good fortune," he said. "You survived the ordeal on the ice. You found the way, and you are right on time."

"Your map was a great help. Your knowledge is amazing," Ica said with admiration. "Is there any part of this landscape you do not know?"

Looking at Ica, Felix wrinkled his forehead. "Señorita, it's you I'm worried about. You have come so far. How will you find your way home?"

Ayar nodded with an equally concerned look on his face.

"As long as there are mountains and valleys to orient me, I'm fine," she insisted. She did not want to admit that she was also slightly worried about finding home all alone.

Don Felix offered potatoes, roasted corn and dried fruit. "You must be hungry. I know what you went through. I have been a pilgrim many times when I was young," he said, grinning with pride.

They sat down on the grass eating and debating which way would be closest and least cumbersome for Ica to take back to Pukamarka.

"Don't go back the same way you came," Felix said. That would be deadly. I'll show you how you reach home without climbing steep mountains." He drew a map of the major landmarks she had to pass. Ica accepted it with gratitude, giving him a big hug.

"You won't get home today," Felix cautioned. "You must stop at the nearest settlement and ask for a place to stay for the night."

Ica nodded.

As they gazed into the distance, they saw an *ukuku* coming their way.

"Who in the hell would end up down here after the fiesta," Felix mumbled, disgusted that someone had found their meeting place.

Ayar and Ica quickly pulled their masks over their faces, nervous that someone might detect them just before Ayar was to disappear in the rain forest. As the *ukuku* came closer, he spoke to them in his high falsetto voice, joking and walking rambunctiously to make them laugh. But the group remained silent, holding their breath.

With a quick movement of his hand, the approaching *ukuku* pulled off his mask, causing sighs of astonishment and relief from the three onlookers.

"Francisca!" Ica exclaimed. "How did you know we were here?"

"I overheard your discussion with the Ortiz family and I knew you would dare to come along to where the paths cross," she responded.

"What a daredevil you are," Ayar said, looking at Francisca with a tinge of humor in his voice.

"Glad you came," Felix said contented. "You make it easier for us to let Ica go."

They continued eating their meal. Francisca added more fruit and water to the menu. Then Don Felix made it known that it was getting late and was time to leave on their separate journeys. He took his leave from Ica and Francisca and walked ahead toward the east. Francisca gave Ayar a hug and returned in the direction from which she had come.

Ayer and Ica knew they had only a few moments alone. Slowly they followed Don Felix at a short distance, holding on to one another, unable to speak. As they came to a split in the path, Ayar hugged Ica with a passionate embrace. "Until soon, my love, until soon," he whispered.

"Yes," Ica answered in tears. "Until soon."

She remained on the spot from where she could see him descend the steep, overgrown, serpentine path. He looked up at every turn he took and she waved good bye until he had disappeared in the thicket far below. From there Ayar followed Felix through several ecological zones down to the immense tropical rain forest.

For a while Ica stood frozen in place. Ayar had taken with him part of her very being. Finally she gathered her strength to turn around and catch up with Francisca.

"Thank you for coming," Ica said, tears flowing from her eyes. Silently they walked together for several hours. As night fell, they reached a small settlement.

"My great aunt lives here," Francisca disclosed.

No one saw them come.

Before they knocked on aunt Benita's door, they took off their *ukuku* outfits, leaving them on a shelf in a hut beside the corral where the animals slept. Francisca took pants and a jacket for Ica from the woven shawl she carried on her back. Except for chief Santiago and their closest friends, no one was to find out about Ica's whereabouts or about her disguise.

Doña Benita was happy to see her great niece and was equally thrilled to meet Ica, who she hoped would tell her interesting stories about foreign countries. In her nineties, she was still intrigued by everything she heard about the outside world. Her great sense of humor had not left her despite a life of hardships.

Please take a seat, Doña Benita said, pointing to two low stools beside the earthen stove. With her fingers she combed through her graying hair. She reached for her shawl and threw it across her shoulders to give a more elegant appearance. Then she put a water kettle on the wood stove to make herbal tea.

"You aren't hungry, are you?" she said laughing as she took the lid from a big pot of vegetable soup. "Many years ago I danced throughout the fiestas and then I ate. Now I only eat," she admitted while chuckling in a contented way. " And because of my good appetite, I made so much soup that there's plenty for all of us."

"Wonderful," Francisca exclaimed, reaching for a plate.

"Just a minute," great aunt cautioned. "First the guest from afar."

She handed a bowl full of soup to Ica who thanked her and immediately started to eat. Then she gave one to Francisca and finally ate herself. Before a second helping was offered, Ica had fallen asleep on the floor. Doña Benita covered her with a thick blanket.

"There go my stories," she said with a bitter sweet expression on her face.

"Auntie, you know how far we have come. One gets tired," Francisca asserted.

"Of course I know, or I would visit you more often," the old lady responded, laughing heartily.

Both talked and joked for some time. Then they, too, covered themselves in blankets and fell asleep on the floor.

The next morning Ica and Francisca rose before sunrise to get an early start.

"Please come again, stay longer and tell me stories," old auntie begged Ica as she said good bye. "You must come soon," she urged, "very soon. I'm old and don't know how much longer I'll be on this earth. I'm at least three times as old as either of you and I'll pray that you both will be as healthy as I am when you are old ladies."

"Thank you," Ica responded laughing.

"You come visit us," Francisca suggested. "You always wanted a hospital that is not too far away. Now we have one."

"That's wonderful," auntie said with a grin. "The next time I'm sick, I'll be there." She gave both a big hug, wishing that the sun would always shine bright on their path. Then she waved until they were out of sight.

"Our *ukuku* outfits?" Ica wondered as they were well on their way.

"We'll leave them in auntie's shed," Francisca said. "Nobody may know what has happened and those who'll find them will be overjoyed."

Enigmas Abound

In the late afternoon Ica and Francisca arrived at the Ortiz home. Francisca continued on her way to Qoripampa. Ica stayed in Pukamarka for two days looking after the leishmaniasis patients.

"I'm glad you are back," Don Ortiz said after Ica had knocked on the door.

"Please tell me what happened since we left," Ica asked.

"The police have been here several times," Don Ortiz informed. "Ayar's disappearance made them even more suspicious."

Doña Lorenza approached Ica, whispering, "We were questioned about Ayar's whereabouts, but no one is aware of your escape or your close ties to Ayar." Looking at Ica with understanding, she confided, "We know how much you love one another. Still, it was wise that you kept your feelings hidden from outsiders."

Ica nodded, smiling for a moment. Then with a more somber expression she asked, "Does anyone suspect where Ayar is hiding?"

"Nobody knows except for Don Santiago and of course Felix. Both can be trusted," Don Ortiz replied in a comforting tone of voice. "But the police are still making their rounds in the villages to the west. They seem to think that's where he's hiding."

"Have they given up looking for the criminals?" Ica asked anxiously.

"It seems so," Doña Lorenza responded with sadness.

Ica decided to visit Don Santiago to thank him for the great help he had given them.

"We *ukukus* must see to it that justice prevails," Don Santiago said responding to Ica's gratitude. "The criminals must be found soon and Ayar will return. I'll keep my eyes and ears open at all times."

"Thank you," Ica said. "I also want to thank you for the costumes you loaned us." In an apologetic tone of voice she admitted, "I left mine in a small village on the way from the sanctuary. Ayar took his to the jungle. I would like to replace both."

"No need to give them back," Santiago said with a smile. "My house is full of costumes. Those *ukukus* who no longer climb to the glaciers leave their outfits with me. Many are still waiting to be used."

For the next two days Ica worked with the healers of Pukamarka. She was pleased to see they had learned well and took good care of their patients, treating those with the cutaneous form of leishmaniasis with considerable success. She took the three patients with *espundia* to Qoripampa.

Back at the hospital Ica's patients, friends and colleagues congratulated her on the courageous work she had done during the flood that came crashing down from Pukamarka's reservoir. All of them prayed that the terrorists would soon be found and that Ayar would return from wherever he had gone. Don Rodrigues and Doña Nilda had learned about his escape from Francisca. They advised Ica to keep this event and her contact with him a secret, since any knowledge of his disappearance could be dangerous for her or anyone else who might know about his whereabouts.

On several occasions officer Redface had tried to find Ica. One day he entered her lab without notice and found her filling small bottles with herbal extracts.

"You must be lonely working without your colleague, the notorious Dr. Yupanqui," he said in a sarcastic tone of voice. Coming closer, he added with a sly grin, "I'm certain you could give me a little hint about his whereabouts. Surely you would be just as happy to see him return as the rest of us."

Ica remained silent. Without looking at him she continued working. Then she placed the pitcher with the herbal solution on the table and looked him straight in the eye. "Officer," she said, "How would you like to do your work plus that of one of your colleagues from morning till night, knowing that the lives of those you try to save rest on your shoulders alone?" Taking a step back, she added, "I'm concerned about him as I would be if any of my colleagues didn't come to work. Wouldn't you be concerned if one of your colleagues remained absent and you had no idea where to find him?" Resuming her work, she said bluntly, "I cannot waste time. As you see, I must do the work for two. Come back when you've found the criminals. In the meantime, don't bother me with your questions."

Redface left without saying a word.

Apart from disturbing rumors and the uncertainty of Ayar's return, Ica's work at the hospital and in the lab proceeded well. Given her concern for the sick and her promise to Ayar to pursue their common goals, she worked until late most nights. Her work also alleviated some of the pain caused by Ayar's absence. As she became more familiar with *espundia*, she became more confident in her role as primary care giver for the people afflicted with this severe illness. Yet, Ayar was always at the back of her mind, where she asked him what to do when things became difficult or a patient was about to die.

Several weeks after the sad farewell on the ridge above the jungle, Don Felix knocked on Ica's door early in the morning. He looked happy. With satisfaction he told her that Ayar had found a decent place to stay on the outskirts of Amarukancha, a small settlement where one of Felix's trading partners lived.

"The locals love him," Felix conveyed. "They are thrilled that Ayar is interested in both, their natural medicine and that of the modern world." He laughed heartily as he continued, "They call his microscope a magic tube. And they have helped Ayar build a large table, which he placed under a roof where he now works with his plants."

Winking at Ica, he opened his bag and handed her a pile of letters. "Here are the details and more," he said with a teasing grin. "I have errands to run and will be back in a week."

Ica reached for the envelopes with joy written all over her face. She did not work late that night. As soon as she had finished treating her patients, she went to her room to be alone with Ayar's letters. She smiled, reading about his experiences with native healers who treated their patients in and around Amarukancha. Most of all he seemed excited to be able to work with natives who lived even deeper in the jungle. "These people may hold the secret of preventing leishmaniasis, or healing it when the first symptoms appear," he wrote. Yet, despite his enthusiasm, his letters did not hide his longing for her. "You are with me every minute of each day," he wrote. "Just as I used to see the sparkle in your eyes in every clear mountain lake, I now see it in every beam of light that dances on the deep green vegetation. Wherever I look in this mysterious forest, I am reminded of you."

In another letter Ayar spoke of her spiritual presence and how it helped him go on with his life and his work. Then he wrote in greater detail about his plans to discover why jungle tribes seemed to be much more resistant to *espundia*. He also wanted to find ways to detect the rate of progression of the disease in people who came from outside the jungle region to Amarukancha to exchange produce. He asked Ica to consider this issue for comparative purposes when diagnosing and treating her patients.

In accordance with Ayar's requests, Ica returned notes to him on the health of the people who came to the hospital from different parts of the jungle. Regardless of whether they were sick with leishmaniasis at arrival, whether the disease appeared at a later date, or whether migrants remained unaffected for some time, she looked for patterns of its manifestation and the speed at which the disease progressed. She also made notes of its frequency and severity in accordance with the regions where people worked, the amount of time they spent there, hours of work, kind of nutrition, and their general state of health.

Their combined research confirmed that people who remained outdoors throughout dusk and part of the night when the sandflies were most active, were much more prone to get the disease than those who stayed inside a house, in any closed place, or under a mosquito net at these crucial times of the day.

Felix returned to Qoripampa as promised in exactly a week's time. "I see you had good news," he said laughing, looking at Ica's happy face. "And how are things going at the hospital?"

"Work goes well," Ica confided. "But I've heard nothing about the terrorists."

"I know," Felix whispered, "The villagers of Pukamarka are still looking for them, but for the police Ayar remains the prime suspect." Moving closer to Ica with his voice lower still, he whispered, "The Ortiz family is being watched by the police. Not a week goes by without them being questioned."

Ica sighed. "We are being observed as well, even the Rodrigues family and Ayar's neighbors and friends." She covered her face to hide her sudden tears. "If only the criminals were found."

Felix touched her shoulders, "Everything will be alright. Ayar *will* return."

Ica forced a smile as he promised, "Next week I'll go back to the jungle to bring him the things he needs, above all your letters."

"I'm glad you can go so soon again," Ica said, now in a more spirited tone of voice.

"I must obey my big sister, good old Doña Lorenza," Felix replied laughing. "She reminds me often that the contact between you and our doctor must be kept alive."

"I don't know how to thank you," Ica whispered.

"Don't worry, he responded with pride. "I travel more frequently than before, but these trips keep me and my donkeys in shape. My trading partners also like it when I come more often."

Ica went upstairs to the attic where she had hidden her letters for Ayar behind a curtain that covered the wall. She added the data about her latest research and photos of the changes that had been made to the hospital since he left. She knew he would be happy to hear that the addition to the hospital resulted in eight more rooms, five of them for leishmaniasis patients.

Ica did not want Ayar to worry, but she needed to inform him that it had become increasingly more difficult to obtain the medication for patients with *espundia*. Pharmacies and hospitals in Qosqo, where they used to obtain the imported drugs, often ran out of them due to increasing demand.

"Ayar will be glad to see that our struggle had not been in vain," Ica said to Felix, as she gave him her notes, photos, and the research materials Ayar had requested and also some clothes and edibles. The package was heavy, but Felix did not complain.

Months passed. Felix left and returned several times. Letters full of love and sometimes sadness, reports on their work, and packages of all sizes passed from the highlands to the jungle and back. Ica continued sending Ayar her findings on the leishmaniasis patients she was treating at the hospital. Ayar sent her vast amounts of data that gave more insight into the disease and its prevention and he also sent her some very special plants that only grow in specific places in the jungle.

In a recent letter he wrote, "I am now living with one of the Machiguenga tribes who use an insect repellent made from the fruit of the *witoq* tree which botanists call *Genipa americana*. Whether this is one of the reasons why these people are much less bothered by leishmaniasis, or whether other factors are also at play, I do not yet know."

Ayar further explained, "It is possible that natives develop immunity to leishmaniasis if they had been previously infected by a less serious form of the *Leishmania* parasite. After the lesions have healed, the natives would have become more resistant to the disease."

Ayar also wondered whether indigenous people from *Leishmania* infected jungle regions had the ability to control the parasite by suppressing it. This means that they would not show any adverse effects from the infection. "If this turned out to be true," he wrote, "more research in this direction could eventually lead to a vaccine."

He also suggested that another reason for the indigenous people's greater immunity with respect to leishmaniasis could be their use of a marvelous plant, called *Uña de Gato* or cat's claw, the *Uncaria tomentosa*, as scientists referred to it. It was known to cure a variety of diseases. "I often see these people drink the tea they make from its bark," he wrote. "I am very interested in this plant. I am sending a sample along with Felix.

In a later letter Ayar wrote, "Lately more migrants have come to this region. I have successfully treated several patients with the cutaneous form of the disease. The leaves and the bark of the cashew tree seem to be a helpful remedy.

And then he revealed a most exciting finding. "Ica, I know you will be surprised to hear that *Galipea longiflora* or *Evanta* is not only effective in treating the cutaneous form of leishmaniasis, but may even heal *espundia* if caught in its initial stages. Isn't this wonderful? My work is the only thing that keeps me from going crazy. I long for you so much."

In his letters Ayar also expressed his concern for preventing leishmaniasis on a larger scale. "We must keep the ecosystems intact. Deforestation causes much harm since it changes the ecological niches of the sandflies and brings many more humans into close proximity with the disease. Spraying with insect repellents is helpful within and around homes, but other solutions must be found for the greater natural environment."

Then he referred to the need for in-depth and long-term research. "Ica, we must find the source of the disease and ways to prevent it, as we have discussed so often. It's important to understand the parasite–vector–host relationship. We must trace the development of the parasite *Leishmania* and its vector, the sandfly *Lutzomyia*. I discovered that the host reservoirs for the parasite in the jungle region where I am, are rats and sloths. Other wild animals seem to be hosts as well. There is so much more to discover here. We certainly don't need cruel experiments where animals are unnecessarily subjected to diseases in the lab. It can all be done in the wild by observing living animals and using those which have died from this disease."

In another letter he seemed enthusiastic as he wrote, "Imagine, Ica, I have finally found the larvae of the sandfly *Lutzomyia*. They are difficult to detect in the wild although they are several millimeters long and can be seen with the naked eye. Yet, the sandfly itself is only one third the size of most other species of mosquitoes. I'm content to be able to learn more about the parasite *Leishmania braziliensis* in the region where I work. What I'm missing here are specific tools which would allow me to better analyze my finds. But I am making progress. Again I must say that intensive long-term research in the wild is necessary to get all the results we need."

Then Ica opened Ayar's most recent letter and read, "Dearest Ica, I am presently trying to cure patients with *espundia*. Over a year ago a family of four came from a small town to collect chestnuts at a place that's about a two days walk from here. The father and his young daughter are now affected by the disease and came to see me. I scraped some tissue from the deep dermal edges of their wounds, stained the material and put it under the microscope. It looks like an infestation of the *Leishmania braziliensis* parasite. For some time I have been using warm compresses on these patients' open wounds hoping that this treatment together with *Galipea longiflora* would help or at least keep it from progressing any further. But last week the little girl's nose showed definite signs of *espundia*. Her father is in bad shape as well. My worst fears for them have come true. Please Ica, if at all possible, send me enough Glucantime or Amphotericin B to treat these patients. Send even a little more if you have enough for your own patients. There are no signs as yet that the other two family members are afflicted. I hope that Felix can come soon. All my love, Ayar."

Ica was worried. Where could she find the medication that Ayar so urgently needed? Apart from the afflicted people who came directly to her hospital, Don Ortiz and Doña Lorenza had recently brought her several more patients who showed the signs of *espundia*. With eight patients at various stages of the disease in her care, she had run out of the pharmaceutical medicine. Even in the city's hospitals supplies had shrunk to where they had barely enough to treat their own most critical cases. This unfortunate shortage was due to an epidemic in the tropical forest that had forced many migrant workers to return to their home provinces to seek help.

Don Rodrigues and Francisca made another trip to the provincial capital trying to find the urgently needed medication. They were lucky. Two shipments of Glucantime had just arrived; one from France, the other from Switzerland. This was sufficient for close to forty patients who had recently arrived in the city's largest hospital. Don Rodrigues was able to buy enough medicine for the treatment of ten people. Ica put aside what Ayar had requested for his two patients. The rest was needed for her eight patients in Qoripampa's hospital.

Given so many patients and scarce medication, the only good news came from Don Ortiz. He reported that engineers and laborers had returned to Pukamarka to work on the internationally funded project. They repaired the damage done to the reservoir, canals and other parts of the irrigation system. Most people had already rebuilt their small adobe houses and corrals which the flood had washed away.

Development work proceeded quickly and in October the irrigation system was ready to provide water for the planting of the new crops. The inauguration was to proceed quietly since the villagers did not want to call attention to the completed work. Most villagers were convinced that the terrorists were still hiding in the province, although the search had been officially halted. To ensure that outsiders did not have easy access to the irrigation works, the local irrigation committee decided that the peasant farmers had to take turns guarding the canals and the reservoir by day and night.

On the evening prior to the inauguration, Doña Lorenza suggested to her husband and several other members of the irrigation committee, that they inspect the reservoir and canals one more time before the night shift observers took over. They agreed and Doña Lorenza decided to come along. As the group climbed uphill, the last rays of the sun gave a deep glow to the yellow and light brown tones of the fields and meadows which contrasted with the green trees and bushes that survived the lengthy dry season. The group members were happy thinking about their fields turning green as the irrigation water would soon flow through the canals giving life to the growing plants.

The rainy season had not yet begun and it was crucial to give the first crop an early start using irrigation water. Early planting would allow peasant farmers to obtain two harvests every year which would not only provide more food and a greater variety of food items for local families, but would also allow farmers to sell part of their produce on the markets. With double-cropping in place, young people's seasonal migrations to jungle regions would no longer be necessary. The villagers had awaited the completion of the irrigation system with great hope.

When the group arrived at the newly repaired reservoir, everything seemed in order. In the calm of the evening, they heard only the sounds of insects humming and birds chirping. Don Ortiz and the group members went around the reservoir scanning the region above it. Here the small river Pumamayu was captured, providing the water for the reservoir. They stopped for a short while looking in awe at this masterpiece of engineering.

As they were about to return home, Doña Lorenza noticed a small, freshly heaped pile of earth, half hidden behind a rock close to the central gate of the reservoir. She and her husband went to inspect the mound. When they came close, they heard a faint ticking sound.

"Get back!" Don Ortiz commanded, as other villagers approached. "A bomb!" He and his wife hurried to where their nephew Marcos waited with other committee members.

"Marcos," Don Ortiz urged, "bring my tools from the shed beside my house. Hurry, a bomb is ticking." He asked two others in the group to alert the police. They ran down to the village.

With the committee members assembled around him, Don Ortiz discussed the steps to be taken to avert another trage- dy. Since he had worked in a quarry for many years, in charge of explosives, he knew exactly what to do. The others had to watch out for the terrorists who would most likely be hiding close by.

Half an hour had passed when Marcos arrived on horseback with the required tools. All in the group hurried closer to the site. But Don Ortiz cautioned them to stay back, as he approached the mound and began to defuse the simple but deadly bomb.

From a distance the onlookers held their breath, some of them shivering at the thought of what could happen to Don Ortiz, to the reservoir and to their village. Doña Lorenza offered a *k'intu* to the Apus, asking for their help. She knew her husband was an expert on explosives, but no one knew the time at which the bomb had been set to go off. Twelve minutes seemed like hours until Don Ortiz got on his feet and walked back to the group. Doña Lorenza took a deep breath. The others complimented her husband on his courageous effort.

"It would have been a devastating explosion," he said, with his voice slightly shaking. "It could have been a second flood."

Dozens of villagers, who had been alerted by Marcos, came to the site to search the area in groups of four to see if other bombs might be hidden. They found none, but decided to remain in the vicinity where the bomb had been planted.

An hour later, with the full moon illuminating the landscape, nine policemen stormed up the hill with the two men who alerted them. The committee members and other villagers decided to observe from different vantage points, each group accompanied by an armed policeman. Don Ortiz and several police officers moved cautiously through the terrain. As they searched high above the reservoir, they heard laughter coming from behind a large rock outcrop.

"The terrorists," Don Ortiz whispered. "They are waiting to watch the explosion."

The police, together with Don Ortiz and a few group members, crawled through the underbrush to where the voices came from. As they peered through the thicket they saw two guards sitting outside a cave conversing with their fellows who were hidden inside.

The policemen were now standing close to the rock outcrop. "Don't move," they called out. The guards turned around and shot at the police. One officer was hit in the arm. A bullet hit Don Ortiz' right leg. The other policemen returned fire. Both guards fell to the ground with multiple gunshots. Two officers handcuffed the guards while the three other policemen with several committee members rushed into the cave. They discovered five more men who had jumped up to get to their rifles which were leaning against the far wall of the cave. The police fired a warning shot. The men froze in place. Committee members from across the terrain had heard the shooting and rushed to the scene. They helped the police handcuff the terrorists. Those unharmed were taken to the valley. Marcos galloped with his horse to the village to get stretchers for the injured.

Five policemen and dozens of committee members remained for most of the night in the area around the reservoir to ensure that there was no more danger.

In the early morning hours, after the injured had received first aid treatment in Pukamarka, the seven terrorists were taken in two police cars to the provincial jail. Don Ortiz and the injured policeman left for the hospital in Qoripampa where Ica and the physician in residence took care of their wounds. Despite their injuries, they were happy to know the culprits were on their way to jail. Intensive questioning within the next two days revealed that the same group had destroyed the irrigation works the previous year.

"These criminals try to destroy everything the government builds with international help," Don Ortiz said with concern. "Our government is far from perfect. They have not managed to bring justice to the poor. But to destroy a project they helped build that benefits the rural population, is despicable." Looking at Ica he said, "Still, we should be content. This time luck was on our side. With the criminals in jail, Ayar is free to return and resume his work among us."

Ica was ecstatic. She wrote to Ayar, telling him the exciting news about the capture. Three days later Felix left on another trip to the jungle to exchange more goods with his trading partners, and most importantly, to take Ica's letter to Ayar and the medication he so urgently requested for his patients.

The news spread quickly. Villagers from Pukamarka to Qoripampa and surroundings were relieved and overjoyed that the criminals had been caught and Ayar was no longer in danger. Ica could hardly wait for his return. It had been so long since their painful good bye. Friends, colleagues and all the villagers, even the Avarons, were busy preparing for

Ayar's arrival. The policemen who had believed him to be the culprit, apologized to the villagers. Those who helped catch the gang were praised for their courageous work. Only Redface remained sour. He was sent by head quarters to a camp for remedial treatment.

Ica worked enthusiastically to get her research data organized. Several weeks earlier she had sent a preliminary report about hers and Ayar's combined research findings to a European institute of tropical diseases. On top of the good news about the capture of the criminals, both she and Ayar received an invitation to present their work at this institute's annual conference to be held in France, all expenses paid. Overjoyed she went to the city with Don Rodrigues to make travel arrangements for their trip to be taken in three and a half months.

After four weeks Felix returned from the jungle - alone. Everyone was sad, and Ica was heartbroken. As always, she received many letters, full of love and valuable new data on the disease. But there was no mention about his return and even the words that were meant to cheer her up, had a sad undertone.

"Felix, what's happening?" Ica asked with grief written on her face.

"Ayar works hard. He must finish his job. He cannot come back as yet. He also has ..... He has some patients with *espundia*," Felix explained, looking the other way.

Ica was devastated. Why would Ayar do this to her, to himself and to everyone who waited so impatiently for his return? His research reports were fascinating. He must be in good health. How else could he work so hard, she wondered.

She asked Felix to wait while she wrote another letter informing Ayar about the French institute's enthusiastic response and their invitation to the international conference on tropical diseases.

"Your work is paramount in finding an affordable cure for the dreaded disease and to prevent it. We will receive international support that can help so many people and allow us to continue our research. Do bring your patients with *espundia* from the jungle to Qoripampa. Please return, I cannot go on without you any longer." She also informed him about the precise travel arrangements she had made for both of them out of Qosqo.

Ica begged Felix to take the letter to Ayar and also to bring him some more Glucantime which he so desperately needed for his patients and which Francisca had been able to buy in the city. "Bring him back with you. The danger is gone and the conference will benefit our patients immensely," she implored.

"I will do my best," Felix promised, trying to comfort her. He agreed to travel one more time to the jungle before the rainy season would be in full swing.

Over a month passed before Felix returned from his trip. Ica spotted him through the window as he approached the hospital. She hurried out to greet him.

"Where is Ayar?" she inquired nervously.

"He had to stay," Felix responded calmly.

"Where is he? What's going on?" she insisted.

"He's working hard," Felix said with a forced smile.

"Where is he working, please tell me," Ica pleaded.

"About eight hours on foot from the settlement where he used to live. It took me a long time to find him, but there he was, working away."

"He must return. We are invited to go to Europe," Ica said irritated. "It's an important conference. His presence is needed. His findings are invaluable." She paused. Looking at Felix she said in a determined tone of voice, "I will go with you. When can we leave?"

"In a few months, after the rainy season is over," Felix responded.

"I will go to get him myself," Ica said with a spark of hope in her eyes. "Please draw me a map of his precise location. Please Felix, please."

"Don't go," Felix insisted. "You would never be able to return in time for your conference or return at all."

"I don't understand you, Felix. Tell me the truth," Ica cried. "It cannot be. This is too much," she uttered in despair. Then in a calmer tone of voice she added, "I know I can trust him."

"He loves you very much. I know he does," Felix responded, handing her an envelope.

Ica walked out into the corn fields to be alone. She opened the large envelope and found extensive reports about the disease, its manifestations, the rate at which it proceeded among non-natives in the jungle in comparison to Ica's data on its progression in the highlands.

There was only one letter. It was beautiful, full of love and admiration for her and her team. He also praised their friends, the Ortiz family and the policemen for their bravery at deactivating the bomb, locating the criminals, and proving his innocence. But then she read the dreadful lines, "Ica, beloved, you are doing such excellent work. Please go to Europe and represent us both. I love you and will be with you in spirit and mind – always. Then please return to Qoripampa. Your patients need you."

Ica cried. This sounded like a final letter, a last good-bye. She could not sleep that night or the following nights. During the days she attended to her patients. Throughout the nights she coordinated their research data, worked on the conference reports and the materials to accompany them. Victor helped her after school and sometimes half through the night.

"Ica, I will go with you," he said, looking deadly serious. "I will, if Ayer does not return in time."

A Mirage in the Fog

Ica sat on her bed by her packed travel bags for several hours, re-reading the many letters she had received since Ayar waved his goodbye and disappeared within the lush vegetation of the forest. The letters smelled of the hot jungle earth, mixed with the odor of the donkeys who transported them, and the bag made of llama wool that contained them. The smell of the wooden box where Ica kept them added to the potpourri of odors, as did the fragrance of the eucalyptus trees coming through the window.

All his letters revealed a longing for her that seemed to increase with the time of their separation. But in the later ones he no longer referred to the joy of reuniting. Instead his words carried an air of melancholy. His love for her remained an eternal bond, profound and intimate. Yet, there was also a painful sense of distance.

Ica clutched the pile of letters whispering, "Why don't you return, Ayar? Why can't we be together? Why Ayar, why?" The thought that something terrible had happened to him did not leave her mind. She shuddered as she imagined that he had contracted a disease, perhaps *espundia*, which they both had been working so hard to combat.

But this could not be. Better than anyone else he knew ways of preventing and curing it. Or was he close to finding a cure, so close that he could not leave? She gave a sigh. Yes, this must be it. This must be the reason. But this comforting idea soon gave way to more doubts.

She remembered the many times when Ayar had assured her that they would always work together, side by side. He explained the ancient Andean notion of duality by which different but complementary forces join to achieve optimum results. Ica smiled for an instant as she recalled how he looked at her when he said that he needed her more than the life-sustaining rays of the sun.

She carefully placed the letters back into the box and slowly walked to the window. She was tired from last night's farewell party with her friends, her hospital- and research teams, and from the many hours she had lain awake hoping that Ayar would arrive.

The door swung open.

"*Mamita*, I am ready! I have packed everything!" Victor exclaimed. His eyes lit up in anticipation of the long journey he was about to take.

Ica smiled at him trying to hide her pain. "You have done a great job, Victor. We are well prepared."

The Rodrigues family offered to take Ica and Victor to the train station in Qosqo, but Ica declined.

"I'm not good company. My thoughts are elsewhere," she insisted. "Besides, we will only be gone for a couple of weeks."

Her friends nodded with understanding, hugging her with tears in their eyes.

Moments later a squeaking bus stopped at the corner of the market place. Ica thought back to when she had stepped off this very bus onto the deserted plaza more than two years ago. She was alone then. Now their friends appeared from all directions as she and Victor boarded the bus. "*Hoq p'unchay kama, apuray qutiramunki!*" they called out, saying good bye and asking them to return soon. The warm wishes of their friends mingled with the grinding noise of the rusty bus that skidded along the earthen road to town. Ica felt torn, recalling her fond memories but also the sadness of this place that had become her home.

As the heat of the day gave way to a cool evening breeze and finally to the fog of the night, the bus arrived in Qosqo, the former capital of the Inca empire. The train was already waiting in the dimly lit station. Few people seemed to travel on this night and Victor had no trouble finding two opposing window seats in an otherwise empty compartment. This was the first time in his life he travelled by train and he could barely hide his excitement as he experimented with the various gadgets along its seats and windows.

With a mixture of hope and sorrow Ica looked out onto the dimly lit platform of the train station. A faint smile moved across her face as she recalled the many times when Ayar had arrived just when she needed him most: When Victor had his accident as they collected medicinal plants; then on the way to Ritipata just before the landslide crushed down. His presence had been invaluable in a storm on Apu Illapa when the giant hail stones pounded from the sky; during the horrible typhus epidemic and at many other times. Even when she was stuck in her work, he always came with support and fresh ideas, always right on time. She knew in her heart that he would also come this very night. But she could not envision how he would make it out of the jungle, or when his beloved face might emerge from the fog in the few remaining minutes before the train left.

As her eyes scanned the station, half hidden within dense fog, she thought she saw a figure move toward the train. Her heart almost stopped as she detected a gait so characteristic of Ayar. She leaned forward across the open window focusing her eyes on the faint figure in the fog. She couldn't see a face. The head seemed covered by a hood. Was this the back of someone's head? But why would the figure approach? She looked more closely, trying to discern whether the person was coming or going. Soon the apparition disappeared behind several old shacks still at a distance. Ica shook her head. Was this person approaching or walking away? Was it even a real person or had her intense longing produced a mirage?

The conductor entered the compartment. "The train will be delayed by twenty minutes," he called out apologetically as he hurried on to inform other passengers.

"Twenty minutes," Ica sighed. "Enough time to see whether the apparition was real." She asked Victor to watch the luggage and got off the train. Slowly she walked in the direction where she had seen the figure disappear. Her body trembled as she approached the shacks.

"Ayar," she whispered. "Ayar, is it you? I *must* see you." But her voice echoed in the otherwise dead silence. She walked around the old huts, partially hidden in total darkness. She stopped and listened, then softly called his name again. But there was no response. In total despair she leaned against the faintly lit side of an iron pillar beside the shacks, crying silently. Her burning wish must have produced a mirage. She shuddered. It had been the image of a man with a hood over his face walking toward her. That's how a leishmaniasis patient would disguise when his face was eroding, she thought. Her whole body trembled. "Ayar," she whispered, "I need you. I need you so much. I must see you. I'll love and treasure you until your last breath, no matter what." She sobbed uncontrollably.

Her mind's eye had not deceived her. Ever since Ayar had received Ica's last letter in his remote jungle hut, he was torn between an intense longing to see her again and the fear that his condition would shock her and convert her love into pity, sorrow, or disgust. Perhaps she would not even recognize him with his face disfigured, and his strength waning. But he needed to see her just one more time, and perhaps..... perhaps he would dare to call her name, hold her, give her the last work he had done and say goodbye. He knew the station well and could find a spot from where he would at least see her. So he left the rainforest, walking at dawn and dusk and throughout the nights, and hiding in the light of the day.

This evening he had reached the station a few hours before Ica and Victor arrived. As he saw them board the train, he left his hiding spot, seized by an irresistible urge to say goodbye, to hold her and kiss her one last time. So he had approached the train, only to stop again behind the old shacks in the fog.

His heart had started to beat faster as Ica stepped from the train, walking toward the shanty huts. He froze as she called his name. And now she stood so close, separated by only a few wooden boards, close enough for him to touch her.

What if she hears me breathe, he thought, half hoping she would discover him. Her sobbing became insupportable. He took a step forward, ready to comfort her, but then retreated hastily. With his hood pulled half over his face, he would frighten her. Perhaps she would not recognize him and run back to the train. This is not the goodbye he wished for. He must remain unseen.

The conductor paced along the platform, announcing the train's departure. Slowly Ica walked toward her compartment. For a few precious moments Ayar fixed his eyes on her beloved silhouette, torn between a burning desire to hold her and his wish to be remembered the way he was before he contracted the dreaded disease.

Victor leaned out the window waving his hands to sign that Ica should hurry back. He partook in her sorrow, yet he was excited to travel to a world so different from his own.

She climbed up to their compartment and sank into her seat. With her heart broken she looked across the deserted station.

Himself hidden by darkness, Ayar could clearly see her cherished face, illuminated by the light of the lanterns on the platform. She appeared calm and serene, with tears flowing from her eyes.

The train started to move, slowly gaining speed, carrying Ica away. Ayar knew he would never see her again. In agony he grasped the iron pillar where she stood moments before, holding it until the train had disappeared in the night with the haunting echo of a last goodbye.

His research notes crumpled in his hands, he finally pulled away from the pillar. Drained of all strength, he swayed toward the back of the station from where he could move unrecognized along dark alleys to the house of his *compadres* Pablo and Placida. They received him with love.

Ayar passed an hour writing to Ica, explaining what had happened to him, asking her to forgive him for his weakness, for hiding, when they needed one another so much. He wrote, "Now I fully understand the people who are torment-ed between love and shame, who hide so tenaciously and cannot be convinced to seek help after the disease has already disfigured them."

He now knew he did the right thing by hiding. He wanted to remember Ica full of love and laughter. She might have insisted on remaining with him to the end, neglecting their work that helped so many people. He also wanted Ica to remember him the way he was before, to treasure their love and boundless happiness.

Ayar was aware that he had to find a way to dispel the immense longing that was tearing him apart. He had to replace it with all the precious memories of the time he spent with Ica. From his ancestors he had learned the secret of *pacha*, the space/time continuum that periodically reverses in the process of a *pachacuti*, a reversal of the world. As the world is turned upside-down, the sadness that existed at one time is converted into happiness within this new time frame, this different dimension of existence. For now they were apart, but this state would not last forever. Eventually Ica's spirit would join him in a place of perfect harmony, in the realm of the condors where their love would burn forever. This knowledge gave him comfort. But the pain was still hard to bear.

He put his letter and research papers in an envelope and asked his *compadres* to keep it until Ica's return. *Comadre* Placida hugged him good bye, crying. Compadre Pablo started his truck to drive his godson to Qoripampa. They talked little during the five hours of their journey, knowing that Ayar needed his strength for the long ascent to the glaciers. On the outskirts of the village they parted with the understanding that their friendship would last forever.

Where the Condors Wait

Qoripampa lay silent in the dark of night. Only one room in the hospital was lit. Ayar stopped for a moment, recalling the joy when finally the obstacles had been overcome and the hospital had been built and equipped. It was Ica who had given him the strength and willpower to persist despite what had seemed to be insurmountable problems.

He passed by the window of their lab. How he would have loved to continue his work here together with Ica and their dedicated crew. Abruptly he turned away annoyed by these thoughts and wishes that could never come true. With his strength and eyesight waning, there was no alternative. His time on this earth neared its end.

In darkness he left Qoripampa on a narrow trail that led toward the snow-covered Apus. Hours passed. Dawn began to lay its silvery veil upon the landscape as he crossed the path that led toward the rock shelter where he had first spent a night with Ica after the landslide and the tragic deaths of their friends. For a moment he reflected on the joy of holding Ica in his arms, as the heat of his body warmed and saved her. He remembered how angry she was in the morning because he had not told her about the fate of her friends. She would have started a search right then, herself at the brink of death. She knew so little about the Andes at that time. But she had become one with the people, the place, and the spirits.

Dawn gave way to a hot, sunny day as Ayar continued his journey toward the eternal snow. Several more hours passed. Then in the distance he saw the peak of the sacred Apu Condornuna, the mountain where the condors reside. Here the Incas and pre-Incan peoples performed rituals for the gods and the spirits of the dead. Intricate patterns of altars, seats, and staircases carved into the rocks throughout the countryside testified to their sacred activities. His heart began to beat heavily as he approached Rimaq Mach'ay - the Speaking Cave - with its beautifully carved altars in its hollow interior. Here he had passed one of the most precious moments of his life.

He stepped through the cave's murmuring entrance and sat down beside the main altar. Moving his hands across its smoothly carved surface, he touched a crevice in the rock. It contained something soft. He pulled at it. Ica's scarf appeared. She had forgotten it as they left the cave in the early morning almost two harvests ago. Holding the scarf to his cheek, beautiful images returned to his mind. He saw Ica and himself, intoxicated with love in a night of splendor. Everything was magic. It was happiness at its fullest. It was here where he knew that he could not live without her. But he had let her go without a goodbye.

He reached into his pocket for pen and paper to leave his last thoughts for her. His fingers touched two crumbled pages. He pulled them out and saw to his dismay that he had forgotten to place them with the rest of his notes for Ica. The pages were most significant regarding his last findings on *espundia*. Confident that Ica would some time return to their sacred cave, he placed the sheets, together with his final thoughts for Ica, into the crevice that had held her scarf.

He hurried out into the hot sun of the afternoon. By accelerating his pace, he tried to escape from the torture of his painful longing. But the images kept flashing into his mind. He envisioned Ica running with him through the meadows. She seemed to fly, as her hair blew in the wind reflecting the golden rays of the sun. They collected herbs, laughing and joking. He embraced her. She caressed his face. He heard her say the loving words, *"askatan munaykuyki sonqochallay!"* The melodious sound of her voice made his heart dance and her ravishing smile let him forget the world around him.

Memories continued to pour into his mind. He smiled as he imagined Ica using their work to help others escape the pain, he and so many of his patients had to endure. He treasured her image that seemed so close. He heard music and envisioned her slender body moving gracefully to the tunes of *huaynos*. Dancing together they floated like clouds through the Andean landscape.

The thought that Ica was travelling far away from him, halfway across the world, no longer tore him apart. Regardless of the distance, now she was with him to stay in his heart and mind. She was so close, he could almost touch her. He had finally achieved himself what he knew so well and had often conveyed to others who were devastated by losing a beloved. He had become one with her mind and knew that he'd be there always, working with her toward a common goal. His sadness was gone as he stepped onto the snowfields of the sacred Apu Condornuna. He knew that at the end of her earthly existence her spirit would ascend to these lofty heights where he would be waiting for her to join him.

The ice field sparkled in the evening sun. Slowly, with little strength left, Ayar ascended the steep inclines. In the distance two condors performed a graceful dance as they approached one another and then parted. He stopped to watch these fascinating birds, the spirits of the Apus, the great ancestors. Then he waved Ica's scarf through the air to let them know that he was coming to stay forever.

Halfway around the world, at the International Congress on Tropical Diseases, Ica's presentation was very well received. Her work with Ayar and their team was awarded a research grant that would allow them to continue with their efforts and also expand their activities. Ica's presentation of Ayar's most recent work in the rain forest was considered a breakthrough. He received an award for outstanding scientific achievements. For a brief time her joy overshadowed her sadness.

Ica took Victor to different parts of northern Europe to visit with members of her extended family who were happy to see her after a long time and to meet Victor. He was invited to stay with Ica's aunt for the rest of his vacation. Ica's decision to return to Qoripampa so soon saddened them. Yet, they understood that the situation there was critical and that she had to return. She knew that something was wrong with Ayar and was eager to hurry back to find him.

She returned to Qosqo, not announcing her arrival in the hope to meet with Ayar alone. Back in the city, she knocked on Placida and Pablo's door.

"*Bienvenida amiga!*" Pablo exclaimed as he opened the door welcoming her to their home. *Comadre* Placida hugged Ica and proceeded to offer herbal tea and freshly baked bread. They ate quietly. No one spoke. No one said what happened since she departed. The silence affirmed Ica's worst fears.

Finally she whispered, with her voice shaking, "I must find Ayar, wherever he is."

Compadre Pablo nodded. "I will take you to Qoripampa tonight. From there we will climb to Apu Condornuna." His tone of voice reflected his own pain. He gave Ica an envelope with a letter and several sheets of research notes that Ayar had left for her. She opened it carefully and read the letter. Overcome with grief, she could not continue reading his notes. With her face in her hands, she remained immobile for hours. Then she asked Pablo to take her to Qoripampa. Doña Placida hugged Ica, sharing in her pain. She handed her a bag with food and drink and kissed her goodbye. Pablo's small truck puffed through the night on the muddy road to Qoripampa. Neither spoke throughout the long drive, but both felt the support they gave one another in their suffering.

Ica was glad that no one stirred so early in Qoripampa. She left her bags in a shed close to the hospital. With her heart broken, her voice choked and her face in tears, she was unable to greet anyone. She also asked Pablo to let her go alone on the path that Ayar had taken to his final resting place.

Pablo understood. "Come back soon. Qoripampa needs you. And visit us whenever you can," he begged, as he hugged her goodbye.

Under a sky dotted with millions of stars, Ica walked along the narrow trail toward Ritipata, a path so full of memories. In the bright night she could discern the many landmarks that have meaning for the people of these high mountains and had now taken on significance for her as well. She crossed the trail that led to the rock shelter, where Ayar had saved her from the thundering landslide and from hypothermia. He was everything she had ever wished for in a man, she thought to herself. But she knew she could not stop and reflect for long. Nor could she continue to cry or delve into memories that were too painful. She had to conserve her energy for the exhausting ascent to the eternal snow to where Ayar had walked just two weeks ago.

In the heat of the afternoon she saw Ritipata in the far distance, but remained on the path that led to Rimaq Mach'ay. Narrow rivulets glistened in the sun as they joined the Rimaq Mayu, the Speaking River that flowed through the gorge to the valley. Ica approached the towering curved entrance to the cave. She trembled as she heard the murmuring sounds that seemed louder and more human than she remembered. In the back of her mind she could not erase a glimmer of hope to find Ayar alive.

Exhausted she fell on the carved seat beside the main altar. Her thoughts went back to the time when she felt so much love and happiness in Ayar's arms. Here they made their vows to always remain together and confirmed them in the presence of the great Apus and of Pachamama who granted them their wish for a while. It was here where Ayar explained that togetherness is in one's mind and that memories remain forever, even if the condors call a loved one to the eternal snows.

Ica leaned forward, resting her head on an altar of stone. A feeling of despair and loneliness seized her. She reflected on the meaning of their sacred union in the presence of the gods, right here in this very place.

"Is there any way to be together forever?" she whispered. "Perhaps I will join Ayar on the ice fields of Apu Condornuna." She sighed, finding relief in this thought, relief from the dreadful pain of a separation that would never end. Exhausted she lay down on the carved bench to take a rest before attempting her final ascent. She fell into a deep sleep.

The splashing sounds of a torrential rain awakened her. It was pitch dark. For a moment she had to orient herself. Frozen and stiff she felt her way along the stone altar trying to locate her small bag. Her hand came across a crevice alongside the altar and touched something that felt like paper. She pulled it out. With difficulty her stiff fingers opened a sheet, folded several times and partially torn. Feeling her way back to the bench she pressed the paper against her body. Could it be that Ayar had left it for her or had other people entered the cave? In her mind she envisioned what his last thoughts might have been.

Finally the rain had stopped and the faint light of dawn penetrated the cave. With her heart beating faster Ica unfolded the paper. At the sight of Ayar's handwriting she cried. Through her tears she read,

"Ica, I implore you not to be sad. Think of me with joy and carry with you the memories of us together - loving, teasing, working, and running across the hills. After the pain of our long separation, I have finally found comfort remembering you without the terrible longing that had always been with me when we were apart. Now I feel your closeness and I cherish every moment of it. I have finally come to terms with my own advice that togetherness does not only take place in the physical dimension, but can express itself most intensely in one's mind and spirit. Ica, I will wait for you. When you are ready to join me, the condors will bring your spirit to the realm of the Apus. In the meantime I know you will be fine. You will continue our work that will help so many who are inflicted with disease, and I thank you so much for it. I will love you forever."

With trembling fingers Ica carefully folded the note that was torn at its corners and put it in her bag. Many small pieces of paper lay in and around the crevice. She wondered whether there had been more pages. Did the birds tear them and carry them off? Glad that they did not fly away with Ayar's note, she slid through the murmuring exit and walked toward the snowfield that sparkled in the distance as the first rays of the sun touched its surface. Soon she would be there and perhaps, if she was lucky, the condors would call her right then to the realms of the Apus where Ayar's spirit was waiting.

The sun stood high in the sky when she stepped on the snow. She advanced slowly. The slippery surface gave way with every step she took. In despair she threw herself into the snow. Ayar's words flashed through her mind and resounded in her ears as though he was speaking:

"Ica, you must wait until the condors call you. You are never alone. I am in your mind. Together we travel everywhere. Go back, Ica, you are needed. The patients are waiting for you."

She tried to shut his words from her mind, but they did not stop ringing in her ears.

"Thank you, Ica. Thank you for doing our work. I will love you forever," she heard him say.

As she closed her eyes, she saw patients with *espundia*, desperate and dying. Scenes flashed through her mind of the times when she and Ayar worked frantically in the lab. She remembered the vows they both made to help every patient, regardless of the sacrifice required. And she saw his animals, his limping dog, his stray cats. All of them needed her care. She thought of Victor returning home, eager to follow in their footsteps, but unable to find either of them.

She rose from the snow. "Yes, Ayar, I will go on, I will!" she called out to the mountain peaks. A clear echo returned, like the voice of an omnipresent spirit.

The condors did not perform a dance, nor did they appear in the sky. But herds of vicuñas watched her curiously as she walked across the snow, then through rubble and finally along meadows down toward Ritipata.

The Power of Memories

The villagers had gathered in the central plaza of Ritipata. From afar Ica recognized the people she had met during the great fiesta in the rainy season. As she approached, they rose to greet her.

"Welcome *doctorita*, please stay with us," they said with affection. They did not ask why she came. They knew that Ayar had joined the ancestral spirits when the condors called him.

The *curandera* Doña Huaman walked toward Ica. "Don't let sadness settle within you," she advised, looking at her with concern. "My husband became sick and left this earth long ago when our four children were young. I raised them alone. But his spirit has always been with us. Each day memories of him have brought me love and happiness." Pointing to the Apus in the distance, she smiled with satisfaction, "Now it will not be long until I can join him."

"I will try to follow your advice," Ica promised.

Doña Huaman looked up in the sky, "*Doctorita*, you must cherish those wonderful memories. They are not of the past. Eternity happens right now, right at this moment and lasts forever."

Ica visited the grave where Juanita, Don Julian, and their young daughters were buried.

"They followed Doña Juanita into the grave," one of the elders informed with sorrow.

Ica touched the tiny stone condor in her pocket which little Sabina gave her to bring luck. She took a deep breath, closing her eyes in pain.

The villagers saw her suffering. "You did all you could. You helped so many of us when the typhus epidemic struck," they said. "And with the new hospital you can help even more. Please stay with our people."

"I promise," Ica responded. "I promise I'll always be there for you. I want to return the hope and strength you have given me."

She remained in Ritipata for several days, finding comfort in the wisdom of the people, treasuring the ground where Ayar was born and where they had gained a deep understanding of one another. Hopeful and ready for a new beginning she descended to the valley. The *curandera* Doña Huaman accompanied her.

The sun had already set behind the rocky peak of Apu Huaman Orqo when they arrived on the outskirts of Qoripampa. From a distance they saw people lined up outside the hospital, patients who had returned from the jungle to their village and those who had never left. As in previous years, many young people had arrived sick, unable to work in the fields or ascend to the high pastures.

Ica was greeted with affection by patients, colleagues, and the Rodrigues family. They hugged her, many in tears, thinking about Ayar's journey to the ice fields.

Then Don Rodrigues said with concern, "We have too many sick people. We don't know where to accommodate all of them. "There was another outbreak of leishmaniasis in the jungle of Madre de Dios. Many patients came here."

In the small room, beside the lab, Ica washed herself and changed her clothes. Then she took her travel bags from the shed where she had deposited them a week ago. They were filled with medicine against the aggressive type of leishmaniasis. "This will last for a while," she said with a ray of hope in her eyes. With her crew she worked late that night and throughout the days and nights that followed, as more patients arrived. The research results, that Ayar had left for her with his *compadres*, were especially useful, as they focused on the early detection of symptoms of the disease and on ways to treat the open wounds of skin lesions, before they progressed to full blown *espundia*, as they did in some cases.

Yet, as she looked carefully through Ayar's last notes, she realized that two pages, which Ayar considered most significant, were missing. "The birds of Rimaq Mach'ay," she sighed. "These little thieves flew away with the pages or what was left of them. Perhaps they dropped them somewhere in the cave. I will find them eventually. I *must* return to Rimaq Mach'ay."

Ica was exhausted, but treated every patient with special care. Those whose condition had progressed too far to be cured, reminded her of Ayar. She gave them love and hope, just as the Andean people had helped her to find spiritual comfort. When she looked at her patients' eroding faces, when she saw their waning strength, their grief and their despair, she understood why Ayar did what he needed to do. Why he followed the call of the condors.

Don Rodrigues, Francisca, the hospital staff and patients were happy when Ica disclosed that the comparative research Ayar had done with her help, had been awarded a grant by the International Congress on Tropical Diseases. It was large enough to allow for an expansion of the hospital and the laboratory, for more equipment, and continuing research and for the purchase of much more imported medicine to combat *espundia*. Ica brought more exciting news. One American and one European team of researchers had announced during the international congress that they were ready to cooperate in the development of a program for *espundia* patients in Qosqo. Above all, the villagers were confident that Ayar and Ica's research would soon result in better prevention of the disease and eventually an affordable cure.

April had arrived and with it came harvest time. Every year, for centuries, the deities responsible for a good harvest had been honored. This year, after the traditional rituals had been carried out, Ica organized a celebration, inaugurating the new addition to the hospital. On this occasion she wanted to commemorate the groundbreaking work Ayar had done for so many years.

Hundreds of people from villages throughout the region attended the celebration. They were keen to express their gratitude, to honor Ayar's tireless work, and his profound dedication to the sick. Ayar stood as a role model to be followed and Ica wanted to ensure that he and his work would never be forgotten.

A sculpture of Ayar, made by village artist Julio Quispe, who had been cured of leishmaniasis, now presided over the central courtyard of the hospital. The people who came from near and far knew that Ayar's spirit would always be with them, giving them hope, both in life and when death was near. During the celebration some people in attendance questioned why Ayar had not cured himself with the foreign medicines that were from time to time available in Qoripampa's hospital.

In his address to the gathering Don Felix informed them that Ayar had indeed asked for Glucantime and other imported medicines at the time when he first noticed that he was infected with *espundia*. With sadness Felix relayed that he had seen Ayar use the medication he had brought him, for a little girl and her father who were also showing the signs of the dreaded disease. In a hoarse voice Felix added, "On my next trip to the jungle it seemed that the little girl and her father had been cured, but Ayar's condition had progressed beyond help." The people in attendance were close to tears.

Ica's days became too busy to concentrate on anything but her patients and research. Yet, in the late evenings when she returned to the Rodrigues' home, she spent time contemplating and reliving the precious moments she had shared with Ayar. Sadness about his physical absence was mixed with the joy of remembering his being. As she sat on the brown velvety couch in the living room, she saw the snow-covered mountain peaks, among them the majestic Condornuna, shining in the moonlight through the window. She felt Ayar's presence which, with the passing of time, was settling ever more deeply into her mind and soul.

Looking across the room she saw grandpa Rodrigues sitting on a couch between two of Ayar's older cats. All three were blissfully asleep. Inti, Ayar's three-legged, chocolate brown dog got up and lay down beside Ica, resting comfortably at her feet with two of Ayar's grey and white stray cats settling down between the dog's legs. What a peaceful picture, she thought. These animals have received love and know how to give it in return.

Listening to the clock ticking in the living room, Ica, too, was ready to doze off, when the door opened and Doña Nilda entered with sheets and pillow cases hanging over her arms.

"Supper will be ready soon," she said with a smile. I just want to finish arranging the room beside grandpa's for our son Rodrigo. He'll soon come to visit."

"Doña Nilda, please let him have his own room. I will move out," Ica said. "Please, I should not occupy his room."

"Impossible," Doña Nilda answered. "You are a member of our family who stays. He only comes to visit. He has concluded his studies in Lima and returned to Qosqo to work, to be closer to his beloved mountains. Whenever he visits, he'll sleep down here."

"What exactly did Rodrigo study?" Ica asked. "I remember Ayar telling me that he was fascinated by weather patterns - hail storms, torrential rains, droughts, and the like."

Doña Nilda took a seat beside Ica. "Yes, ever since he was a child, he had been interested in the weather, the mountains, the glaciers and the water that comes from their peaks. He was fascinated and intrigued by the hydrology of the mountains. He climbed up to the glaciers with Ayar, who was his friend and age-mate. Francisca sometimes joined them. These three had their differences, but always remained friends, sharing interests and work. Each year, after the dry season was over, they put markers at the point to where the glaciers had receded. With one exception they had receded every year," she said with great concern. Then, in a happier tone of voice she added, Rodrigo's love for nature lasted throughout his youth, so he studied Meteorology, Climatology, Glaciology, and who knows what else.

"Now I remember," Ica said. "Ayar mentioned Rodrigo's studies when we looked at the snow-covered mountains which seemed to shed a little more of their snow and ice each year."

"Yes," Doña Nilda said with sadness. "The two had much in common. Rodrigo will be shocked to hear that Ayar's spirit has already gone to the realm of the condors.

"Glaciers, oh those glaciers," grandpa sighed. He got up and moved toward Ica and Doña Nilda, taking a seat beside them. Pointing to the snowy peaks to the east, he said, "I always tell people, watch the glaciers, watch them closely." In a barely audible voice he revealed, "They are the ones that let us know what will happen; first up there and then down here." He raised his eyebrows. "It will be serious. But few people want to listen. Ayar and Rodrigo knew what was coming, and so did Francisca."

"Grandpa," Doña Nilda said, "Tell us more."

He nodded, then addressed his daughter-in-law. "Nilda, you must still remember what these mountains looked like half a century ago when you were a child. Did you see their snowy ponchos reach below the path that now leads to Ritipata?"

"I remember," she affirmed. "That path was built about three decades ago. Before that time permanent snow covered that land."

"When I was a child, the snowline came down even lower," grandpa resumed. "I have watched it retreat for over eight decades. Slowly the water in some mountain lakes and rivulets dried up and the grasses, bushes and trees that grew in their vicinity became stunted. Many disappeared all together and so did some varieties of herbs."

Doña Nilda nodded.

Ica looked at grandpa with concern. "I know it's serious," she said. "Ayar told me often that the biodiversity of medicinal and other plants in this region is no longer as rich as it used to be. Where will all this lead?"

Grandpa sighed. "If the trend continues much longer, humanity as we know it will cease to exist."

"Grandpa!" Doña Nilda exclaimed, shaking her head. "Don't say such things. Let's wait until Rodrigo comes home. He may have more to tell us after all those years of study."

"I know grandpa is right," Ica interrupted. In his last letters Ayar often referred to this situation. He observed that the larvae of the sandflies are now found at higher altitudes than previously and in altogether new regions. This means that the climate is changing and the terrible *espundia* will no longer be restricted to areas such as the jungle."

"Ica, you have your work cut out for you, both now and in the future," grandpa said. Holding her hand, he uttered in a hoarse voice, "We are glad you are with us. We are happy you continue Ayar's work. You were sent to us by a higher power."

"That's nice of you to say, grandpa," Ica said with a smile. "I'm just doing my work, our work."

"Supper is ready!" Francisca called from the kitchen. Don Rodrigues had arrived home. The potatoes, vegetables and a dessert made from the *capulí* fruits of the late rainy season tasted delicious.

"Enjoy it while you can," Francisca said with a bittersweet look on her face. "I just returned from a meeting with peasants from three of the adjacent districts. Bad weather had destroyed much of their crops. Some had to deal with floods, others with droughts. We may have to share our crops with many other people."

"Climate change brings new challenges – lost crops, new diseases." Don Rodrigues added. "But if we work together as we always have, we'll be able to cope." Looking at Ica with a smile, he said "With you in our midst, what can go wrong?"

"I'm drawing on Ayar's knowledge and experience and on his spiritual support. He helps me so much," she responded.

"He helps us all," grandpa said. The others nodded in agreement.

Victor returned from Europe to move to the next grade in Qoripampa's school. He thanked Ica for the wonderful experience she had given him. "I'll accompany you to California next year when you present your doctoral research," he said. With a grin he added, "I will work so hard, you won't be able to do without me." To show her that his interest in herbs and healing remained strong, he spent all his free time assisting her and was determined to follow in hers and Ayar's footsteps.

Shaken that Ayar's spirit had been called by the condors, Victor was surprised to find Ica working away cheerfully and asked her how she had overcome her sadness. She took him up to Huaman Orqo, the peak that dominated Qoripampa.

There they sat down on a rocky outcrop facing one another.

"Victor," she said with an air of contentment about her. "You see, I continue working with Ayar. I work with his ideas, his concern for patients, his enthusiasm and his love. We are not apart." She looked up to the snow-covered mountains as she explained, "With every step I take I feel his energy emanating from the landscape, from the snowy peaks and the very earth I tread. I feel the warmth of his life within me. He gives me the strength to continue when I'm exhausted." She looked at

Victor with a smile, "Perhaps you cannot understand this yet, but that's what happens when one truly loves someone. Ayar's body rests with Pachamama, but he never really died. His spirit is always right here with us and it is everywhere we go."

They continued walking past stone altars and rocks, carved to irregular, yet pleasing shapes. "I now understand the wisdom of your ancestors," Ica resumed. "The wisdom Ayar knew so well. The wisdom the *curandera* Doña Huaman conveyed to me. The wisdom about love that transgresses death."

"I know," Victor said with an air of deep understanding, "You have now become one with his spirit."

About the Author

In the course of almost 30 years Inge Bolin has done research and applied work in the jungles and highlands of Peru. Through both peaceful times and the turbulent years of the Shining Path, she has encountered indigenous beliefs and practices concerning health and healing, life and death. She came into contact with patients displaying the ancient and devastating disease, leishmaniasis, which is on the increase. The fate of these people inspired her to write this novel.

Her ethnographies: " Rituals of Respect - the Secret of Survival in the high Peruvian Andes," and "Growing up in a Culture of Respect - Child Rearing in Highland Peru," both published by the University of Texas Press, and her published articles deal with many Andean themes. She is a Research Associate at Vancouver Island University and continues to work together with the volunteer organization "Yachaq Runa," which she founded in Cuzco in 1992 and deals with Andean Medicine, Nutrition and Ecology.

Printed in Great Britain
by Amazon